DEATH
RETURNS

Book 3

The Death Card Series

By

J.S. Peck

BEJEWELED PUBLISHING
LAS VEGAS, NEVADA

Bejeweled Publishing
6480 Annie Oakley Drive, Suite 513
Las Vegas, Nevada 89120

ISBN: 978-0-9824607-5-7
First Edition: June 2019

COVER ART DESIGN: Kelly A. Martin
INTERNAL DESIGN: Jake Naylor

DEDICATION

I dedicate the entire Death Card series to my talented sister, Judith Keim, who has taken time away from her successful authoring to help and support me.

"You have been the wind beneath my wings by believing in me and my talent for writing mysteries. When I've been in doubt, all I've had to do was pick up the phone, and you'd patiently share advice and encouragement. I honor and love you as my twin sister— I'm forever grateful."

Table of Contents

PART 1 - SANTA FE

CHAPTER 1	1
CHAPTER 2	9
CHAPTER 3	15
CHAPTER 4	25
CHAPTER 5	33
CHAPTER 6	37
CHAPTER 7	45
CHAPTER 8	51
CHAPTER 9	57
CHAPTER 10	65
CHAPTER 11	71
CHAPTER 12	79
CHAPTER 13	85
CHAPTER 14	89
CHAPTER 15	95
CHAPTER 16	103
CHAPTER 17	117
CHAPTER 18	121
CHAPTER 19	127
CHAPTER 20	131
CHAPTER 21	141
CHAPTER 22	147
CHAPTER 23	155

PART 2 - LAS VEGAS

CHAPTER 1	163
CHAPTER 2	169
CHAPTER 3	173

CHAPTER 4   179
CHAPTER 5   183
CHAPTER 6   187
CHAPTER 7   195
CHAPTER 8   201
CHAPTER 9   207
CHAPTER 10   213
CHAPTER 11   219
CHAPTER 12   231
CHAPTER 13   235
CHAPTER 14   241
CHAPTER 15   249
CHAPTER 16   255
CHAPTER 17   259
CHAPTER 18   263
CHAPTER 19   267
CHAPTER 20   273
CHAPTER 21   277
CHAPTER 22   283
CHAPTER 23   287
CHAPTER 24   293
CHAPTER 25   297
CHAPTER 26   303
CHAPTER 27   307
CHAPTER 28   313
CHAPTER 29   321
CHAPTER 30   327
CHAPTER 31   333
CHAPTER 32   337
CHAPTER 33   341
CHAPTER 34   351
CHAPTER 35   355
CHAPTER 36   361
CHAPTER 37   373

DEATH
RETURNS

Part 1

Santa Fe

CHAPTER 1

" When will our plane be here?" Isabella asked with excitement as we stood in the middle of the airport.

"Soon, sweetheart. It shouldn't be too long now."

I was here with the oldest of four little girls who were to have been auctioned off at the Purple Passion Lounge as part of their human trafficking scheme. She'd become attached to me when I helped them escape and had taken to calling me Mama because she wanted me to be her new mother. However, that was not going to happen for all sorts of reasons, which she had difficulty understanding. It had been Jacklyn from the agency handling human trafficking who had reached out to me with a special request. They had found some of Isabella's relatives in Santa Fe, New Mexico. They couldn't afford to come to Las Vegas to pick her up, and she refused to go there unless I went with her. The agency's job was to reunite children with their relatives to provide them with a family of their own people. They'd asked if I would take her to Santa Fe to meet her relatives despite it being unconventional.

I had agreed to what they'd asked—with one condition. If I found that Santa Fe was not a good situation for Isabella, I wanted to be able to bring her back to Las Vegas. Since her parents had refused to take her back, I wasn't about to leave her defenseless with strangers. Jacklyn and I'd agreed we'd cross that bridge if and when we came to it. The bigger problem was that, as an intuitive, I didn't feel good about anything we were headed to.

Looking around, I had to smile because I didn't know who was more excited about visiting Santa Fe— Isabella, me, or my dog. I could feel eyes on us. We probably looked like a motley threesome. Even at 11, Isabella turned heads with her Mexican beauty—light coffee skin; dark, silky hair; and shining black eyes over a smile as wide as her face. She was petite, and when she held Sweet Pea in her arms, I could barely see her behind the dog.

On the other hand, I probably looked like the nervous wreck I was with my uncontrollable long hair flying around my face, now creased with worry. I hadn't been able to reach Mike, the new love in my life, to tell him of my sudden change in plans. I was frustrated by how many times I'd tried to reach him to no avail. Of course, that was part of his being a private detective on assignment— not always available when I'd like. Now that Mike and I were developing our relationship more romantically, I knew he'd worry if he discovered I'd left Las Vegas without knowing where I was. Since we'd done investigative work together, he had become very protective of me. Although I didn't feel I needed his protection, letting him know what was happening was easier.

I felt someone at my elbow and looked to see a rather large woman pointing at Isabella. "Are you her mother?" the woman asked.

I said, "No. At the same time, Isabella said, "Yes." The woman looked confused. "Yes," I amended, not wanting to get into a public disagreement with Isabella. "Why?"

"Mexicans and dogs aren't allowed on the airplane." I looked at her in disbelief.

"Ah, there you are, Mabel," a voice behind me said with relief. Once he saw my face, he said, "Oh no. What did she say?"

"Something insulting, I'm afraid."

"I'm so sorry. Please don't mind her. She has Alzheimer's and often says the most bizarre things. I hope she hasn't offended you."

"Just my daughter and my dog," I said, annoyed. I looked at Isabella, who wore such a pleased expression on her face that I was puzzled. I reached out and patted the man's arm. "It's okay. I know you have your hands full."

"Thanks for understanding. Come on, Mabel; they're calling our flight." They headed toward their gate.

I turned to Isabella, grinning from ear to ear. "What?" I asked.

"You told that man I was your daughter, Mama."

"No, I didn't, honey."

"Yes, you did. You said, 'Just my daughter and my dog.'" I thought about what she told me and realized I'd said that without thinking. "Oh my, Isabella." I hugged her and whispered, "But you know that's not true. You know we're here together, so I can take you to Santa Fe to meet your family, right?"

"I know," she said sadly, lowering her head.

As I turned away, my huge Dooney & Bourke traveling purse fell off my shoulder and landed with a thud, scattering some of its contents. My tarot cards spilled, and there it was—the Death card on top—a sign for me that there would be an upcoming murder or death of someone I knew or would soon meet.

"Give it a rest," I mumbled. Still, the card sat there, waiting for me to pick it up. Again, a feeling that Santa Fe held more in store for us than simply meeting Isabella's family came over me. With a sigh, I collected and stuffed everything back inside my bag. Our flight was called, so we tucked Sweet Pea into her carrier and boarded with the others traveling first class.

Once on the plane, I explained to Isabella we'd land in Albuquerque, New Mexico, where we'd spend the night. Then we'd rent a car the following day and drive the hour or so north to Santa Fe.

"Oh, Mama, I'm so excited! I've never been on an airplane before!" I decided not to scold her for calling me Mama. It would be a waste of time, anyway. "Mama, am I going to see Indians in Santa Fe? Real, live Indians?"

"Yes, Isabella, I bet you will. Let's Google all about them on my iPhone and see what we can find out."

Isabella looked at me with stars in her eyes. "Okay."

I did my magic, and she hung on my shoulder as I read aloud, "Of the 19 Native American communities in New Mexico, eight are near Santa Fe. All eight are Pueblo Indian tribes, and their communities are called pueblos."

"Can we visit a pueblo, Mama?"

"I think that's a great idea," I answered, pleased by her curiosity yet disturbed by a sudden fear that washed over me. I envisioned myself standing on a cliff, calling out for Isabella. Goosebumps ran up and down my body and made me shiver. What were we getting ourselves into?

It was a short flight, and before we knew it, we were wheels down, ready to land in Albuquerque. It was a beautiful city, and we headed to the Hyatt Place Albuquerque Airport Hotel and settled in our room because it was too late to wander around the city.

"Oh, Mama, this room is so pretty. Look outside and see all the lights."

Watching Isabella run and jump on the bed with Sweet Pea tickled me. Both hopped off when they heard the knock on the door announcing our food. Her eyes were as big as saucers as Isabella watched the server roll in the tray table with plates and silver covers to keep the food warm. She became entranced by someone in uniform pulling out her chair and serving her. I had to smile. I was sure she'd want more of this kind of attention in the future. After dinner, we took Sweet Pea for the final walk of the day. Then, I readied Isabella for bed and tucked her into the queen bed closest to the bathroom. Sweet Pea snuggled next to her.

I picked up the local newspaper to read in silence while Isabella nodded off. As I perused the newspaper pages, I saw an article about a murder in Santa Fe. As I read the story, goosebumps rippled across my entire body. I felt this murder was tied to Isabella and me, but how? The thought wouldn't leave me, so I tore out that page and tucked it in my purse.

I wondered about the status of Isabella's family. Were they U.S. citizens or immigrants "protected" under Santa Fe's sanctuary policies? Would she need a visa or have to apply for a green card? Would that be a problem for Isabella when she was there as a visitor? I'd have to check with the agency to find out how they'd handled other cases because

I wasn't sure what would be best for her. How was this all going to work out?

I changed into my pajamas and climbed into the other bed. I wasn't sure I'd be able to sleep, so I was surprised to wake up eight hours later to face a dancing little girl with Sweet Pea in her arms. I opened my arms. "C'mon girls, climb into bed for a hug before we begin our day, okay?"

Isabella settled in next to me and looked at me with brooding eyes. "Mama?"

"Yes, sweetie, what is it?"

"I don't want to live with anyone else. I don't even know those people, and I don't like them."

"Now, Isabella, how can you say you don't like them until you've met them? That's what we call being prejudiced—when we prejudge someone by deciding about them before we even meet them. Do you follow what I'm saying?"

"Yes, Mama, but I still don't want to live with them."

"Well, let's take one step at a time. We'll meet them briefly tomorrow and see what happens, okay?"

"Okaaay." Doubt in her voice.

"Who wants to take a swim in the hotel pool?"

"I do!" shouted Isabella, pulling on my arm. "C'mon, Mama, let's go!"

Even though I didn't particularly like swimming in a public pool, I was happy to do so for Isabella's sake. She jumped into the shallow end like a pro and bobbed up and down with excitement. She looked at me with pride.

"Watch what I can do, Mama," and she dunked her whole head underwater. Isabella jumped up quickly and pushed the hair out of her eyes. She laughed. "Can you do that?"

I chuckled. "Not with this hair. We'd never get to Santa Fe."

Death Returns

Without hesitation, she nodded in agreement, wearing a wide smile.

After we showered and dressed, we nibbled on the freebie breakfast muffin and drank our juice before we dashed back upstairs to get our baggage and check out. We were excited about driving north to Santa Fe to see what awaited us.

CHAPTER 2

When we left Route 25 and headed into Santa Fe, the outskirts seemed like those of any small city anywhere until we came closer to the center. Stucco adobe houses in natural earth tones seemed to pop out of nowhere, turning the area into a magical fairyland.

Isabella rolled down her window and leaned out. "Mama, I don't see any Indians. Where are they?"

"Remember, they live in their pueblo, so we'll have to go there to see them. We will, I promise you."

"Sometime soon, okay?"

I pulled over to the side of the road to look at the map I had gotten at the rest area to find the best way to our hotel. We would stay at the Eldorado Hotel & Spa for a few days. I called a real estate agency and inquired about whether there was a house I could rent for a month—it would be less costly than staying at the hotel. Happily, we were going to meet with the agent the next day.

As the valet helped me out of the car and removed our bags from the trunk, Isabella stood tall and marched through the door the other valet held open. She looked like a little princess and had the confidence of one in all her swagger. I chuckled and wondered if I had opened Pandora's Box by bringing her here.

It was a beautiful day with a cloudless blue sky. The air was refreshing and much purer than in Las Vegas. After checking in, we headed down San Francisco Street, which led into the historic Santa Fe Plaza in the center of the small downtown. Isabella made the short journey longer by peering into each shop window. She marveled at the displays of clothing and jewelry and then turned to me with a smile, pointing out one piece or another. I knew how she felt because there were so many stunning items to see—particularly the Indian jewelry, which stood out with its turquoise stones and beads.

When we finally reached the Historic Plaza, I looked at my walking map and searched out the Palace of the Governors. There, Native Americans were allowed to line up against the wall to sell their wares under the portico. As we headed there, I explained to Isabella what we would see. "As a special treat, you may pick out a piece of jewelry. I'm sure there'll be a lot to choose from, so take your time to look at everything before you decide, okay?"

"Oh, yes, Mama, I will. Come on, Sweet Pea, let's hurry."

The Indians came into view where I expected them to be. I felt a lump in my throat, and my eyes watered. There was something about being close to any Native American that made me feel as if I'd arrived home. I must have lived as one in a past life. Isabella ran ahead with no trepidation and began her search at the far end of the line. I smiled as she talked to each vendor and picked up a piece of jewelry.

I felt eyes on me, and I looked to find a person staring at me, whom I guessed was the oldest seller. She beckoned me forward with an outstretched hand and her fingers dancing. As I moved closer, her toothless smile widened. Knowing it'd be hard for her to rise, I knelt before her.

She touched my cheek, wiping away the tear that had escaped. "You've returned home, my daughter, haven't you?"

I looked deep into her eyes. "Yes."

"What have you brought us?" the wise woman asked as she eyed Isabella headed our way.

"An extraordinary little girl, Grandmother," I answered with the traditional formality of speaking to an elder. "We are here to meet her family."

The wise woman looked at me intently and started to say something but stopped as Isabella neared. When Isabella saw me kneeling before the older woman, she stepped forward and knelt beside me.

"C'mon here, child, and let me look at you," the older woman commanded.

Isabella immediately obeyed and knee-walked forward. Isabella traced Grandmother's face. "Mama, her skin is the same color as mine. Her eyes too."

"Call her Grandmother, Isabella, as a formality, okay?"

Isabella nodded and rolled the bracelets that lined the arms of the older woman. "This one is so beautiful, Mama—look!"

The woman smiled and picked up a smaller version of her bracelet from her store of items for sale. It held a large turquoise stone on a bear's figure, symbolizing strength and courage. She handed it to Isabella.

11

"Oh, how beautiful! This is the one I want, Mama."

I reached for my wallet to pay for it and felt Grandmother's hand pushing mine back. "No, my daughter. She must always wear this; it will help keep her safe. Do you understand what I'm saying?"

When she touched me, I felt lightheaded and again envisioned standing on a cliff, calling out for Isabella. "Yes, Grandmother, I understand."

Grandmother smiled. "Isabella, you must meet my granddaughter. She's close to your age. I think you two would get along just fine."

"Oh, yes, Grandmother. I'd like that. Where is she?" Isabella asked as she searched the crowd for her.

"Back at the pueblo, but she'll be here tomorrow. Maybe you could come by here again."

"Could we, Mama, please?"

"Of course. What time should we be here, Grandmother?"

"Anytime. My granddaughter will be here all day with me."

I leaned down, kissed the older woman on both cheeks and rose to go. I looked back and smiled because Isabella had followed my actions. Grandmother looked pleased. Sweet Pea had been sleeping next to the older woman and seemed reluctant to leave, but Isabella picked her up, and we left. I realized we'd be late to meet the realtor if we didn't hurry.

The real estate office was high-styled, which usually meant they dealt with wealthier clientele, which could mean higher-priced dwellings. I wanted to rent a place for a month and wondered if I'd have to pay a premium.

We introduced ourselves to the receptionist, who picked up the phone and announced us to Nancy, the realtor I'd spoken to previously. She came rushing from the back and smiled at us. Then she immediately bent down and patted Sweet Pea. "What a cute dog! I hope we find a place that allows one—even one as cute as this."

Seeing my concern, she said, "No worries. We'll come up with something for sure. We always do."

Hearing what I had in mind, Nancy shook her head. "I don't have anything yet. However, I'm still waiting to hear back from an owner I called earlier. He's a dear friend of mine, and he's leaving for Europe for a visit. I'll let you know as soon as I hear from him."

As we rose to leave, the phone rang. The receptionist answered it. "Nancy, this is the call you've been waiting for."

"Don't leave yet. Let's see if this is it," Nancy said.

We sat back in the waiting area while Nancy went to her office to speak to the caller. Ten minutes or so later, she returned smiling.

"Well, we might be able to work something out for you. My friend leaves the day after tomorrow for his trip, and he's looking for someone to take care of his place while he's gone. I know you were looking to rent a place for only a month, but he'll be gone for six weeks. Can you extend your time here in Santa Fe to house-sit for six weeks?"

"That might work …."

"You'll want to see the house before you decide, so if you have time now, let's all hop in my car and peek."

I looked at Sweet Pea and hesitated. Nancy said, "She can come with us too. Right, girl?"

The house was a few blocks from the center of town, within walking distance of the plaza. It was a beautiful stucco house set back from the road with a driveway beside it. No garage. The front door was painted turquoise and decorated with red chili peppers, which we'd seen on many doorways around town.

The front door was opened by a man in his early 60s who looked much like Mike with his rugged figure, tanned skin, dark hair, and smiling eyes. He made me realize how much I missed Mike. The inside was much larger than it had appeared from the front. It had three good-sized bedrooms, a dining room, a living room, and a heavenly gourmet kitchen. The rooms were neat and clean, and a stunning deck overlooked a beautiful garden at the rear of the house.

We agreed that Isabella and I would move in the day after he left. Once we returned to the office, I would sign the paperwork—a simple agreement between the owner and me with Nancy as a witness. I wasn't concerned about how my money would be divided between Nancy and her friend. Relief flooded through me to have found such a place.

Now, if only I would hear from Mike.

CHAPTER 3

O n our way back to the hotel, Isabella and Sweet Pea dragged. "Let's return to the hotel and rest before we meet your family, Isabella."

"Do I have to, Mama?"

"Go back to the hotel?" I asked, uncertain what she meant.

"No, Mama, do I have to meet them? You're my family, not some strangers."

"We both know that's not how it works. The only reason I'm here with you now is I promised the agency I'd take you to meet your family since they couldn't come to Las Vegas. You do understand that, don't you?"

"What if they don't like me? What happens, then? What if I don't like them?"

We stared at each other. In a soothing voice, I answered, "We'll just have to cross that bridge if it comes to that."

Although I'd had a makeshift family after my parents died and my grandmother moved in, at least I'd had the opportunity to spend time with her before my parents' death. And when she'd visited, I'd taken to my grandmother right away, which had bothered my mother. So much so that I wondered whether that was why she didn't let my grandmother visit us very often. I'd come to learn my mother was embarrassed and afraid of my grandmother's psychic abilities. She didn't want me to follow in her footsteps. The remembered tension between my grandmother and my mother took time for me to become comfortable with my grandmother as my guardian.

I empathized with Isabella's uncertainty about fitting into her new family. Maybe she'd find someone like Grandmother in her own family who would be kind and loving to her. Yet, perhaps it wouldn't be that difficult because hadn't Isabella taken to the old Indian?

I called Isabella's uncle for directions to their home. He sounded angry, and I wasn't sure whether he was upset with me or if something else was bothering him. We agreed to meet at 4 o'clock. After I hung up, the phone rang again, and I was delighted to see it was Mike. "Hi, there!"

"How are my queen and her princess?"

I chuckled. "Well, now you have two princesses to fuss over."

"What do you mean?" he laughed.

"Since you left for Boston, the agency called to ask if I'd take Isabella to meet her family in Santa Fe, so here we are."

Mike sounded surprised. "Well, that's nice, I guess. Right?"

"Yes, it is. It's a much-needed break from all that happened in Las Vegas. God knows I need some time to recover. I've found a house to rent for the next six weeks, which should give Isabella enough time to adjust to Santa Fe with her new family. I hope you can come and stay with us."

"That sounds nice."

"Is everything okay back there?"

"Yeah. Brian and I are working undercover, meaning we have no cell phones. That's the only reason you haven't heard from me." He sighed. "We're still going to be here for a bit, I'm afraid, but I'll do whatever I can to visit you soon. How is Isabella doing? Is her family nice?"

"We're going to meet them for the first time in an hour. I'll let you know."

Mike whispered into the phone, "I miss you, Rosie." There was mumbling in the background, and then Mike said, "Sorry, I've got to run. Brian says hello."

"Goodbye," I said to the disconnected phone, silent in my hand.

Hearing Mike's voice stirred my thoughts. I realized now that any relationship with Mike now included Isabella for whatever time she and I had left together.

I called Isabella. "It's time to go, sweetheart."

"Can Sweet Pea come too?"

"Sure, why not?" A dog can often be a good soothsayer and an indicator of whether or not a person is all right.

We hopped into the car and set out. As we approached their address near the rental house, the houses were tiny, some in poor repair. I turned into an extra-wide driveway between two places. Neither was numbered or identified. When I pulled the car up farther, a woman stepped out onto the porch of the shabby house on the left. She looked none too pleased to see us.

Isabella got out and came around to my side of the car. She took in everything around her. I opened my door and stepped forward to greet the woman. As I did, the front screen door swung open and slapped shut as a reasonably large man with a frown marched onto the small wooden porch and stood beside the woman. Then he stepped down and came closer to us. His eyes gleamed as they came to rest on Isabella. I disliked him from that moment and didn't trust him at all. Isabella instinctively pulled back from him.

"What have we here?" he asked as he eyed Isabella up and down.

Then all our attention was drawn to the car where Sweet Pea barked, growled, and scratched at the driver's window, trying to escape. "Are you Miguel?"

"Naw, he's in the house on the other side of the driveway."

I shivered and hustled Isabella around to the other side of the car. Sweet Pea had made enough racket to draw Miguel from his house. He stepped forward and smiled when he saw Isabella. "You look just like your mother."

Isabella immediately responded, "No, I don't."

Miguel and I were surprised by her response, but neither of us said anything. Miguel looked at me, scowled, and said begrudgingly, "I guess you might as well c'mon in."

It was clear that Miguel didn't want me there, but I gamely followed him anyway. I was anxious to see where Isabella might end up living. Even though the house was tiny, it was neat and clean. A tantalizing aroma wafted from the kitchen, where Maria prepared something delicious. She was short, round, and plump, with a baby bump covered by a white chef's apron tied around her full waist. She smiled at us and encouraged Isabella to come forward for a hug. A girl and three younger children raced from one of the back bedrooms. They stood and stared at us. The girl was the oldest and looked around eight or nine years old.

"This is Angela," Maria said when the little girl came forward to examine Isabella. "The others are Armando, Riccardo, and little Miguel."

Isabella spoke rapidly in Spanish to Maria, who looked hurt by what she'd said.

"Isabella, what did you say?" I demanded in a quiet voice.

"I told her that I'm not going to live here," she answered, an ashamed expression on her face.

"Let's just take one step at a time, hear?"

Isabella nodded. She turned to the girl and demanded, "How old are you, anyway?"

"Nine years old," Angela answered, her chin held high. "Going on 10."

"Oh," Isabella said. "Well, I'm 11. Want to see my dog?"

"Oh, yes!"

I smiled at Maria as we shared the thought to let the girls be and see what happened. Maria asked, "Rosalie, would you like a cup of tea?"

"Yes, please." I was relieved we'd have some time together.

Maria gave Miguel a pointed look, and he suddenly clapped his hands. "Time for you guys to go back to playing in your bedroom."

They raced off, the oldest boy leading the way. I smiled at the proud expression on Miguel's face as he watched them go. Then he turned back to Maria. "I've got to get back to work," he said, kissing Maria. He looked my way and struggled to be polite. "Thanks for dropping Isabella off."

"But ..." I began.

Maria reached forward and touched my arm, forestalling further conversation. She said, "Miguel works for the biggest landscaper in town." Miguel smiled with pride and left without another word.

We carried our tea into the small living room and sat down. After a few sips, I began the conversation. "Maria, as you know, the agency asked me to bring Isabella here to meet you. They have also assigned me a say about whether it's in Isabella's and your best interest to have her live here with you. I hope you understand what I'm saying, and I hope that doesn't offend you."

"No, I understand. I wouldn't want Angela left with people she didn't know either. I must warn you, though, that Miguel feels very strongly she's his responsibility now, and he doesn't want anyone outside the family to interfere."

I nodded. I'd already gotten the message—it would be hard to win Miguel's friendship. On the other hand, I felt Maria and I could work together to come up with the best solution for Isabella—whatever that was. "To begin with, we should have Isabella get acquainted with all of you through short visits. Is that okay with you?"

"Yes, that's fine," she smiled.

"I'm curious to know about Isabella's family in Mexico. Is there anything you can tell me?"

Maria sighed. "I met Isabella's mother when I was dating Miguel back in Mexico. She's his sister and used to be the beauty in town. She became pregnant when she was very young and was forced to marry the man who was the father."

I sighed with empathy.

Maria drew in a long breath. "He's not a very nice man. You should probably know that it was Isabella's mother who sold her. It was not only for the money to be able to feed the younger ones but also so that Isabella could escape. She told us that the man who'd contacted her said that Isabella would be trained to be a servant and that she could earn a good living and send money back home to her. She found out later that wasn't the real deal at all."

I saw the pain in Maria's eyes at what she'd confessed. "She refused to take Isabella back for her own good because she thought Isabella had a better chance of having a successful life here in America rather than return to their situation."

How many mothers would have the courage to do that? I wondered.

Maria continued, "I hope someday, maybe when she's older, Isabella will understand her mother's sacrifice. Right now, I know she's angry, and, honestly, she has reason to be."

I remained silent, taking it all in. Maria gave a crooked smile as she placed her hand on her stomach and announced, "I will be bringing another baby into this world very soon. My last, for sure."

I smiled at her tenderly. "Maria, I need to ask you about your status here in the United States. When did you and Miguel come here? Do you have green cards? I need to know how it'll work for Isabella, that's all."

Understanding, she nodded. "Our children were born here and are citizens, and Miguel and I are working toward citizenship. Honestly, I'm not sure how it'll work for Isabella."

We heard screeching and laughter. We looked out the window and saw the girls racing around to escape Sweet Pea, who had something hanging from her mouth. Silky dogs were known as "ratters." I hoped that wasn't what Sweet Pea had dug up. We watched her drop whatever it was on the ground and run after the girls. It was good to see Isabella acting like a little girl rather than the world-weary person I knew she sometimes felt like.

Cars pulled into the street and parked along both sides. People got out and congregated around their vehicles before they entered a small stucco house at the end. I felt goosebumps as I envisioned a man dead, and I thought of what I'd read in Albuquerque. I made out some yellow tape on the ground.

"I read in the newspaper that a man was murdered here in Santa Fe. Did you know him?"

"Yes. He lived just down the street there, where everyone is going. There was a service for him today. Now it's just his wife and two small children left. Very sad."

"Why was he murdered?"

"I don't know, but I heard it was about the border crossings. Miguel is the one to ask, though. He can tell you more."

"Gosh, murder is a pretty harsh consequence for crossing the border, don't you think?"

"Well … there are some in Mexico taking advantage of those wanting to escape to the United States by overcharging a fee for their help. Many times, they never really help at all; they take their money. I don't know if he was involved in that or not."

"Oh, I see." Goosebumps covered my body.

The girls headed in with Sweet Pea at their heels. Both were laughing, and Isabella looked at me and smiled.

Getting her acclimated to her new family would be easier than I thought. I felt a pang of jealousy. Maria turned to her daughter. "Angela, be a good girl and prepare the boys for dinner."

I saw how it might work then. It wasn't uncommon for larger families to have the oldest girl to help care for the household and younger children. With Isabella being older than Angela, would that mean everything would fall on her if she became part of their family? Lost in thought, I'd missed what Maria had said.

She asked again, "Would you like to join us?"

I looked at Isabella, who shook her head no. "Not this time, Maria, though we'd like a rain check if possible."

"Of course."

"We'll spend lots of time getting together, right, Maria?"

"Of course."

"Perhaps you'd let Angela join us for lunch on Saturday. By then, we'll be settled in the house I've rented. We can pick her up around noon if that's okay with you?"

Maria smiled. "That would be nice."

We said goodbye and backed out of the driveway under the stare and scrutiny of the neighbor. Sweet Pea saw him and growled. I shivered all over and knew he was someone I'd have to deal with down the road.

I turned to Isabella. "Well, what do you think?"

"I like Angela well enough, and they seem nice, but I'm not going to live there," she stated in a determined voice.

I didn't say anything and wondered how this would work out. I heard Isabella when she whispered in Sweet Pea's ear, "Mama, and you are my family."

Sweet Pea whined and licked her face before turning to me with a puppy smile.

CHAPTER 4

T hat night, Isabella and I dined in the hotel's fancy restaurant. Again Isabella was enchanted as the waiter pulled out her chair, settled her in it, and placed a large, white cloth napkin in her lap. She looked at me and beamed. I smiled back. I was emotionally drained by all that had happened that day and by what I was sure to come. I wasn't comfortable with Isabella living in Santa Fe—why did I feel that way? She'd seemed happy enough playing with Angela. Who was I to say no?

We left Sweet Pea in the room the following day and climbed the stairs to the pool on the roof. I sat on the side and acted as a lifeguard for Isabella and another little girl whose mother was busy reading a novel, not paying attention to her daughter. Every once in a while, the mother tore herself away from her book, glanced at her daughter, and smiled at me. "Thanks so much for keeping an eye on her." Then she'd go back to her reading. I wondered whether I could ever relax as she was doing without keeping an eye on Isabella.

I wanted to check with the local authorities to see what they knew about Maria and Miguel's next-door neighbor. I believed he was nothing but trouble, and I wasn't willing to turn Isabella over without knowing she would be safe.

After swimming, we dressed, ate a quick breakfast, and scooped up Sweet Pea to meet Grandmother and her granddaughter. When we arrived, Grandmother was sleeping, and a beautiful Indian girl with long braids sat beside her.

The girl immediately jumped up and shouted, "You must be Isabella! My name is Veronica." She made a disapproving face. "I know, it's a terrible name, so just call me Nica."

Isabella and I laughed.

Grandmother stirred from her nap and greeted us. "Good morning, my daughter." She held her hand out, and I sat down beside her.

Nica became enthralled with Sweet Pea, and after she played with her a bit, she asked, "Grandmother, can I show Isabella and Sweet Pea the Indian Museum?" She turned to Isabella, "My mother works there, and I want her to meet you. Is that all right, Grandmother?"

"Leave the dog with us and go, my children."

"Is it safe for them, Grandmother?"

"The museum is nearby, and Nica knows her way around Santa Fe. She's been trained in the old ways to be aware of all around her. They are safe for now, my daughter."

"I know I worry too much. I don't want anything to happen to Isabella," I said wistfully as I watched them walk away.

Grandmother looked deep into my eyes and pulled me close to her. She silently hummed a chant, and I sank into her. It felt like old times when my grandmother held me tight and talked in a low, soothing voice, telling me I'd always be protected and loved.

"Tell me, daughter, what's on your mind?"

I told her a little about Isabella's story and my concerns. She listened and nodded now and then with sorrow in her eyes. "Grandmother, I read about a murder that occurred here, and it turns out the man lived just down the street from Isabella's new family. Is this place going to be safe for her?"

Grandmother became lost in thought and didn't answer me for several minutes. Then she said, "My daughter, within each of us is the wisdom necessary to survive. Mother Nature always provides for us if we let her. Sometimes we've already closed our choice to live. We have to wait and see."

I looked at her and said nothing—I couldn't. I told her I wanted to meet with the police and find some answers to my questions about the murder. She nodded pleasedly and said, "Go, my daughter. Isabella and the dog are safe here with me."

I found the police station not too far from the center of the Historic Plaza and entered. A typical-looking policeman greeted me in navy pants and a light blue shirt with a shiny badge that immediately caught my eye. "I need to speak to somebody about the murder the other day."

Another man came from the back offices. He looked more like a cowboy than anything else—he was tall and wore a big Stetson cowboy hat and cowboy boots that echoed with each step on the tile floor. His pants were blue jeans, and his shirt was identical to the one worn by the policeman in front. However, instead of a typical police badge, his was an old-fashioned sheriff's badge.

"Sheriff? This here lady wants to speak to you about the murder."

"How can I help you, Miss?"

"Well, it's a long story …."

"Come back to my office then, and let's get started."

As I followed him, I looked him over. He had an air that reminded me of Mike—very sure of himself—and I instinctively knew I could trust him. I thought he was part Indian because of his tan skin, dark hair, and dark eyes that gleamed with intelligence. His body was muscular and trim, and his broad shoulders narrowed to a small waist. His hands were rough from work. No sissy there, I thought.

"My name's Coyote, by the way. And yours?"

"Rosalie Bennett. You can call me Rosie, though … everyone does."

"Okay then, Rosie. What can I do for you?"

"I've brought a young girl here to meet her aunt and uncle and their family. Next door to them is a man who seems to be trouble. I wanted to see if you could enlighten me about who he is and whether he's someone I should be concerned about."

"What's his name?"

"I don't know," I said, embarrassed. "I can tell you where he lives, though."

"Okay, we'll start there. What's the address?"

Once I gave him the address, he looked up surprised. I knew he was curious about how I was connected to

Isabella's family, but I remained quiet. He frowned in thought. "Is that the murder you're talking about—the one just down the street from there?"

"Yes. I read about it in the newspaper. I have the clipping right here," I said as I pulled the article from my purse. "Is Isabella going to be safe there? What's that murder all about anyway?"

"Still working on it," he said, shutting off any further conversation. "Who did you say are the aunt and uncle of this little girl?"

Once I repeated their names, he nodded. "I've seen Miguel around town. He works for my friend's landscaping company. He seems okay. However, the neighbor next door you're worried about is someone we've been watching. He's a troublemaker. We've been called there several times for disturbing the peace, but we have nothing conclusive enough to put him away. I'll keep an eye on him, though."

I wrote down my telephone number and pushed it toward him. "I'll be here in Santa Fe for six weeks, and I hope you can do something about that awful man. Thanks for your time, Coyote. I'd better head back to the Palace of the Governors and Grandmother..."

Coyote suddenly smiled. "By any chance, do you mean that wise old lady who sits there?"

"I do. Why?"

"That wonderful woman is my grandmother. Be warned. If she's taken with you, there's a reason for it," he said with a chuckle. "She must have something on her mind ...."

"What is it?"

"I've no idea," he said. "Even if you ask, she may not tell you."

"Oh, my," I said. We smiled at each other, lost in our thoughts about what Grandmother was up to. I rose and said, "Thanks again, Coyote."

"I'll call you," he responded.

I felt more at ease knowing he had his eye on that awful man who lived next door to Maria and Miguel.

When I joined Grandmother, she smiled. "You met my grandson, Coyote?"

"Yes, Grandmother."

She wore a pleased expression. "Come sit, my daughter."

"Where are the girls? Have they come back yet?"

Just then, Sweet Pea barked, and I looked to see the girls coming our way. "I thought I would get us all lunch. Can you leave here?" I asked Grandmother.

"We can go next door to the little restaurant. The food there is good."

"All right. Let me help you collect your things. Will this spot still be here for you when we're finished, or must someone stay?"

With a queenly wave, she said, "No, this is mine. Little Squirrel will watch my things for me."

Little Squirrel looked at us and waved us away, confirming she'd take over.

Our lunch was prepared the Tex-Mex way, the fusion of Mexican and American cuisine, and was perfect. We sat outside on the restaurant's wooden deck and listened to the girls as they planned to spend more time together. Then, we heard heavy footsteps bound up the stairs and headed toward us. Coyote approached our table. "Rosie, may I see you for a moment, please?"

We stepped to the side of the deck. "What's the matter?"

Looking embarrassed, he said, "I thought I recognized your name, so I looked you up in our computer files. I had no idea you were the one who solved the Grim Sleeper serial killer case in California."

"Certainly not," I laughed. "And it wasn't just me. My grandmother was the lead, and we played only a small part ..."

In his eagerness, he interrupted me. "Would you be willing to assist me now and then for the time you're here? I have several cases I'm working on, and I could use your help."

I was flabbergasted. Did I want to do this? It was true I was going to be at loose ends at times while Isabella was getting situated here in Santa Fe, but still ...

"I'll take whatever time I can get," he said as if he read my mind.

"Let me think about it, okay?"

"Sure. If you can meet me tomorrow, I'll show you something I'm working on now. Then you can decide if you want to get involved."

"I'll see what I can do." A part of me was already excited because I'd taken great satisfaction from my role in solving several murders in Las Vegas. Maybe I could be of service in Santa Fe too.

"Fair enough. Anytime works for me. You have my number, right?"

"I can't guarantee anything, you know."

"No problem. I think you'll do just fine."

Coyote followed me to the table and kissed his grandmother's leathery cheek. She grabbed his arm and pulled him toward her. "Take care of this woman, Coyote, you hear?"

"I officially ask Mother Earth, Father Sky, and the Great Spirit to walk in our shoes," he chuckled. "May you do the same, old woman," he added affectionately before placing an additional kiss upon her wrinkled, weathered face.

I saw their ease with each other, and it reminded me of my time with my grandmother. How lucky I'd been to have had her in my life.

Coyote tipped his hat, and off he went. I looked away from him and saw Isabella stare after him, lost in thought. She met my eyes and smiled. "He's a real Indian cowboy, isn't he, Mama? I didn't know Indians could be cowboys."

Nica smiled at her. "That's not all Indians can do. Wait until you see …."

CHAPTER 5

I t was time to wrap my mind around moving into the house I was renting. I had already paid for another night at the hotel, so we wouldn't sleep at the rental house until the next day. Today, we'd go grocery shopping and bring food and other essentials for our stay there.

"C'mon, Isabella, it's time to go shopping."

We left Sweet Pea behind and headed to the largest food market—Albertson's on Guadalupe Street. Getting out of the car, the hair on the back of my neck stood up, and I felt goosebumps crawl along my arms. I didn't notice anything out of the ordinary. As I walked slightly ahead of Isabella, I heard noise from the side of the building. I peeked around the corner into the alley and saw Maria's crazy neighbor arguing with another man.

They heard me gasp, and they turned toward me. "Who's that?" the other man demanded of the neighbor.

I didn't hear what he said, just his taunting laughter. I hurriedly backed out of the alley and pushed Isabella away before they saw her. I rushed her inside. "What's the matter, Mama?"

"Nothing worth seeing, sweetheart,"

When we came out of the store with groceries, I heard several popping sounds. For a second, I thought someone had set off fireworks. Others around us heard them as well, and a man came running from the alley side of the store and called out, "Someone, call an ambulance. There's been a shooting!"

"Isabella, get in the car right now." I pushed the grocery cart to the back of the SUV and began to unload our things. I felt someone at my elbow and shrieked when I turned and saw it was Maria's neighbor.

"If you tell anyone you saw me there with that man, I'll take your little girl and hurt her. Do I make myself clear?" He looked me up and down and added, "Or maybe it'll be you. I can think of many things I'd like to do to you …."

"Get away from me right now, or I'll scream," I threatened.

"I wouldn't do that, lady."

"Don't even think about hurting us, do you understand?"

The neighbor looked surprised at my boldness and seemed excited, like a challenge. I felt sick. Another man approached us.

"Are you all right, ma'am?"

"Just a misunderstanding," the neighbor said in an oily voice.

"That's for sure," I said, disgusted. "Now, if you get out of my way, I'm leaving."

34

Both men stepped back, and I got behind the wheel. My hands began to shake, and my heart raced with adrenaline. I could barely breathe. I backed out of the parking lot and drove to the rented house with whirling thoughts. I was in trouble. What should I do?

I felt sure we'd be safe staying at the hotel for the night. Still, I needed to be on guard to keep Isabella from harm. If Mike and Brian knew what'd happened, I could hear them now … "How do you do it? What trouble have you gotten yourself into now?" Sometimes it seemed they were right, and trouble followed me.

I needed to talk to Coyote about the best way to handle things. When we got to the house, I telephoned him. I began to give him a brief description of what had happened when an urgent phone call for him interrupted us. "Can't talk now, Rosie. I'll have to talk with you later."

That evening, once again, I indulged Isabella by having our last dinner in the expensive restaurant at the hotel. It would be our last bit of elegance before being alone with no one to wait on us. While dessert was being served, I saw Coyote talking to the maître d, who turned and pointed us out before he escorted him to our table. All eyes turned toward him as he made his way to us. He looked like a handsome cowboy straight from a classic Western movie. He made a show when he removed his cowboy hat, held it to his heart, and bowed low. "May I join you, fine ladies?"

"Certainly, sir," I answered, barely able to stop myself from swooning over such a romantic gesture. Isabella's eyes widened with appreciation at being included in his request, and I chuckled. She was not the only one taken with her 'cowboy Indian.'

"You said you'd be here for a while, Rosie, but you didn't say exactly where you'd be. I only have your cell phone number. I thought I'd better find out where you're staying so I can keep an eye on you."

My heart fluttered that I might need protection. I gave my address, and Coyote said, "That's Earl's place. Great location, near everything, but you'll still need to be careful. We've had a few break-ins, so keep a light in the front room at night. That'll help."

Noticing my concern, he added, "Santa Fe is like every other place these days with all the drug addiction and problems. Just be aware of all around you."

"Any news on the neighbor yet?"

Looking at Isabella, he gave a slight shake of his head. "We'll talk about it tomorrow when you come in to see me." He smiled at Isabella. "So you've met Nica?"

Isabella said excitedly, "She's my best friend!"

Coyote and I looked at each other and sensed that'd never change—they'd be friends forever. Some things you know …

CHAPTER 6

I t would be easy to say the food I'd eaten kept me up all night, but it wasn't. I was filled with worry. Maria's neighbor and his threat loomed large. How would I explain to Maria and Miguel that I could not have Isabella stay with them? Not yet, anyhow. Not with him nearby.

Isabella jumped onto my bed and tugged on my arm. "Time to get up, Mama. It's our moving day."

"Are you going to take a last swim this morning?"

"No, Mama. It's Saturday, and we're picking up Angela for lunch. I want Nica to come too. Can she, Mama? Can she, please?"

"We'll see whether she's with Grandmother today and if it's okay with her."

"Then it'll be a real party, Mama!"

I forced myself out of bed and into the shower. Isabella was already packed and had made her bed as well as she could, with Sweet Pea in the middle. I didn't bother with my hair and drew it back in a ponytail. I knew Isabella's patience wouldn't last long enough for me to do much more than that.

The valet pulled our car around for us, and we headed to the rental house, where a new chapter of staying in Santa Fe was enfolding.

I loved the house—it was comfortable and homey. It had a large master bedroom suite where I'd sleep and two smaller but good-sized bedrooms with their own Jack 'n' Jill bathroom between. Isabella picked the one closest to where I'd be. Sweet Pea would have a choice of where to park herself at night.

The kitchen was a spacious true chef's kitchen with double everything. I'd be happy here in Earl's kitchen because he had everything anyone could need or want. White cabinets, black granite countertops, cutting boards everywhere, and spices too numerous to count. What I liked most about the kitchen was the center island with stools underneath the wide granite overhang. All in all, the house was going to work out just fine.

When we settled in and scoped out the backyard, it was time to check on Nica and pick up Angela for lunch. Isabella had changed her clothes three times and ended up in one of the outfits she had picked out the previous spring when we'd first shopped together at Nordstrom. I looked at her with pride. She was something with all her beauty, brains, and, most of all, her loving spirit. It amazed me her good attitude was intact despite all that'd happened to her.

Grandmother was in her usual spot when we parked the car, and Nica was with her. "Good morning, Grandmother."

"Greetings, my daughter."

"We were wondering if Nica could join Isabella and her cousin for lunch."

Nica was already on her feet and jumping up and down with excitement. "Yes, Grandmother, please say yes!"

Grandmother smiled. "You may go, my child. Bring the girls back here afterward. I believe you have an appointment with Coyote."

I hadn't said a word to her about meeting him, and I had a feeling Coyote hadn't either. Grandmother was so much like my grandmother had been with psychic abilities that she made me feel at home. "Thank you, Grandmother."

The nearer I got to Angela's house, the more I filled with dread. When I pulled into the joint driveway, I was relieved that the neighbor was nowhere near. "Girls, stay here while I get Angela." With one push of the button, I locked all the doors, unwilling to take a chance the neighbor might show up.

Angela heard us arrive and was already halfway out the door. Maria stood behind her and held out some money. "No, Maria, Angela is our guest. We'll be back in a while and talk then, alright?"

Maria nodded. "Behave now, Angela. Do you hear me?"

"Yesss, Mama," she replied before racing to the car.

We entered a small café on Canyon Road where they served Mexican food and hamburgers. After we were seated, I asked Angela, "Do you and your brothers often play outside?"

"Sometimes," she responded without interest.

"Are you friendly with your neighbors who live next door?"

"No, my mother says to stay away from them because they're bad people."

Nica and Isabella caught the end of what Angela had said. Nica spoke up first. "Are you going to have them arrested? My uncle can do that, you know. He's the sheriff!"

"I don't know," said Angela.

"I think you have to catch them in the act, right Mama?" asked Isabella.

"Yes, you're right. You can't have people arrested without cause and proof."

"Maybe we can become detectives like Mike. He'd know how to get proof," Isabella bragged.

"Now that is NOT a good idea, girls. I don't want you girls getting involved by playing detectives. Do you hear me?"

"Yes," they echoed one after another.

"Promise me? Pinky promise?" The three girls held their pinkies out to me and made their vows.

Talking stopped when our juicy hamburgers arrived with choices of Mexican toppings and a pile of French fries. As I sat and observed the three girls interacting, I knew from experience that sometimes three people in a group could be a tricky dynamic. Two can join together and thrust the other one aside. Then something happens, and the twosome changes until it constantly shifts back and forth. It was interesting to watch them because I had a deep sense it wouldn't happen with those three girls. Intuitively, they seemed to accept who each was and their position, not needing to compete.

When we got back to Angela's house, we all went inside. Angela wanted to show the girls something in her bedroom, and that gave me a chance to talk to Maria. Her brow was sweaty, and she huffed and puffed as she guided me into the small living room. She plopped awkwardly in the most oversized chair and drew in short panting breaths. "Whew!"

"Maria, are you all right? Is the baby coming?"

"I've called Miguel, but he hasn't answered. He's working on a big project up north. I've also called my sister to come, but she hasn't answered either. The baby isn't due for a week, so they probably aren't expecting my call."

At first, I thought Maria must have spilled her drink because there was a puddle by her feet.

But then she frowned. "Oh no, my water broke!"

"What can I do?"

"I can't leave the children alone," she moaned.

"I'm calling 911, and then Coyote to come here to stay with the children." A calmness overcame me, and I spoke as if I had plenty of knowledge of how birthing a baby worked. I knew very little about it.

Maria groaned and puffed while she nodded in agreement. Then she knelt on the floor and gasped, "There's no time!"

Coyote arrived at the same time as the ambulance. When the EMTs got inside, they found Maria lying on the floor with me holding her hand, which she squeezed tightly enough to numb my fingers. The medics immediately placed a sterile pad beneath her and took over, but Maria refused to let go of my hand.

Coyote herded all the children back into their separate bedrooms after wandering out. Then he came, sat beside Maria, and held her other hand. He spoke to her in Spanish and said something that made her smile. She gave one last push, and a pink, squalling bundle emerged.

Tears rolled down my face as I exclaimed, "It's a beautiful little girl, Maria. A perfect little angel."

She smiled with pride and relief that the baby had safely arrived. As the EMTs continued their ministrations, she took her newly wrapped daughter in her arms and kissed the top of her little head. The baby's arms waved furiously as she cried, and then she nestled against her mother's chest and quieted down. I was overwhelmed as I watched them because it was one of the most beautiful, tender things I'd ever witnessed. I looked up and saw Coyote staring at me. He reached across Maria's body and wiped the tears from my face, taken up with the moment. He pulled his hand back and looked surprised by what he'd done.

Miguel came barging through the door. "Maria? I got your message!" Seeing us surrounding his wife, he asked, "What's happening here? Are you all right, Maria?" He stopped short when he realized what had happened. He stepped forward and looked down at his beaming wife.

"Come meet your daughter, Miguel."

He knelt beside his wife. "I'm so sorry I missed your call, Maria. I was working on the heavy equipment today. It was so noisy, and I never heard the phone …."

A medic stepped forward. "Ma'am, it's time to take you to the hospital so they can weigh the baby and examine you both to ensure everything is all right."

Maria's face scrunched in concern. She looked around, and I knew what she wanted. "Before she goes, can the children please see the baby?" I asked.

The medic agreed, and I went to get the girls while Coyote released the boys from their bedroom. They rushed forward but were held back by Miguel. They stood in awe at seeing someone so small, then raced off. The girls gingerly came forward and knelt beside Maria. Each touched the top of the baby's head—almost as if anointing her with a blessing. They looked at each other and smiled. "What will we name the baby, Mama?" asked Angela.

Maria pointedly looked at me. "I think we'll name her Rosa. What do you think?"

"Oh, yes," agreed Angela, "that's a beautiful name."

"Miguel? The name Rosa?" asked Maria.

All eyes turned to him, demanding a response. "Yup, it's fine," he agreed without much enthusiasm, aware that Maria was honoring me for helping her at a time of need—when he hadn't been there. I couldn't blame him for feeling out of sorts.

"Miguel, you go ahead with Maria. I'll stay with the children," I offered.

He brightened. "Maria's sister will come as soon as she can."

"No worries. Take all the time you need."

Before the ambulance crew took Maria out on the stretcher, I bent over her and kissed her cheek. She squeezed my hand, and I knew I had a friend in her. "You are such an inspiration," I whispered.

While we watched the ambulance pull out, Coyote received a call. He was getting ready to leave and take Nica with him. "Are you sure you're going to be all right?" he asked. "Those boys sure are a handful."

"Ah, my good sheriff, you may have forgotten, but I have two little girls who know how to handle them. Besides, any gringo worth her salt knows to order pizza."

"Right you are," he laughed, and off he went.

CHAPTER 7

Maria's sister arrived shortly after the pizza was delivered, but not before I'd had a chance to peek into Angela's bedroom, where a twin bed and a crib were set up. The room was small enough that putting in another bed would be impossible. I had to remind myself not to jump ahead.

After we had eaten the pizza and I helped to clean up, Isabella and I left. We were anxious to get home to let Sweet Pea out since she'd been housebound for a long time. I saw something dark covering the doorknob as we approached the front door. I couldn't determine what it was until I got closer, but what I saw made my heart fall.

"What is it?" Isabella asked in alarm.

"A crow." Despite what most people believed, the crow wasn't the harbinger of death in Native American cultures.

Instead, seeing a crow was good luck. But a dead crow? What was that message?

"Mama, what does that mean?" asked Isabella, worried.

"I don't know, sweetheart. We'll have to check with Coyote or Grandmother. Maybe they can tell us. I'll clean it up while you let Sweet Pea out."

I called Coyote to tell him what'd happened. His response was instant and thoughtful. "I don't like this one bit. Just leave everything as it is, and I'll come over and check it out."

"I'm afraid that's not possible. I've already cleaned up the mess. But what does the dead crow mean?"

"Someone is unhappy you're here. Any ideas?"

"Just that crazy neighbor."

"Are you going to be okay?"

"Yeah. It's probably just a joke."

"As long as you're sure you don't need me …"

"No, have a good night."

"Be careful, and call me if you need me—no matter the time."

It had been a long day, and I wanted nothing more than to get into my PJs and cuddle with Isabella on the couch. I wasn't the only one who was tired. When I tucked Isabella in bed and put Sweet Pea beside her, I heard her say, "I love you, Mama."

My eyes filled. I leaned over Isabella and kissed the top of her head. "I love you too." Sweet Pea smiled her doggy smile and tucked her nose farther into the covers.

I sat in bed with my book open, the words blurring. Why had I ever agreed to do this? Leaving Isabella behind would be one of the hardest things I'd ever do. I felt my grandmother around me and heard her say, *"Your mission, Rosalie, is to be the wind beneath her wings."* My grandmother often appeared when I needed clarity; this time, her wisdom was no exception.

Terrible nightmares that conjured up my fears about every aspect of being in Santa Fe haunted me. I saw dead crows flying … I was standing on a mountain calling out for Isabella … Grandmother kept reaching for me. Still, I couldn't get to her … Mike was angry and kept pointing his finger at me … Coyote was throughout my nightmares, and crying babies were everywhere. When I awoke, tears had dried and crusted around my eyes. I felt utterly lost and overwhelmed.

I forced myself to leave my bed and made coffee in the kitchen. The phone rang, startling me. It was Mike.

"Good morning! How are my queen and her princesses?"

"I'm so glad you called. How are you?"

"Things are moving along. I think I'll be able to break free soon and head out to Santa Fe to be with you for a few days." There was a pause. "I sure have missed you, Rosie."

"I've missed you too," I said, wiping away a tear.

After ending the call, I peeked into Isabella's room to check on her. She was still asleep. Sweet Pea saw me and hopped off the bed, ready to go outside for her daily business. When I opened the French doors to the backyard, I felt such peace wash over me that I shoved thoughts of the dead crow from my mind. I stepped off the deck and wandered to where Sweet Pea was busy sniffing around a small tool shed. I wasn't sure it was part of Earl's property.

"C'mon, girl. Leave that alone."

Sweet Pea looked at me and didn't move. Each time I stepped closer to her, she stepped closer to the shed until we both were in front of it. I held my breath, flung open the wooden door, and peeked inside. Several empty plastic water bottles were scattered on the floor. I headed back to the deck, and Sweet Pea reluctantly followed me. She periodically paused and looked over her shoulder at the toolshed.

When Isabella joined me on the deck, I asked, "What would you like to do today?"

"I wanna see where Nica lives. She invited us. Do you know where she lives?"

"No, I don't. But I can check with Coyote."

I reached him on his cell, and he greeted me enthusiastically. "Everything okay?"

"Yes, no more disturbances."

"I guess we can't meet today, right?"

"What do you mean?"

"Aren't you helping Miguel with the kids?"

My face burned. I hadn't even given that a thought. "I don't know. I'll have to call him."

"Just let me know, okay?"

I punched in Miguel's number and held my breath. He picked up.

"Good morning, Miguel. It's Rosie calling to see if I can give you a hand with the kids today. I'm assuming Maria's not home."

He gave a short, bitter laugh. "Did you forget Maria is Mexican? The hospital gave her and the baby a once-over and sent them home."

"May I talk to her, please?"

A few minutes later, Maria said, "Hi, Rosie. I actually could use your help. I wonder if you and Isabella could come for a little while and help with the boys. Later, my sister will be here to get dinner."

"Sure thing. How's the baby?"

"She's fine … even slept through the night. I think the later babies know they have to," she chuckled.

I agreed we'd come in time for lunch. I'd bring sandwiches from one of the cafes. Before that, we'd visit Grandmother to see if she had greater insight regarding the dead crow and who might be behind it. Also, we'd get directions to their Pueblo.

We left Sweet Pea behind—much to her dismay—for there'd be enough confusion at Maria's without her there. We found Nica sitting with Grandmother when we arrived at the Palace of the Governors. The girls raced toward each other and hugged. Grandmother and I just smiled as we watched them.

"Good morning, my daughter. Come sit."

I flopped down and leaned into her, comfortable beside her. I asked, "So, Grandmother, although you're always here, where exactly do you put your head at night?"

She patted my hand. "We live in the Pueblo of Tesuque, about 10 miles north of Santa Fe. It's at the Sangre de Cristo Mountains base in the Pojoaque Valley." At my look of confusion, she added, "You can't miss it. Many signs will guide you there. It's become quite a tourist attraction."

I quietly asked Grandmother's permission for Nica to join us for lunch. Grandmother agreed and said, "Nica, do you want to join Isabella for lunch at Angela's house?"

"Oh, yes, Grandmother!"

I kissed Grandmother on both cheeks, and the girls did the same. As we drove away, I remembered I hadn't asked Grandmother about the crow.

CHAPTER 8

When we got to Maria's house, it was plain to see she was exhausted. "The boys behave so much better for their father," she sighed.

I watched the boys run around full of energy, and I could understand why Angela was also losing patience with them. We heard Rosa cry lustily, hungry, wanting to be fed. We all stopped and looked at each other before we inched our way closer to the bassinet. We watched as her tiny arms waved wildly, and her little face got all red and puckered up. She looked so demanding and out of sorts that we all laughed.

"Who's ready for lunch?" I asked.

"I am!" cried each little boy.

In a very grown-up voice, Isabella said, "Mama, I've got this. You sit with Maria and the baby. We girls will handle everything."

Maria and I listened to the girls giggle in the kitchen. It was a pleasant sound that pleased Maria as much as me. "I haven't heard Angela laugh so much in a long time. The girls are good together, aren't they?"

After lunch, Maria began to nod off. "Why don't you take a nap? I'll watch the kids," I suggested.

"I think I will," she agreed, relief in her eyes.

We carried the bassinet into her bedroom, and I covered Maria with a blanket I took from the bottom of the bed. I went to find the girls. "Why don't you take the boys outside to play?"

"Yeah, let's go," Isabella readily agreed.

"Stay in the front yard where I can see you, okay?"

"I get the ball first," yelled Armando, the oldest boy.

"Then it's my turn!" demanded Riccardo, next in age.

"Me too," said little Miguel.

The girls looked at each other and just shook their heads.

While they played ball tag outside, I got out my laptop and read my emails. I wanted to ensure Sarah at *Women Living Well* magazine received my article for the following month. I was relieved to see she had.

I had a disappointing email from Romano, my dear chef friend from the Purple Passion Lounge. We were paired in creating a high-end restaurant and a new building for the agency that helped human trafficking victims—the same agency I was working with regarding Isabella's case. Both buildings were under construction on the land that once held the Purple Passion Lounge.

Romano wrote that clearing the property for the new building to house the agency was delayed. Since I was the overseer for that part of the project, I would need to monitor what was happening, or the whole thing wouldn't meet our deadline. I sighed and closed my computer.

I rested my head against the couch and began to nod off. It was so peaceful … until it wasn't. I came fully awake at a loud cry of agony. I jumped out of my seat and ran to the front door. I saw little Miguel on the ground, screaming and holding his right knee. The other kids circled him but parted as I raced forward to discover he had scraped his knee. I knelt, held him close, and tried to quiet him. Angela explained he was probably overtired because he usually napped every afternoon. I watched as little Miguel put his thumb in his mouth and began to suck it, confirming what she'd said.

I picked him up and started to carry him inside when I felt a chill and looked to see the dreaded neighbor watching us. "Can't control those kids, I see," he hollered, trying to goad me.

I ignored him and continued toward the house. The rest of the kids silently followed me inside.

After putting little Miguel down for a nap, I felt drained. How did Maria do it? Even more so, how was she able to handle two more children?

Maria awoke from her nap, and since I knew her sister was on her way, I corralled Isabella and Nica to go back to Grandmother.

We dropped Nica off and headed back to the rental house. "Can I take Sweet Pea for a walk, Mama?"

"Just out back, sweetheart. I don't want you to wander."

"Okay, Mama."

The phone rang. I was glad to see it was my dear friend and lawyer, Susannah, from Boston, calling. I'd asked her for information regarding Isabella's plight. "Rosie, I have news regarding Isabella's status in the United States. There are specific laws in place regarding her situation as a child-trafficking victim. As you know, agencies hold these children in unique or foster homes until they locate their family or some family members. Hold on; I've got some notes here.

"Let me read some of them to you. 'The United Nations established a resolution adopted by the General Assembly wherein it encourages the states to use the most suitable forms of alternative care, keeping in mind their cultural background and religion.' As in the case of Isabella, 'they are encouraged to reconnect them to their family, but only if they are not at risk of being denied a nurturing environment. Each case should be viewed as a case-by-case situation.' And we know Isabella wouldn't be safe if returned to her mother in Mexico."

"Oh my," I said, contemplating what Susannah said.

Susannah continued, "This is quite long and fascinating in its details—all to do with the alternative care of not being raised in the original family home. I'll send you a copy. That is the first bit of information my contact gave me. She's looking into more."

"Thanks, Susannah, I greatly appreciate it."

"So that you know, you need to be aware that most of these children have their trauma to deal with. Many have been abused in all sorts of ways, including sexually. Has Isabella shown any signs of abuse?"

"I'm observing her. I've noticed she stays out of Miguel's way—you can tell she wants nothing to do with him. Isabella proclaims she doesn't miss her parents or Mexico the few times she's spoken to Maria about it. However, I've noticed her sadness when she's around her aunt. I think Isabella misses her mother, although the circumstances in Mexico were far from ideal. She refuses to talk about it, and when I've tried to bring it up, it only makes her confirm that I'm her mother now."

With concern in her voice, Susannah said, "Hearing that, I must say, as a lawyer and your friend, that's an issue for both of you needing to be addressed very soon because it's obvious how close you two are becoming. Let's hope Isabella will be assimilated into her new family quickly."

I agreed.

CHAPTER 9

A fter dinner, I researched the Tesuque pueblo while Isabella sat and watched TV with Sweet Pea nestled beside her. She amazed me. It was strange that Isabella appeared so well adjusted—so strong and sure of herself, exuding love and an unusual peace. Her understanding of life was usually found in someone much older.

The more I read about Tesuque, the more I became excited about seeing it. Tears slid down my cheeks. What was it about being close to the Native American culture that made me so emotional? It was as if a part of me had been lost and found again. I wiped away my tears and continued reading.

The following day, we piled into the car, and I shared some of what I'd learned about the Tesuque Pueblo with

Isabella. I told her to be on the lookout for Camel Rock, the entrance to the Pueblo.

Soon, I heard her yell, "There it is, Mama!" As she pointed it out, she rose from her seat. "Oh, it does look like a camel, doesn't it?"

I laughed, and we pulled into the parking lot. "Grandmother said they would be waiting for us in the plaza."

As soon as we exited the car, Nica ran toward us. Grandmother was seated on the small wall surrounding the fountain in the center of the square. She waved as she waited for us to come closer. Again, she reminded me of my grandmother.

Grandmother stood up as we drew near. The girls chattered away while Sweet Pea dutifully sat and waited. "Good morning, Grandmother. What a beautiful morning it is. Have you been waiting long for us to arrive?"

"Good morning, my daughter. Being out in nature is always pleasant—she assures us we are never alone."

"What a beautiful place this is! Look at those old buildings. It looks like one big apartment building, the way some places are stacked on top of one another. Do you live in one of them, Grandmother?"

"No, my child," she chuckled. "Coyote bought several newer condos farther in. I live in a large one with Nica and her mother. My daughter's husband died of the disease a few years back," she added as if to explain why she lived with her daughter.

"Disease?"

"Alcoholism."

"Oh."

"Do you want to see where we live, especially since Isabella will spend some time there?" she asked.

58

Goosebumps covered my body as I thought about my vision of calling out for Isabella. I was pretty sure my dream took place here.

Grandmother saw my hesitation. "Is there anything wrong, my child?"

"No," I answered, pushing away my worry. We followed a small dirt path and roadway from the plaza's center to a small development that would be hard to see from a distance because the houses fit into the landscape so well. The condos were stucco, single-story homes in the earth tones popular in Santa Fe. They looked like replicas from the past, but as we got closer, it was easy to see they were pretty new, with enough age to give them an added charm.

"Here's ours. Coyote is around the corner. Come on in."

When we entered, Isabella peeked in from behind me. "Look, Mama; their fireplace is the same as ours was at the hotel. Oh, look at all the beautiful pottery, Mama. So pretty." She turned to me, smiling.

I was as excited as she was to see such a charming place, filled with different aspects of what Mother Nature provided as the basis for all the creativity wrought here. It, indeed, was spectacular in all its simplicity.

"Do you want to see my room?" asked Nica.

"I want the full tour," I said as I followed behind her. I looked inside her bedroom, saw twin beds, and wondered whether she shared this room with Grandmother.

Then, Nica said, "Grandmother's and my mother's rooms are down the hall."

I felt such relief to know when Isabella did visit, she'd have her own space, so to speak, unlike at Angela's house.

We returned down the hall into the kitchen/dining room area, where Grandmother was brewing tea. "Sit, my daughter. Girls, why don't you take Sweet Pea outside?

Nica, you can show Isabella some of your favorite places. Here, take some water with you."

She had already poured some into a bowl for Sweet Pea, who happily lapped it. The girls grabbed their bottles of water and rushed out. Sweet Pea hurriedly took a few more laps of water and then raced to the open door with her leash dragging behind her.

"I've steeped some special tea for us."

"That sounds wonderful," I said as I picked up my cup and took a sip. "What kind of tea is this, Grandmother? It has a funny taste."

"Wait! Don't drink it all before I explain. It has some special herbs. If you're willing, it will show us our past life together. Are you ready for that?"

"I've been wondering about that myself. The girls are okay, then?"

"Yes, Nica knows her way around. They'll be fine."

"Then let's do it."

We held hands—her gnarled fingers in mine—and each took several sips.

I saw us together in a flash, plucking herbs from a forested area. She was my mother, and I was her daughter, about nine. She kept pointing out what to pick and what not to do. "You need to pay attention, Little Bird. You need to keep your head out of the clouds and stop daydreaming, do you understand?" she asked me as she continued bending toward the ground and her task of gathering herbs and mushrooms.

"Yes, Mother."

"And watch your little sister too. I don't want her eating Anything bad."

"Yes, Mother."

"I know it's not easy for you. You are like your name—not part of the earth, always flying in the clouds in your mind."

"It's so difficult to concentrate, Mother, when so many people are inside my head."

"Shhh. Don't say that to anyone else, hear me?"

"I know. You have taught me well."

We went along and picked more herbs until suddenly, she turned and faced me. "Where's your little sister?"

"Right there!" I said as I turned around and saw no one in sight. "Little One, where are you?" I hollered.

Knowing she shouldn't be that far behind us, we began to run back the way we had come. When we reached her, we stopped in shock when we saw her lying on the ground with staring, lifeless eyes as a poisonous snake slithered away. When I looked down at her, I saw the face of Isabella, and I began to scream.

Then all went black.

"Wake up, my child. All is well." She squeezed my hand. "I'm so sorry for upsetting you like that. When I first laid eyes on you, I knew we'd had a past life together. I wanted to make sure it was what I thought it was so we could move forward to clear any karma between us. I've waited a long time for you to appear," she said, holding me close. "Tell me what you saw, and I'll do the same."

What we both experienced in our visions was nearly identical. It became clear that the three of us were entwined in this lifetime too. That allowed Grandmother and me to save my sister—Isabella—from any danger at this time in her life. That made sense since I felt compelled to keep Isabella safe at any cost. If all turned out well, the karma for each from that experience would be cleared, especially for Grandmother, who had blamed me for her daughter's death instead of taking some responsibility for what'd happened.

Grandmother pulled me from my chair, led me to the couch, and held me close. She placed her arm around me and guided my head against her shoulder while I tried to stop my tears. She made soothing sounds and sang an old Indian tune that comforted me. "My daughter, you must remember, we are here to experience all of life, even the sad parts. So please know how much I love and honor you for your journey. I am here beside you to help you however I can."

She began humming the same Indian tune again. "Grandmother, I need you to help keep Isabella safe," I pleaded.

"Don't let your negative energy of worry over Isabella seep into her being. You have lived many lifetimes believing and knowing that all is as it should be. Do you understand, my daughter?"

I nodded and knew she was right. Then the girls and Sweet Pea burst through the door, and Isabella immediately sensed something had happened. "What's wrong, Mama?"

"Not a thing, sweetheart. Just reminiscing about living here in the past," I answered without cloaking my words.

She stopped and stared at me. "I've been here before, too, haven't I?"

Grandmother squeezed my hand tight. "Yes, sweetheart, I believe you have been."

"Good. I thought so." She came forward and hugged us.

Nica joined us, smiling. "It's a group hug, Grandmother."

"Yes, it is, my child." Grandmother picked up Sweet Pea from the floor where she had been dancing around and enfolded her in our group.

After we pulled apart, I collected myself as best as I could. "How about we go back to the plaza and shop?"

We went from one store to another and bought a few items. I wondered why I'd needed to experience what happened when Isabella had been Little One and I, her older sister. She caught me staring at her. "What? What is it, Mama? You look so sad."

"Nothing, Little One," I answered, unconsciously using her former name.

Isabella ran off to join Nica. Grandmother rose from where she sat on a bench outside the store, grabbed my hand for support, and leaned toward me. "My daughter, looking back at the past is to understand your choices better today. Spending too much time thinking about the past keeps you locked in its energy and doesn't allow you to live your moments freely today. Do you understand?"

I nodded and hugged her. "Ready to go to Santa Fe?"

CHAPTER 10

We climbed into the car with Grandmother's basket and a roll of jewelry for sale. We waited for Nica, who'd returned to the house to gather some clothing because she would spend the night with Isabella and me. The girls were hoping to have Angela join them, but I wasn't sure she'd be able to with the new baby. Her mother might need her help.

I parked the car beside the Palace of the Governors and helped Grandmother out. I returned to the car after getting her settled and saying goodbye to the girls and Sweet Pea. My thoughts of the past floated in my head. I looked up, and my heart stopped. The neighbor was leaning against my car.

"Hi, pretty lady."

"What do you want? Get away from my car."

"Or what'll you do? Call your boyfriend sheriff to come and rescue you?"

I ignored him. I entered the car, locked the doors, and turned the key. He came around to the driver's side and tapped on my window. He looked at me with menace and said loud enough to hear, "Remember what I said …."

I tore away in anger. What a repulsive man! Yes, I certainly would tell the sheriff about this. There had to be something he could do about this man. I drove to the police station only to discover Coyote had been called out for a dispute between two neighbors fighting over water rights. With nothing else to do, I drove back to the house.

When I pulled into the driveway, I searched the front door, half-expecting to see another dead crow. But there was nothing. I'd been holding my breath and slowly exhaled, feeling lighter. When I reached the front door, I saw it was slightly ajar. My heart began to pound. I poked at the door with my shoe, and it opened more without making a sound. I stepped into the small hallway, waited, and listened. I heard movement in the back of the house, but I was close enough to the open front door to escape if necessary. I took a deep breath and hollered, "Anyone home?"

I heard more movement. Next came the sound of the sliding glass door opening, followed by someone running off the deck. I moved cautiously forward and hoped it had been just one person. When I entered the kitchen, I saw my large Dooney & Bourke bag on the floor, turned upside down, its contents spilling. Whoever it was must have thought it was my purse with my wallet inside rather than my carry-on with extra items. As I neared it, I saw the tarot cards upended on the floor, and right on top was the Death card. I shivered and knew I'd been warned—there would be another death.

I reached for my cell phone to call Coyote but thought better. I quickly searched the house, and it appeared nothing was taken. It was too late to apprehend the intruder because I felt sure he was now long gone. What could Coyote do anyway? I opened the refrigerator to grab a bottle of spring water and was surprised to see the empty fridge. I realized the break-in had been about more than money— he was after food. The phone rang and pulled me from my thoughts. I smiled when I saw it was Mike calling.

"Hey, how goes it?" he asked.

"It's going all right, I guess ...."

"Did you get Isabella situated with her family?"

"That's going to take some time yet, I'm afraid."

He'd heard me express doubt about Isabella's situation before, so now he said, "You need to remember what you're there for, right, Rosie?"

"I know. How's your case going?"

"It's like gum to a shoe ... we can't seem to get it done. We've come so close but haven't been able to get enough on the guy we know committed the crime. We had his place wired, and we've been tailing him and have done all the other things we need to. It's a matter of time, though, and he'll slip up."

"Good. Does that mean you'll be here soon?"

"That's why I'm calling. I should be there in a couple of days."

His words put a smile on my face. I went outside to sit on the deck. I drew in several deep breaths as I collected my thoughts. I looked around, and my eyes came to rest on the toolshed in the corner of the property. Was my intruder inside, enjoying the food he'd taken from the refrigerator? I left my chair and slowly descended the deck steps toward the shed. As I got closer, I heard the noisy crunch of the small stones on the driveway. I turned and saw Coyote get out of his truck.

"Hi, Rosie."

"Good afternoon, Coyote."

"I heard I'd missed you this morning at the office, so I thought I'd stop by on my way back into town. What's going on?" He eyed me carefully. "You okay?"

I told him about the break-in, and afterward, he looked at me with concern. "Were you heading for the toolshed when I arrived?"

I blushed furiously. Even I knew it would have been a dumb thing to do alone. "I wanted to make sure nobody was living there and could bother me again," I said defensively.

He considered me. "Well then, let's go down there together and look, shall we?"

I breathed a sigh of relief. "Sure."

As we walked stealthily toward the shed, I was glad to have Coyote there. When we reached it, he was ahead of me and swung his arm wide, holding me back. Then in one swift movement, he kicked open the door and swore. "Shit!"

"What? What's the matter?" I pushed Coyote aside and peered in to see that someone had set this place up as his home. Articles from my cupboard and refrigerator were stacked against the far wall, and empty wrappers were on the floor. There was an open sleeping bag on the floor—a large teenage boy asleep on top of it.

"Damn it, Stalking Deer, get up!" demanded Coyote, lightly kicking at the boy. "Wake up, Redmond!"

The boy stirred and looked surprised to see Coyote looming over him. "Whaat?"

"You heard me. Get your lazy ass up right now."

"I'm not going back to the reservation, and you can't make me," the boy yelled.

"Being out alone won't solve your problem, Redmond, and you know it. Now get up. You're coming with me."

"Where to, Uncle Coyote?"

"Maybe a few days in jail will keep you safe and give you enough time to straighten things out …."

"You can't make me," he growled.

"You heard me … move!" roared Coyote.

I watched as Coyote stacked all the food items in his nephew's arms and guided him back to my house to return most of what he'd taken. I followed them with a few loose things. I was impressed that Coyote would tend to this detail.

Afterward, I stood on the deck as they returned to the shed, and Redmond gathered his belongings and followed Coyote to his truck. Redmond hopped inside, and Coyote tossed his things into the open bed. I walked toward the truck, and Coyote turned to me. "Call me if you need me."

CHAPTER 11

I t was time to check in with Maria. I didn't want to arrive at her doorstep with Isabella and Nica and ask whether Angela could have a sleepover with them. That wouldn't be fair. I picked up my phone. "Good afternoon, Maria. How is everything going?"

"Fine, Rosie—the baby's sleeping through most of the night, so we're all getting more rest."

"That's wonderful. Good sleep makes such a difference—I know how I get when I don't have enough sleep," I chuckled. "I'm calling to see if you'd let Angela spend tonight with Isabella and Nica at the house for a sleepover."

She hesitated.

"I don't mean to pressure you."

"I know she'd like that. Right now, though, she's helping me with the little boys until my sister arrives. What time were you thinking?"

"I can pick her up around 3:30 or so. Does that work for you?"

"That'd be good."

"I'm going to the store to pick up some milk and other things. Can I pick up anything for you while I'm out?"

"No, thank you, Rosie." I knew she didn't want to be obliged to me. "If you change your mind, just let me know, okay?"

"Thanks, Rosie."

I grabbed my purse and carefully locked up the house. Without giving it much thought, I drove to the only grocery store I'd been to. I looked around, hoping I wouldn't see the neighbor anywhere near. Luck was with me, and I went inside.

I've learned much about an area by the food the grocery store sold and promoted. Being the largest grocery store, it held almost anything anyone could want. I saw many Mexican ingredients and a large variety of ethnic food. I loaded my cart with various things, many of which I wouldn't usually buy. Since the girls were having a sleepover, some sweet stuff, and special treats were in my basket too.

I pushed my grocery cart to my car, quickly unloaded it, and left it with the others to be picked up later by one of the kids responsible for collecting them. As I backed out, I heard a commotion from behind the building. Not wanting to get caught in whatever happened there, I immediately stepped on the gas and headed out of the parking lot. As I neared the exit, an older boy ran in front of my car, and I swerved to the left, only to have the man who chased him run into the front of my car. I jammed on the brakes, came to a squealing stop, and looked up in time to see the boy smiling triumphantly as he ran away.

Filled with dread, I hurriedly got out of the car. The man lay on the ground, gasping as he tried to fill his lungs with air. I saw he wasn't hurt, and he confirmed this by holding up his hand, signifying he was all right. I stared at his hand and saw an odd tattoo across it. "Do you want me to call the police?" I asked.

His eyes widened, and he frantically shook his head. "I'm okay," he puffed. "No police."

He noticed me staring at his hand as I tried to make out the tattoo. He jerked his hand back and hid it. The more I studied him, the more he scowled at me. "It's okay now; you can scram," he panted and turned away with a slight limp.

"Are you sure you don't want me to call an ambulance?"

"No, just go!" He called over his shoulder, "I'm fine."

A few curious customers had gathered, and I made my way back to the car. Adrenaline coursed through my body and made me feel weak and sick. I'd have to be sure to report this to Coyote, but first, I needed to drop off the groceries at the house. I'd pick up the girls and Sweet Pea from Grandmother before we collected Angela for the sleepover party. It should be quite a night with the three of them chattering like magpies.

The girls reminded me of my sister-friends, and I felt this could be the same for Isabella, Nica, and Angela—something I'd love for them. And the nice thing was they'd all live close to each other. I was beginning to see that Isabella's living here in Santa Fe would have its perks.

When I tucked the girls into bed much later than usual that night, I bent down and kissed each one, beginning with Isabella. Her sweet voice said, "I love you, Mama," repeated by Nica and Angela. My eyes watered at their sweet voices of love.

"I'm leaving the nightlight on in the bathroom, so if anyone needs to get up during the night, you'll be able to see where you're going, okay?"

There was a chorus of "Thank you" as I shut their bedroom door and gave them privacy.

I had been soundly sleeping when I awoke with a start. I heard the girls as they raced out of their bedroom and headed to the kitchen. I smiled as I listened to their giggles. I rose, threw my robe around me, and went to join them. After fixing them bacon and scrambled eggs, I brewed my coffee and took a cup with me outside to the deck. I left the sliding door open and heard them whispering. The gist of what they said was something about the mean man next door. I stepped back inside and said, "Remember your pinky vows, right?"

The girls' eyes rounded as they wondered how I knew what they'd been discussing. All three nodded without saying a word. I poured a second cup of coffee and went outside to plan my day.

When I'd picked up Angela the previous afternoon, Maria had invited Isabella to spend the day with them at the house. My first thought had been to say no, but then I'd realized it was the right thing to do—let Isabella spend some alone time with her aunt, uncle, and cousins. We'd agreed that I'd pick her up at 7 o'clock after they had eaten supper. When I'd talked to her earlier, Isabella seemed hesitant about spending the day with them but finally agreed to the plan.

Later, when I dropped off Nica with Grandmother, I knew she was disappointed not to go to Angela's house, but I could do nothing about that. I drove on to Maria's, and as I pulled into their driveway, the neighbor eyed us as we got out of the car. He made a lewd gesture, which I ignored and hoped the girls hadn't seen.

Maria greeted us at the door with her finger on her lips, signaling us to be quiet. "C'mon in," she whispered. "We had a tough night last night, but the baby is finally asleep now."

I peeked inside the bassinet in the living room and saw a little rolled-up pink bundle, eyes closed.

I turned to Isabella. "Isabella? You have your cell phone with you, don't you?" I asked. "Call me if you need me."

"Yes, Mama."

"Have fun and behave." Isabella hugged me tight and tilted her face up for a kiss. I whispered in her ear, "Love you."

When she turned away, she wore a broad smile, something Maria didn't miss. Isabella grabbed Angela's hand, and they headed into her bedroom. When Maria's eyes met mine, there was a flash of complete understanding between us, as only mothers can experience. I knew without any doubt that Maria was my friend. I hugged her and left to meet with Coyote.

"Good morning," I said to the policeman at the front desk, and he flashed me a smile. I continued toward Coyote's office.

"Good morning, Coyote."

"Hey there. Come on in."

Sitting across from him, I watched his expression darken when I relayed what had happened at the grocery store. When I mentioned the man's tattoo on his hand, Coyote pulled one of the file folders piled on his desk toward him and drew the same design as the tattoo I'd seen. "Did it look something like this?"

"Yes, it sure did. Like a scorpion. What does it stand for?"

"It represents a gang set up by one of the cartels who served as border commandos for them. When they started just a few years ago, that group set up their own sting operation to eliminate the former group's members. That's how they got their name—the Scorpions—and believe me, they are as deadly as any living scorpion. Some of them have entered the United States to get rid of anyone in that former group because they felt money had been withheld from them. That's what we think might have happened to Raoul, the man down the street from Miguel."

"Sheriff!" the deputy called out as he burst into the room. "We just received a call that a man's been shot behind Albertson's Market."

"Wait! I'll go with you," I said to Coyote.

He looked confused, not sure what to do with me. "Okay, just keep up with me. Come on!"

I hopped into his vehicle and buckled up, and he pulled out of the parking lot with his siren blaring. Something inside me stirred and made my blood course with excitement. I couldn't deny it—I loved being a part of it.

Another car with the deputy and his partner followed close behind us. The ambulance had already been called, so we all arrived together.

"What have we got here?" called the ambulance driver, who ran behind Coyote.

"I'm not sure. Let's see."

I followed and gave them plenty of space to do their job. I stood inside the yellow tape that the deputy and his partner had already secured to block off the area against any voyeurs.

The medic was on the ground examining the man, shaking his head as he touched the victim's neck and searched for a pulse. When I peeked around him, I was shocked. The same man had run into my car the day before. The medic turned his head away from the victim, and I saw that the victim had been shot execution-style, leaving a clean bullet hole in his forehead. I took a deep breath in to steady my light-headedness.

The medical examiner arrived and pushed me aside. He also knelt beside the dead man and began to examine the body. Coyote turned from where he stood over them and looked at me. He raised his shoulders in question, and I knew what he wanted to know. I nodded yes; it was the man I'd told him about. I waved to Coyote and mouthed goodbye. I called Uber only to discover that one curious Uber driver was already at the scene, steps away from where the body lay.

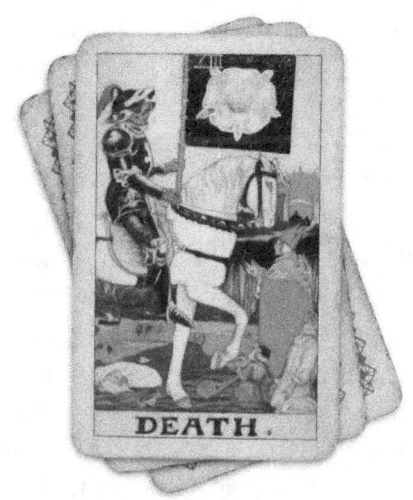

CHAPTER 12

L ater, when I arrived at Marie's to pick up Isabella, Miguel answered the door. He begrudgingly opened the door and motioned me in. "Isabella, your ride is here!"

Maria spoke to him in Spanish and stepped forward, shaking her head at his rudeness. "Rosie, please come in."

"Did everything go okay?"

Isabella rushed forward into my arms, obviously upset. "How come you never answered me, Mama?"

"What do you mean?" I asked, alarmed. "I texted you, but you never answered."

"Oh my. I never heard the phone beep, sweetie. Let's check it to see what's happened." I reached into my pants pocket to retrieve it and realized it must have slipped out of my pocket. I hoped it was in the car. "I'm so sorry."

Isabella stared at me and looked forlorn. Angela followed Isabella out and hugged Isabella goodbye. She turned to me with her arms raised for a hug. "Good night, sweetheart," I said and hugged her.

I turned to Maria. "Thanks for everything. I'll call you tomorrow, all right?"

"That'd be good." Then she hugged Isabella.

My phone was on the floor halfway under the driver's seat when we got to the car. I picked it up and checked it to see that, yes, indeed, Isabella had sent me several texts. Again, I hugged her and said, "I'm so sorry."

Isabella got into the back seat, where Sweet Pea enthusiastically greeted her. She squealed with delight, which made me chuckle. As I drove to the house, I looked at the front door and saw something hanging from the knob. It looked like another dead crow. If it were, this time, I'd call in Coyote.

True to his word, Coyote arrived and reviewed the dead crow in all its unpleasantness. He shook his head in dismay as he picked up the bird and the loose feathers. After refusing a cup of coffee, he collected the trash bag and said good night with his parting words, "Call me if you need me."

I awoke the following day to my cell phone chirping away. When I rolled over and looked at the clock, I was surprised to see it was already 7 a.m. I had slept soundly without any dreams—a nice treat.

"Good morning, Mike," I said in a cheery voice.

"Good morning, baby. I've got some good news. I'm finally done here. I have a few loose ends to complete, so I should be there tomorrow or the next day."

"That is good news. Send me your itinerary, Mike, and I'll pick you up at the airport."

"Sounds great, but renting a car in Albuquerque might be easier for us both. The woman who makes all our travel arrangements will check that out, and I'll let you know, okay? I'm looking forward to seeing you," he said in a husky voice.

"Me too. It's been too long," I agreed, my heart thudding with excitement.

"Gotta run, Rosie. Stay out of trouble until I get there, hear? Love you."

"Love you too."

"Is Mike coming here to our house, Mama?"

"Yes, sweetheart, he is. Isn't that nice?"

"Yeesss, Mama, it is!"

My mind began to race ... how could I have Mike stay here? I now had Isabella to think of. What kind of mother, even a temporary one, brings her boyfriend home when a child is involved? It was fine when Mike stayed at my townhouse in Las Vegas. He'd been my security guard and slept in his separate bedroom. But now that things were changing between us, what was the correct protocol?

I went into my bedroom and called Maria as I promised to do. I knew how important it was for Isabella to spend more time with her family. Maria suggested it was Isabella's turn to spend the night with them. I had to admit that if Isabella lived there permanently, she would be lucky to have Maria as her foster mother. I just wished Isabella had more space so she'd feel she belonged there. Miguel? Was he capable of loving her as much as he did his children? Was I worried about nothing?

I went back into the kitchen. "Isabella? Come here, sweetheart. I need to talk to you."

"What is it, Mama?

"Maria has invited you to spend the night with them. I'm going to drop you off around 5 o'clock, and then you'll eat dinner there and have an overnight with Angela afterward."

"No, Mama. I don't want to go there tonight, pleeease."

"Isabella, I'm afraid you don't have a choice," I stated in a low but firm voice. "You know the agreement we have. I'm here in Santa Fe with you so you can get to know your aunt, uncle, and cousins. They are your family," I reasoned.

"No, Mama, you and Sweet Pea are my family, not them," she insisted.

I drew in a long, frustrated breath. "Isabella, I need you to stop that! You are here because your real family is here. They're nice people, and they want you to live with them. Please understand that, and don't make this more difficult than it is."

Her dark eyes drilled into mine, never wavering. "I asked Grandmother what it means to be a family. She told me it means people who are part of your heart or soul. So, Mama, you are my family … not them."

I looked at her, speechless. She stared at me. Then her voice wobbled, "Don't you love me, Mama?" She plopped down in the chair beside me, hunched over, and began crying earnestly. When she got up, her nose dripped, and spittle flew from her mouth as she choked out, "Don't you want me?"

My eyes filled as I reached out and took her in my arms. "Of course. I love you, Isabella, and I'd be honored to have you as my daughter," I spoke softly as my heart broke into pieces, "but the problem is how the laws are set up; it's impossible. I'm afraid you and I don't get to choose."

"Why not, Mama?"

Why not, indeed? I thought. I pulled her down onto my lap. She sat stiffly and then began to pull away in anger. I reached around and gently pulled her head against my shoulder. Out of nowhere, I began to hum the same Indian song that Grandmother had sung to me. I felt her start to relax against me as I stroked her hair. "Hush, Little One. We must let things work out as they will be, understand?"

"I'll go, but I don't want to!" she said crossly.

I left Sweet Pea the following day and drove to Maria's to pick up Isabella. After saying thank you and goodbye, we climbed into the car and took off for the rental property. When we drove into the driveway, much to our surprise, Mike stood on the front porch, studying something dark in his hand. My heart fell when I saw what it was. Instead of running and wrapping my arms around him, I gingerly stepped forward. "Hey there, Mike."

He jumped a mile. I'd scared him. He hadn't heard us pull up. His eyes lit up when he saw me, and he instantly scowled as he looked first at me and then at the dead crow he held in his hands.

"You don't seem surprised to see this. What's this all about, Rosie?" he demanded. "Has this happened before?"

"Yes," I nodded. "Come inside, and we can talk about it there."

"First, let me throw this thing in the garbage. Is it out back?"

"I'll show you where it is and the outside faucet so you can wash your hands and give me one of your best hugs."

He smiled. "Lead the way."

Seeing that Mike was upset, Isabella remained leaning against the car. As Mike passed her on his way to the back, he said, "Hi, Isabella; how are you? You look like you've grown!

83

After washing his hands, Mike moved close enough for our bodies to melt into one another. With smoldering eyes, he lifted my chin. Mike bent down, and our lips met urgently, sending sparks all along my body, resting in my feminine. His kiss expressed all the hunger for me he'd put aside while he had playacted as my boyfriend and security guard. Being wrapped in his strong arms and held close felt so good. I sniffed his neck and breathed in his scent—the great outdoors with a touch of pine. After another long, delicious kiss that was so unlike our perfunctory pretend kisses, we pulled apart and returned to the front. I knew we must look a sight because Isabella grinned at us.

I explained to Mike about the dead crow and what it meant. Then, he emphatically declared, "I don't like the idea of you girls being here alone. It's not safe. I will cancel my hotel reservation and stay here as long as this happens."

"What about Brian? Is he with you?"

"He's decided to stay in Boston. He may come later. So that settles it then, right? I'll be staying here."

"But ..." I was wondering about the protocol of having him stay in the house with Isabella here.

"I mean it, Rosie, and I don't want to hear you say, 'I don't need anyone to protect me.' This is not the time for that. No messing around with this stuff."

"I agree," I said, much to Mike's surprise.

"Okay, then. I'll get my suitcase and bring it in."

CHAPTER 13

After Isabella was tucked in for the night, Mike and I cuddled on the couch, getting used to each other more romantically. It wasn't as awkward as I thought it might be. Mike had already agreed to sleep on the couch. He'd been the one to suggest it.

"How long are you able to stay?" I asked, wondering whether he'd soon be pulled away again by his most prominent client.

"I'm taking some vacation time for the next few days. Why? Trying to get rid of me already?" he teased.

"Hardly," I chuckled.

It felt good to have Mike's arm around me as he pulled me closer. I became caught up in the moment and nestled into him, feeling loved and safe. Our lips were hungry for each other, and our kisses took my breath away. Finally, I pushed against him, "Oh my, enough of this. It's a good thing you're sleeping on the couch tonight."

Mike laughed. "We could change that, you know."

I got up and looked at his handsome, smiling face, and it was hard for me to think he was the same man I'd first met when he became my security guard and protector. He was so relaxed and carefree now, unlike the reserved, self-controlled man who'd seemed mysterious—as if he were holding onto an underlying story yet to be told. Yes, although we needed time to get to know each other better, I liked what I saw.

I kissed him. "Sweet dreams, Mike."

The following day, I awoke to the delicious smell of coffee brewing. I rolled over and stretched with pleasure, loving that Mike had everything under control again. I heard Sweet Pea's paws dancing on the tile floor, and I knew she was as happy as me to have Mike around again.

I got up, wrapped my robe around me, and headed to the kitchen. "Good morning, sleepyhead. Here you go, my queen, your coffee."

"Thanks, Mike."

"Where are you going?" he asked as I approached the sliding glass door.

"Outside on the deck. It's too nice to stay inside. Come join me."

"So what exactly has been going on here, Rosie? I can tell there's been more than finding dead crows on your door. I want you to level with me, hear?"

I told him about Maria's next-door neighbor and the times I'd been in contact with him. Mike rose out of his chair and demanded in a loud whisper, "You didn't tell me this before … why?"

"Calm down; there's more." I was determined to tell him everything, including that the neighbor had been in the alley and possibly mixed up in the shooting at Albertson's. Then I explained that he'd threatened me to keep quiet about what I'd seen and not to go to the police.

Mike was thoughtful. "So what did the police say? You did go to the police, right?"

Then I remembered I'd told Coyote about the shooting at Albertson's. Still, we'd been interrupted when he'd received a phone call, which had made it impossible for me to go into the details of the neighbors' threats against Isabella and me. When I'd dropped the girls off with Grandmother and had gone to tell Coyote about more dangers, he'd been out of the office settling the water dispute. Then the deal with his nephew in the shed took priority. I realized I hadn't fully disclosed all the threats to him yet. My face flushed.

"Rosie?" Mike prodded.

"I told Coyote about most of them, but each time, we were interrupted, so I'm not sure how much he knows about all the threats."

"Who is this dude, anyway?" Mike snapped. "Doesn't he know how to do his job and get all the details of a disturbance?"

I immediately went on the defensive, which made Mike raise his eyebrows. "Coyote's the sheriff and a good one, too," I said. "I think you should meet him. I think you'll like him."

"What does that have to do with his investigating methods? What does he say about the dead crows? You have spoken to him about that, haven't you?" It was apparent he was frustrated with me.

"Hold on, Mike! You're putting me in the position of defending myself and Coyote too." I stood up and faced him.

Mike's expression softened. He lowered his voice, "I'm just worried about you."

"Mike, I don't want you to worry about me. You need to treat me as your partner—your equal partner. Instead, you act like I'm your responsibility and you are my boss. That doesn't work for me. We work together or not at all!"

Mike ran his hands through his hair and glowered at me. I returned his stare, unwilling to back down. Finally, he stepped forward and wrapped me in his arms. "God, Rosie, I just want you safe, understand?"

"Of course, I understand because I want the same for you." I pulled back from him so we were eye-to-eye. "Maybe now you'll begin to understand I want the same for Isabella as well. I'm determined not to have anything bad happen to her, you know?"

"I know," he said as he pulled me closer.

"Do you?" I asked in a voice muffled against his shirt, wondering whether he knew what that might mean.

He didn't say anything, but he tightened his arms around me.

CHAPTER 14

I sabella wandered out, and I wrapped her in my arms. Mike fixed his special eggs for us, and when we sat down, I said, "There's the Loretto Chapel downtown that I thought we'd all like to see. It has a mysterious staircase featured in an Unsolved Mysteries episode. They don't know who the builder was, the type of wood used, or its construction's physics."

"How come they don't know that?" asked Isabella.

I reached for the brochure on the kitchen counter and read, "*When the Loretto Chapel was completed in 1878, there was no way to access the choir loft 20 feet above. Carpenters were called in to address the problem, but they all concluded access to the loft would have to be via ladder, as a staircase would interfere with the interior space of the small chapel. Legend says that to find a solution to the seating problem, the Sisters of the Chapel made a novena to St. Joseph, the patron saint of carpenters. On the ninth and final day of prayer, a man appeared at the chapel with a donkey and a toolbox, looking for work. Months later, the elegant circular staircase was completed, and the carpenter disappeared without pay or thanks. After searching for the man—they even ran an ad in the local newspaper— and finding no trace of him, some concluded that he was St. Joseph himself, having come in answer to the sisters' prayers. The stairway's carpenter, whoever he was, built a magnificent structure. The design was innovative for the time, and some of the design considerations still perplex experts today. The staircase has two 360-degree turns and no visible means of support. It is said that the staircase was built without nails—only wooden pegs. Questions also surround the number of stair risers relative to the height of the choir loft and about the types of wood and other materials used in the stairway's construction."*

"That sounds cool. I want to see it!" exclaimed Isabella. I turned to Mike. "I think you'd like to see the chapel too. Then we could walk to Coyote's office, which isn't far from there."

Mike nodded in agreement, then reached over and tousled Isabella's hair. "When are you going to introduce me to your family?"

A cloud covered her face, and with dark eyes flashing, she announced, "You're looking at it." She got up from the table and stomped away. "You're so stupid, Mike," she called over her shoulder.

"Cripes, what did I say?" asked Mike, looking first at me and then at Isabella's back in confusion.

I rose from the table and bent to kiss the top of Mike's head. "You'll see ...."

After Mike's shower, he found me still in the kitchen with a second cup of coffee. "Are you going to get ready?"

"Sure," I said. "There's still some more coffee. Want a cup?"

"Naw, one is enough for me. Where's Isabella?"

"I imagine in her room. I'll check on her, shower, and be with you shortly."

I knocked on Isabella's bedroom door. "May I come in?"

"Yes, Mama."

"Hi, sweetheart. Are you almost ready?"

"Yup," she answered with a smile.

"I'm going to take a quick shower, and then I'll be ready too."

I watched Isabella braid her hair and noticed she wasn't wearing her bear bracelet. "Isabella, where's the bracelet Grandmother gave you?"

"Oh, I didn't feel like wearing it today."

I fought down the fear of anything happening to her. "It's so pretty, and remember Grandmother said you should always wear it."

"Okay, Mama, I will. I promise I'll never take it off, okay?" she smiled.

I smiled back and gave her a thumbs-up before holding my pinky up in the air. Maybe I was making too much of everything surrounding Isabella's safety. It was time to loosen up a bit.

I hurriedly showered, dressed, and put on the new necklace I'd bought while shopping at the Pueblo. It was beautiful in its simplicity. The saleslady at the store called it "Indian Pearls," a simple necklace of silver beads strung like pearls with each bead shaded, emphasizing its roundness. It was beautiful and the perfect necklace to hold a slide to give it a different appearance. I looked forward to finding just the right piece for it. Maybe today I'd see one I liked.

We paid and stood in line to enter the Loretto Chapel. When it was our turn to go inside, we followed a short hallway into the chapel, which opened up to high ceilings. The chapel was magnificent, but what we mainly had come to see was the spiral staircase, which drew everyone to it. It seemed impossible that it was natural and functional. It might as well be called the floating staircase, for it appeared angelic as if it had been dropped from heaven.

I watched Isabella as she stepped forward and touched the winding staircase, putting her hand on the handrail and looking up in awe. When I went to move her back from the roped-off area, she turned to me with a radiant face. "This is the most beautiful thing, isn't it, Mama? It's like being close to heaven."

I held her hand and looked up. "It's as if angels live up there, right?"

"Yes, Mama, yes."

Afterward, we wended our way to meet Grandmother before seeing Coyote. As soon as Mike saw the Indians gathered at the Palace of the Governors, he said, "That's so cool they're allowed to sell their wares there. What a great idea."

I took Mike's hand and led him to Grandmother. She studied him. When he came closer, her eyes lit up, and she smiled broadly. He returned the smile and said, "Good morning, Grandmother. Your spirit is bright today."

She chortled and said, "And you are very handsome. What brings you here?"

Mike remained silent until Grandmother lifted her brows in question. "My queen," he said, a slight bow toward me.

She smiled. "Good choice," a phrase so unlike her Indian expressions that we all laughed.

"Come, my daughter, join me," Grandmother said.

I complied, and Mike said, "I'm going to look around, okay?"

"Sure."

I watched Mike approach the small girls. Isabella was no longer irritated with him and proudly introduced him to Nica. "This is Mike, Mama's boyfriend. He's going to help us with Angela's bad neighbor."

"Ooooh," Nica said, obviously entranced. She became starry-eyed as she reviewed Mike's good looks, much as Isabella had done with Coyote. Mike bent down and talked to the girls, and they nodded. Then he patted each on the head and went to look at all the jewelry for sale. The girls tagged along behind him. Each time Mike picked up a piece, he'd show it to them, and they either nodded in agreement or pushed his hand away.

Then Mike and the girls headed our way. Mike grinned as the girls ran ahead with Isabella shouting, "Mama, you must see these. They are so beautiful, and you get to choose!"

Mike held out both closed hands to me. "Here, my queen, pick one."

"What if she doesn't pick the one you chose for her?" asked Nica.

"I'm sure she'll pick the right one for her," answered Mike with a knowing glance toward me.

I closed my eyes to see which one had the more incredible energy in my mind's eye, and I immediately tapped his right fist. I was floored when he opened it to let me know what he held. It was an exquisite pendant slide, a high-end piece with inlaid mother-of-pearl, onyx, and turquoise. It was a figure of a bear, the shape not unlike the one Isabella had on her bracelet.

"Oh, Mike, it's stunning, absolutely gorgeous!"

"We helped pick it out, Mama. Isn't it beautiful? That's the one I thought you'd pick."

Mike just smiled. "I wanted you to have something to remember me by, Rosie."

"What do you mean?" Worry creased my brow.

"When I'm not with you, I want you to be able to look at this and know I love you," he said tenderly as his face heated up. I was surprised to hear him voice any endearment in front of the others because he was such a private person.

"Thank you, Mike. This means so much to me."

"Did you know the bear stands for strength and power—the power to protect yourself?" He looked deep into my eyes, and I understood he was trying to keep me as safe as I was trying to keep Isabella safe. In a flash, our minds met, and the energy of love flowing between us didn't need words.

"It's like mine, Mama!" exclaimed Isabella as she held up her arm to put her bracelet next to my more significant piece. A mischievous grin crossed her face. "Don't you want to see the other piece?"

I laughed. "Sure, why not?"

Mike opened his other hand and inside was another beautiful but uncomplicated piece in the form of a sun with a large turquoise in the center. As pretty as it was, it could not compare to the bear.

"Oh, that's very pretty, but I love the piece I have."

Mike smiled as I unclasped my necklace and slid the pendant onto it. Mike went back to the artist who created both pieces. When I saw Grandmother's eyes widen in appreciation of its artistry, I knew how stunning my piece was.

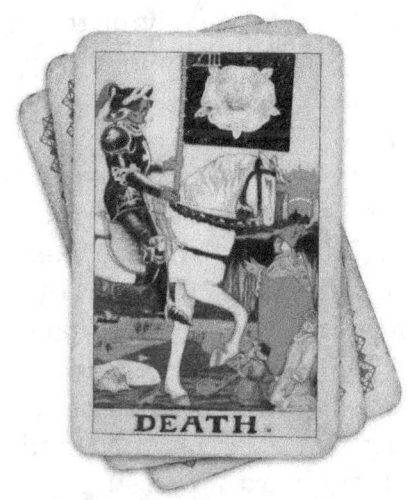

CHAPTER 15

We told Grandmother that we were headed to see Coyote. She flashed me a look. "Nica would like to have Isabella stay here with us today. Is that all right with you, my daughter?"

I chuckled, knowing she was being polite in asking. The girls had already made their plan to be together. "That'd be lovely, Grandmother." I stuffed a few bills in her hand. "That's for lunch."

Grandmother nodded in appreciation. We said goodbye and walked to Coyote's office. When we arrived, the policeman, who now seemed a fixture at the front desk, eyed Mike appraisingly as we approached.

"Coyote's expecting us," I said.

He tipped his head toward the back. "He's there. Go on back."

Mike assessed the setup of having the police and sheriff offices in the same small building, and when we reached Coyote's small office, he stopped and gestured me into the office before him.

Coyote stood up when he saw us and moved around his desk. He looked first at me and then at Mike.

"Hi, Coyote. I'd like you to meet Mike." I stepped aside to let Mike squeeze through closer to Coyote.

"Hi there," Mike said as he shook hands with Coyote.

"Welcome to Santa Fe," Coyote answered.

They were about the same height—6'2"—and looked alike with their tanned skin, dark hair, and eyes. It amused me to watch each apply extra pressure to their handshake. I chuckled to myself. You had to love testosterone.

Mike asked Coyote, "I have some questions about a few things happening here. Can we talk?"

At hearing that, I said. "I'll leave you two alone. I've got a few errands to run. I'll meet you back at Grandmother's spot in an hour. Does that work for you guys?"

I wanted to find a small market to buy prime beef tenderloin steaks for tomorrow night. I didn't want to return to Albertson's because of all that had happened there, but it was the only place large enough to have what I wanted.

I exited the car, grabbed an empty basket, and entered the store. After piling the grocery cart with what we needed and some extra treats, I checked out. While I waited in line, I saw Coyote's nephew— the one who had been my intruder—talking to a man in the parking lot. It looked as though the man had passed him some money. Then the woman behind me pulled on my sleeve and asked, "What type of flowers do you think my friend will like?" giving me a choice between two bunches of flowers that she held out to me.

When I looked back outside, Coyote's nephew was still there, but the other man was gone. Chills covered my body. It would have been difficult for anyone to identify the man from that distance, especially since his back was to me. Although I couldn't recognize him, something about him seemed familiar. Coyote's nephew was also gone when I got through the line and ready to leave.

I decided that the easiest way to introduce Mike to Isabella's family was to keep it simple by having Angela join us for dinner that night. I called Maria, and she agreed. Later, Isabella, Mike, and I pulled into Miguel and Maria's driveway. The neighbor came outside and hung around when he saw us, curious.

Mike got out of the car and shouted, "Hello."

The neighbor yelled, "What do ya want?"

"We're here to see Miguel."

"Well, he ain't home," he said with disgust.

"Mike," I whispered, "Don't even bother with him."

"That's the man I was telling you about, Mike," said Isabella. She came around the car to stand next to him. She grabbed his arm and pulled him forward.

"It's okay, Isabella," he said soothingly. "Let's go inside now so I can meet your family."

Isabella bristled at Mike's words. He reached over and grabbed my hand, and we moved forward. When we reached the entrance, Maria opened the door and looked tired but pleasant. Angela squeezed through the doorway past her mother and pulled Isabella inside.

I drew Mike forward. "Hi, Maria. I'd like you to meet Mike. He's here in Santa Fe with me for a few days."

"C'mon in. Miguel just got home."

So much for the neighbor telling the truth. "How's the baby, Maria?"

"She's interested in everything and looks all around, not wanting to miss anything," she answered proudly.

"Wait until you see her, Mike—she's beautiful."

We heard loud laughter and giggles from the boys' bedroom when we entered. Then we listened to the girls making baby talk to Rosa in Angela's bedroom. Heavier footsteps came toward us from the short hallway. When Miguel saw us, he frowned and asked Maria something in Spanish in an unwelcoming tone. There was a flurry of words between them, which I couldn't understand. Mike twitched beside me, and I realized he probably knew what Miguel had said, but he never let on.

Maria's face was flushed as she turned to us. In English, she said, "I'm so sorry. Won't you have a seat?"

Mike stepped toward Miguel with his hand extended. Miguel looked at it and did nothing—his rudeness was not lost on anyone. There was an uncomfortable silence while Maria glared at Miguel until he relented and held out his hand for a shake.

"Nice to meet you, Miguel. I understand you're Isabella's uncle, is that right?"

Reluctantly, he responded, "Yes."

"Well, Isabella is lucky to have you and Maria as her family here. Do you intend to send her back to her mother in Mexico?"

"No, she's mine now," he stated in a possessive voice.

"Oh," Mike said.

I called the girls, and they sensed the tension in the air and looked between Mike and Miguel. As we were leaving, Angela went first to her father and then to her mother with a kiss.

Isabella raced to the door and hollered over her shoulder, "Bye." Again, there were a few more awkward moments because of Isabella's easy dismissal of her aunt and uncle.

I said goodbye to Miguel and hugged Maria again, whispering, "Thank you for being you."

She patted my arm in understanding and appreciation. Mike herded me outside, and we slowly walked silently to the car. I knew Mike was unhappy, but he never said a word. He probably didn't want to spoil our special night.

We drove to the same restaurant where I'd taken all three girls. Once again, we ordered hamburgers and French fries. Both Angela and Isabella were relatively quiet at dinner without Nica there. Out of the three, Nica was the chatterbox. Mike made them giggle with his joke. "Do you want to hear a pizza joke? Never mind, it's pretty cheesy."

Not too much later, we took Angela home and returned to the rental house. Isabella sat with Mike on the couch in the living room. I watched them from the kitchen while straightening up a few things.

Mike asked Isabella, "So tell me about Angela. How old is she?"

"She's nine going on ten. Her birthday is soon."

"I see you two get along okay. You're lucky to have a cousin like that, you know?"

Isabella studied him. "I know. And Nica too."

"Yes, the three of you are quite a trio," laughed Mike. "So what about your Aunt Maria and Uncle Miguel? Are you getting used to them?"

"Aunt Maria is really nice but always busy with the new baby. Angela's brothers are always running around and getting in trouble," she said in annoyance. She thought for a second. "Angela has to help out a lot. She even does the laundry sometimes. No ironing, though."

"Really?"

"Yup. Angela is learning how to cook meals too."

"That sounds kind of fun, don't you think?"

"I guess …"

"What about Uncle Miguel?"

"I don't like him." In response to Mike's questioning look, she added, "I don't want to talk about him."

"You'll probably get used to him in time, don't you think?"

"I don't know," she answered, shrugging her shoulders.

"I think you're lucky to have a family like that. You can be a big help there too."

"So that you know, I'm not going to live there. We're just visiting." Isabella eyed Mike, determined to make her point. "Mama and Sweet Pea are my real family."

"Rosie said you had a nice overnight there, though—that you had fun with your cousins."

"It was okay. Angela and I had to sleep together in her bed, and she kept hogging the blanket," she said, disgruntled. "They don't have room for me there."

"They don't?" asked Mike, not understanding the dynamics.

I rescued both of them. "Isabella? It's time for bed, sweetheart."

"Okay, Mama," she said, relieved to end her conversation with Mike.

She politely kissed Mike on the cheek before she headed to me. I gathered her in my arms and held her close. Even from where he sat, I knew Mike could hear Isabella's sweet voice saying, "I love you, Mama."

"I love you too, sweetheart," I responded, giving her a final squeeze.

After Isabella left my side, Mike studied me. He became quiet and didn't say a word.

I broke into his thoughts. "How about some Amaretto and soda on the deck?"

"Sounds good."

When I handed him his drink, he made room for me on his chaise lounge. He kissed me thoroughly on the lips, and I eagerly returned it. Then he became serious. "Is there really no room for Isabella at their house?"

"Well, that's just one of my concerns. There are more ..."

"Like what? I mean, besides the neighbor?"

"Well, I think it's asking a lot of them to take on another child financially. Isabella makes number six, and that's a lot of mouths to feed and care for. And too, a part of me would like so much more for her than they can afford, but I have to be careful not to hurt their pride."

"I can understand that. It's hard to feel indebted to someone because of money. Just remember, Isabella is not your responsibility."

I let out a long sigh. "I can assure you that I feel she is."

"So Rosie, what are you going to do?"

"I don't know."

"You'll do the right thing; I know you will."

"What is the right thing, Mike?"

"Whatever you decide, my queen," he answered as he pulled me into his arms.

CHAPTER 16

T he following day, I woke again to the aroma of brewing coffee. I searched for Sweet Pea, but she was long gone. I stayed in bed and contemplated the conversation Mike and I had the previous night. It should have been simple for me to introduce Isabella to her family and have her live happily ever after with them, right? Yet the reality was a far cry from that. Why was I making it more complicated than that? I took a deep breath as I came to terms with my feelings. The simple answer was that I loved Isabella, and I wasn't sure leaving her here was best for her. What about Maria? She certainly had her hands full as it was. Could she handle another child? Did she want to? I knew she'd be a good mother, but then there was Miguel. What about him? I sighed.

My cell phone rang and interrupted my thoughts. It was my dear friend Romano calling. "Hi there, Romano; how are you?"

"Hello, my darling Rosebud. We've got a problem."

"What is it, Romano?" I was sure it had something to do with the construction project Romano, and I were heading up. What's going on?"

"The architects said for us to remain on schedule, you must approve the new blueprints in person. They told me I could sign off only on the restaurant's construction—that I'm not allowed to sign for you on the office building. When can you fly back to take care of this?"

"How come they changed it?"

"The first drawings were too close to the property line. They had to move it back quite a few feet, which meant some of the layout had to be redesigned."

"Well, I guess I can make a quick trip back. How are your plans coming for the restaurant?"

"Divine ... just divine," he answered with pride.

"You must be so excited. I'm happy for you."

"Let me know when you're going to be here. Why don't you plan to come for dinner? I want you to meet my partner anyway."

"That sounds wonderful, Romano. Thanks for letting me know what's going on. I'll call you with my plans as soon as they are in place."

Maybe this little break would allow me the space to step away from Isabella's situation and give me a different perspective on a solution. I got out of bed and went into the kitchen. It was empty. Mike sat alone on the deck, and I joined him.

"I just got a call from Romano. He needs me to fly back to Las Vegas so I can approve the new blueprints for the agency's office. The architect's original drawings were too close to the property line, and they had to move it. Because of all the changes, they need my signature again."

"So how are you going to manage that, Rosie?"

"I'm not sure yet."

"It makes sense for Isabella to stay at Maria's for the next few days. Don't you agree?"

"Yes, I do. It'd be a good test for all of us." I studied him. "Then why don't you fly back with me, Mike? You'll be able to see what we're working on. Can you take the time?"

"Why not? That'll give us some time alone," he said as he gave me an intimate glance.

My heart raced with the thought. Alone with this handsome man—oh my! "I'll see if I can arrange to fly out tomorrow and return the day after that. Does that sound okay?" I bent and gave him a long, tender kiss.

"Where are you going, Mama? I want to come too!"

"You're going to stay at Maria's. It's only for a few days, and we'll be back."

"You're going to leave me there, aren't you?" she spat in disgust.

"No, sweetheart, I'd never do that."

"I don't believe you! You're going to leave me there and never come back!" she hollered.

"That's not true, Isabella, and you know it," I stated in a low, stern voice.

She turned her back to me and pouted, stifling her tears. "Isabella, look at me!" I commanded. She slowly turned my way. "I want you to look me in the eye. I promise we'll be back before you even realize we left. You'll be fine with your cousins."

As tears slid down her cheeks, she examined me, looking for truth. Her voice was just above a whisper as she held her finger up. "Do you pinky promise?"

"I do, and I'll do even better than that—I'm going to leave Sweet Pea with you. You know I'd never leave my two favorite girls behind forever, right?"

Isabella thought about that. Then she came forward and wrapped her arms around my waist. "I love you, Mama."

"I love you too."

Once I had called Maria to make the necessary arrangements, we packed our things and loaded them into my rental car. We agreed to leave Mike's rental in the driveway and hoped it wouldn't be bothered.

Isabella—sad to be left behind—was quiet on the way to her cousins' house. As we pulled into the driveway, we saw the neighbor hanging around outside. It looked as if he had nothing better to do. I collected Sweet Pea's leash, food bag, and toys from the back seat. I walked Isabella and the dog to the door, where Maria greeted us. Sweet Pea followed Isabella inside, which allowed Maria and me to talk for a moment.

"I can't thank you enough for letting Sweet Pea and Isabella stay with you for the next few days. I hope it'll give us a better idea of how this might work out— particularly for you, Maria."

She nodded. "I know it's not easy for you to leave her here. We'll take it one step at a time, okay?"

I hugged her tight. I whispered, "You are the best, Maria. You're so sweet and caring …."

"As are you, Rosie," she replied with a smile.

I turned away, comforted by knowing Isabella was in good hands. When I got into the car, Mike said, "I talked to Coyote this morning, and he'll check on Isabella while we're gone."

Looking at the neighbor who stood watching us, Mike said. "I don't like that guy ... or trust him, either."

I patted Mike's arm. "I know exactly what you mean."

The flight to Vegas was short and sweet. After we landed, we hailed a cab. When we pulled up to my townhouse, I had flashbacks of the shooting that'd taken place there, and goosebumps crawled along my arms. I shook them off and carried my bag inside. I telephoned Romano to tell him we'd soon be on our way.

After I got off the phone, Mike pulled me toward him and drew me closer. His smoldering eyes studied mine as he placed his palm behind my head and tenderly pulled me toward him, his lips searching mine. He nuzzled my neck with yet another tender kiss. The kiss promised all that was to come. I sighed in pleasure, and it made him smile.

"Okay, enough of that," I laughed, pushing him away. "We don't want to be late for Romano, and you certainly don't want to miss whatever he's fixed for us. Trust me."

Randy met us at the door when we arrived at Romano's house. I smiled because it was easy to see that Romano kept him well-fed. He was handsome in a wholesome way—much like Romano—filled with energy and sparkling eyes, and his whole demeanor exuded a joy of living. He quickly set both Mike and me at ease.

Romano came around the corner and threw open his arms. "Ah, my darling Rosebud, I've missed you!" he exclaimed as he hugged me. He looked at Mike and smiled. "It's good to see you again. Come in, come in. Make yourselves at home. Randy will get you your drinks while I finish in the kitchen."

The evening was a huge success. Mike slowly relaxed and enjoyed being in Romano's and Randy's company.

After we finished a superb dinner of sautéed shrimp in a delightful lemon cream sauce over angel hair pasta—served with a salad of fresh greens—we all sat back, satisfied. Then Randy brought in a unique coffee with brandy to accompany our after-dinner conversation. It was only natural for it to turn to Santa Fe.

Romano asked, "My darling, what's happening with Isabella?"

I filled them in on my predicament while trying to settle Isabella into her new family.

Romano blew me a kiss from across the table. "How long will you be in Santa Fe, Mike?"

"For a few more days at least."

"I'm glad you'll be there with her," said Romano, worry on his face.

When it was time to leave, I received real kisses from both men and a package of baked goodies from Romano. Mike and I departed with the glow of warm friendship still with us.

After we got home, it was easy to see that Mike was as tired as me. We climbed the stairs, and each went our way to prepare for bed. I finished first and crawled into bed to wait for him. That was the last thing I remembered until I smelled coffee brewing the following day.

When I realized what'd happened, I threw on my robe and raced downstairs. Mike heard me enter the kitchen and turned to me with wide arms open. I hurried into them. "Mike? Why didn't you join me in bed last night?"

He chuckled. "My sleepy queen, you were sleeping so soundly, I didn't have the heart to wake you."

"I'm so sorry."

"Don't be. We have this morning…."

"Ah, yes, we do. My meetings aren't until this afternoon."

Mike fixed his special eggs, and as we ate, we kept peering down at our feet, expecting Sweet Pea to be there. We looked at each other and laughed. After breakfast, Mike reached for me and pulled me against him. I felt his readiness as I leaned into him, and we headed upstairs to my bedroom. My heart pounded in anticipation, and my stomach fluttered with thoughts of what was to come. It would be our first lovemaking, and although I was excited to come together finally, I was also nervous. I wanted it to be everything I'd dreamed about.

Mike gently lifted me onto the bed and bent over me. "My beautiful queen, let me," he said, pulling apart my robe and exposing my readiness for him.

He began to disrobe me and slowly explored my body with his kisses, and later, I returned the favor. That was the beginning of learning how to pleasure each other in familiar and new ways. In Mike's arms, I felt safe and loved. It was lovemaking at its best, and I screamed my pleasure as we climaxed together. Not much later, we repeated our lovemaking slower, drawing out our pleasure as long as possible.

Earlier, I'd asked Mike if he'd join me in my two meetings, and he'd agreed. After we made love again and showered together, we dressed to leave. First, we went to the architect's office and spent a full hour reviewing the plans and new revisions. I requested two changes. The first was to add a bathroom in the intake area, eliminating access to the private living space in the back. My second was to enlarge the eating area in the kitchen so it would hold more than four seats. We needed the larger space since the agency was dealing with more human trafficking victims than ever before. Sitting with the victims around a kitchen table for intake discussions was a softer approach that I hoped would help put them at ease.

Afterward, we drove to my meeting with Jacklyn, the head of the agency, who was overseeing Isabella's case. I dreaded meeting with her because Isabella still wasn't settled in with her new family. On the other hand, I was curious to learn more about how their entire system worked, especially since I had doubts about leaving Isabella in Santa Fe.

"Good afternoon, Rosalie. Nice to see you again."

"Jacklyn, nice to see you too. I'd like you to meet my friend, Mike."

"Nice to meet you, Mike. Won't you please come this way? We'll meet in my office."

As we followed Jacklyn, I saw exactly why they needed more space. I noticed three tiny offices with desks stacked high with folders and closed doors that indicated the kitchen and bathroom areas. Jacklyn's office was the largest of the three, with a small round table and four chairs. It seemed as if every square inch was used in this small building.

"Here you go. Have a seat right here," Jacklyn said.

Mike guided me to the table's far side so I'd face Jacklyn, and then he sat beside me. "Thank you for seeing me on such short notice, Jacklyn," I said.

She smiled. "It's my pleasure. It's been what, a couple of weeks since you left?"

"Yes, that's right."

"Since you're here, am I to assume everything is all set for Isabella in Santa Fe?"

My face heated. "Not exactly."

"Why don't you tell me what's going on, Rosalie, and we'll see what the next step should be."

"It's probably taking a bit longer than you expected," I said, trying not to be defensive. "However, I do have some concerns …

"Go ahead. This is a safe place to discuss your feelings, Rosalie."

"Isabella's family there is lovely in many respects, especially Maria. She is a real gem, someone I like very much. Her husband, Miguel, is a different case. He's hostile to me, and when I first met him, he said, 'Thanks for dropping her off.' He's very fierce, and Isabella doesn't like him. She stays far away from him."

"What about the children?" Jacklyn asked.

"Angela is a year younger than Isabella, and they're developing a nice relationship. She's the one asked to step up to complete many of the household chores and take care of her three little brothers. Their new baby, Rosa, is just days old, and she shares one of the three bedrooms with Angela. The little boys share the second bedroom. And, of course, Maria and Miguel have the third bedroom. What worries me is there is no room for Isabella… no space of her own. When she stayed overnight there, she shared a twin bed with Angela. I know money is tight for them, and I can't imagine it would be enough for Isabella even if they put in bunk beds for the girls. She's at the age where privacy becomes very important. I'm sure you understand."

"Yes, I do."

"I'm also worried about Maria. In the past few weeks, she's gone from having four children to now having six. That's a lot for her, even with Angela's help."

I watched as Jacklyn folded her hands in her lap and sat back in her chair. "I can tell there is something more you want to talk about. What is your main concern for Isabella? What is holding you back from letting them straighten out their situation?"

The blood rushed to my face. Jacklyn was right. I was barricading them from moving forward on their terms. I swallowed and felt my mouth go dry. I opened a bottle of water placed before me and took several gulps, then collected my thoughts and pushed on.

"I'm not telling you anything new when I say Isabella is strongly attached to me, calling me Mama and expecting me to be her mother, right?"

"Yes, so much so that we thought it would be beneficial for you both if you were the one to introduce her to her real family. We hoped your doing so would release you from her as she integrated into the family. I can see from the expression on your face that's not happening."

"No, it's not."

"Would you like to be pulled off the case, then?"

"Absolutely not. If it won't work out in Santa Fe, what happens to Isabella?"

Jacklyn looked upset. "Well, then we'd have to put her in child custody, which we don't like to do unless necessary."

"Do you mean foster care?"

"Yes, she'd be part of that system."

"I understand," I whispered, troubled.

One of the other women knocked on the open door. "Jacklyn, this is the phone call you've been waiting for."

"Tell them I'll be right there. Rosalie, are we all set here? You'll continue to get Isabella situated as we discussed?"

"Yes, I'll be in touch. Thank you so much for your time, Jacklyn."

"We thank you for your time and efforts to settle this little girl," she said, giving me a dutiful, quick hug. She shook hands with Mike and left, leaving us to follow.

Mike held my hand in the car as tears formed in my eyes. He looked at me and didn't say a word. What was I going to do?

Back at the house, we changed into more casual clothes. Mike fixed margaritas, and we toasted each other with kisses and a clink of glasses. Then we put our feet on the coffee table and relaxed on the couch while soft, romantic music played. I'd almost forgotten what it was like to have "vacation" time to do nothing but what I wanted to do. No children, pets, or dead bodies to interrupt my peace.

Pretty soon, we were in each other's arms, kissing and panting with the need for each other. We pulled apart, both pleasantly surprised at how evenly matched we were in our desire. Mike continued to surprise me with his sensitivity, knowing I was feeling down about Isabella's situation.

The doorbell rang and interrupted us with the arrival of our takeout Chinese. We ate greedily, enjoying every bite. We laughed at each other when we tried to pick up some of the smaller pieces of food with our chopsticks and couldn't. It felt good and natural to be together. I began to relax into that comfort of not worrying about anything.

I heard my cell phone ring, and I ignored it the first and second times. When it rang the third time, I got up to answer it. Strange … it was Coyote calling. My heart began to pound with worry.

"It's Coyote," I hollered to Mike before answering it. "Hi, Coyote; what's going on?" I asked as Mike came to stand by me. I put the phone on speaker and said, "Mike's here too."

"Rosie, I have some bad news. The girls are missing … all three of them."

"What do you mean, missing? Since when?" I looked at Mike, who squeezed my shoulders in support.

"Maria said they went outside to play with Sweet Pea. She got busy with the baby, and when she looked at the clock, she realized they'd been outside for a long time. When Maria heard Sweet Pea frantically barking and scratching at the door, she opened it and yelled for the girls. She got no response. Then she went outside to see what was going on. Sweet Pea kept running to the driveway, making circles around where the neighbor usually parked his truck. As Maria looked down the road, she saw his truck driving away, but she couldn't see if the girls were with him. That's when she called me."

The first thought that came to my mind was how difficult it must have been for Maria to have made that call. "How did Nica get involved?" I asked, confused.

"I wondered that myself. When I talked to Grandmother, she said Nica told her you were picking her up and would call her later. She didn't know you were out of town."

"Oh, my God, what a nightmare! The girls aren't safe, and there's that horrible neighbor!" I screeched. "We're on our way!" I said as Mike nodded in agreement. I looked at my watch. "We should be able to make it there around one or two in the morning. We'll call you as soon as we arrive."

Mike was already on the phone, making airline reservations and calling a cab. I threw all the leftover food in the refrigerator so it wouldn't rot in the trash bin. I'd worry about the rest of the mess later. I ran upstairs, threw everything I'd brought back into the suitcase, and changed my clothes. Mike raced past me to do the same.

Before we knew it, the cab had arrived, and we were inside, both slumped back against the seat. Mike held my hand and squeezed it. "Don't worry, we'll find them, I promise."

"They just have to be okay, or I'll never forgive myself."

Mike brushed away my tears. "Don't go down that road. Calm down and relax. Maybe something will come to you."

As much as I tried to open myself up for insight, nothing came. Perhaps it wasn't supposed to if this was to mimic the past that Isabella and I'd shared.

Pretty soon, I snapped out of my panic mode and became pragmatic. After all, Isabella had been inventive enough to find her way to me in Las Vegas. She was a little girl smart beyond her years in many ways. Nica knew her way around the area, and her training in the Indian ways would be an asset. Although Angela had a mind of her own, I knew that if Isabella told her to do something, she would obey without question. I had to believe that when the three of them pooled their thoughts, they'd make positive choices to keep safe. I needed to stay in that state of mind or go crazy.

Once we were on the airplane, I settled back in my seat and willed myself to relax. I was somewhat startled to wake up from an unexpected nap as we landed in Albuquerque. Mike had dozed off as well. When he felt me move against him, he asked in a groggy voice, "Are we there already?" I smiled. His hair was tussled, and he looked about ten years old.

As soon as we were inside the airport, I telephoned Coyote. He picked up on the first ring. "Anything yet?"

"Nope, nothing. Do you have any idea where the girls might be?" Coyote asked.

"What about the neighbor? Anything there?"

"We pulled him in for questioning, and he claimed he knew nothing about the girls. I'd watch out for him, though. He wasn't at all happy to be dragged into this."

"We're just getting into our car now and headed your way. See you at around 1 o'clock. I'll call you when we get there."

"Okay, we'll find them ..." he trailed off.

CHAPTER 17

We pulled into the rental house and dragged our suitcases out of the car. Mike called Coyote, and while talking to him, I felt the urge to go to the shed at the bottom of the garden. Even though it was late, a full moon provided enough light for me to see my way. When I reached the shed, the door was opened a crack. It was dark inside. "Isabella? Are you in there?"

I felt someone behind me, and before I knew what'd happened, a hand covered my mouth. I knew who it was as soon as I was grabbed.

"You think you're so smart trying to involve me in kidnapping your little girl, don't you?" he asked drunkenly. I struggled and reached for the hand that smothered my mouth. I grabbed his baby finger and pulled it back far enough to hear it snap. He immediately let go of me. "You bitch!" he yelled while clinging to his hand.

As soon as he dropped his hand from my mouth, I hollered, "Mike! Mike, down here!"

I'd barely gotten that out when my assailant shoved me hard and forced me further into the shed. "I knew you were trouble the first time I saw you in the alley. You're just not going to quit, are you?"

Everything happened in seconds. The neighbor pushed me up against the shed wall and leaned into me while covering my mouth again with his grubby hand. His breath smelled of alcohol, and his whole body stank of old sweat. His eyes bored into mine. "You know, you're one hot sex kitten …."

There was a crash as Mike rushed through the door. Now it was the neighbor's turn to be shoved against the wall. Mike grabbed him by the collar, turned him around, and swung his fist into the neighbor's face. Blood spurted from his nose, forcing the neighbor to catch it with the dirty sleeve of his shirt. Mike kept his forearm across the neighbor's throat. The neighbor was too drunk to resist.

"Where are the girls?" Mike yelled. "What did you do with them?"

The neighbor's eyes widened. "I didn't do anything with them!"

"You threatened Rosie that you'd hurt her little girl, didn't you?"

He bobbed his head up and down frantically. "Please…"

"Give me one reason why we should believe you had nothing to do with them missing."

He gulped in fear. "I asked if they wanted a ride, but they said no. I don't know nuthin' else, honest."

"What do you mean you asked them if they wanted a ride? Where were they going?" I screeched.

"I dunno, I dunno," he pleaded.

"Which way were they headed?" I demanded.

"I guess into town."

Mike turned to me. "Grab my phone and call Coyote. Tell him to meet us here."

"What are you going to do with him?" I asked.

"He's not going anywhere. Go to the house and bring me my handcuffs ... hurry."

I could tell the neighbor had no fight in him with Mike's big body towering over him. He was hunched over and pulled at his baby finger, trying to set it back in place. His nose still oozed blood. He looked a mess, and Mike grimaced as he turned his face away.

I raced up the hill. Mike had packed his handcuffs in his briefcase, most likely out of habit. I grabbed them and started down to Mike as Coyote pulled into the driveway.

"C'mon, Coyote, this way!"

As we ran to the shed, I filled Coyote in on what the neighbor said. When Coyote stepped into the hut, the neighbor's eyes widened. He held his hands up, saying, "I didn't do nuthin', honest, sheriff!"

"What do you call attacking Rosie? Why are you following her anyway? She's not the one who had you questioned. I did. What's going on here?"

The neighbor's face darkened and filled with guilt.

"Well?" prompted Coyote.

"Nuthin' going on," he mumbled. He looked at me, and chills ran along my body. I held my tongue, for now, more concerned with finding the missing girls.

"I'm taking you in for assault. You can sleep it off in a cell," said Coyote disgustingly.

A siren announced the sheriff's deputy. After trudging up the hill and watching the patrol car pull away, we looked at each other and silently headed inside the house.

I made coffee, and we sat together at the kitchen table to plan our strategy.

"Okay, guys. Where do you think the girls were going? What or who do you think interfered with their plans? If they're hiding, where do you think that might be?" I asked.

Mike piped up. "If they're hiding, it would be somewhere they felt safe. You two know this area better than I do."

We sat bleary-eyed until Coyote spoke. "Let's meet at first light in the morning and trace their steps from Maria's house. Our heads will be clearer, and you, Rosie, can speak with Maria. Perhaps she'll think of more to add to what we already know."

Collectively, we sighed, knowing he spoke the truth. I watched Coyote as he walked to his car, his shoulders drooped.

CHAPTER 18

T he following day, we got up after a restless night. I had slept in Mike's arms all night, which comforted me and enforced the idea that all would turn out well. I dashed into the shower that I'd been too exhausted to take the night before. I wanted to wash off any remaining smell or touch of the neighbor. Mike went to do the same. After I dressed, I smelled coffee brewing and hurried to the kitchen. I was surprised Mike had found time to toast some English muffins, and we munched them and filled our travel coffee mugs to take with us.

When we arrived at Maria's, Coyote was already there. Maria opened the door, and when she saw me, she burst into tears and talked excitedly in Spanish. I gathered her in my arms. "I'm so sorry, Rosie, I'm so sorry ...."

I held her tight. "Maria, the girls are okay. I know they are. We need to find them, that's all."

She studied me. "Are you sure?"

I nodded, knowing I was right despite having no concrete evidence. Maria pulled me to where Mike, Coyote, and Miguel were standing. I said hello to Miguel, and he mumbled something but refused to look at me. Mike looked at Miguel, then me, and wondered what was happening.

"Rosie, we think it'd be best for you to return to the house because that might be where they'll head. Maria will be here if they find their way here instead. Are you okay with that?" Coyote asked.

I thought I'd have a better chance of finding them if I could walk around the area and sense them, but maybe he was right. At my silence, the guys took that as a sign of assent.

"Great, then. You take the car, and I'll ride with Coyote," Mike said.

I looked at Maria. "Are you going to be okay?" She nodded as she wiped away a few tears.

"You have my phone number, and I have yours. So call me if you need to talk or think of something."

She stood looking forlorn. "Remember what I said, Maria. The girls are all right. We need to find them, is all."

As I started back home, I drove by the Palace of the Governors despite knowing it was probably too early to talk to Grandmother. As I neared, I saw her sitting alone in her usual spot. When she looked up and saw me, her face split into a smile, and she waved me forward. I parked the car and eagerly went to her.

Her hand grasped mine, and she pulled me down beside her. I nestled against her, and she began to hum the unique Indian tune I loved so much. She whispered, "So the time has come, my daughter ... the time when the past meets the present."

"Yes, Grandmother, but I know they are safe. I can feel it. We need to find them."

Grandmother continued her singing, not speaking. Then she stirred. "You need to be strong because this is only a test. Do you understand what I'm saying?"

"You mean there's more to come?"

Grandmother's only answer was pulling me closer as she continued her song. I felt my grandmother's spirit around me and heard her say, *"One step at a time, darling girl. One step at a time."*

My heart fell. I brushed away tears, nearly overwhelmed by the love that surrounded me. After a few minutes, I rose, said goodbye to Grandmother, and kissed her on each weathered cheek, covered with tears.

I drove home with my mind whirling. I brewed a second cup of coffee and took it into the living room, where I played soft music and began to meditate. I knew the girls were okay, but where would they hide? Yes, Nica knew her way around Santa Fe and could tuck them in a safe spot where they wouldn't be found. Angela probably didn't have a specific place in mind other than her house. "Isabella? Where are you?" I asked the space around me.

I closed my eyes and asked my angels to protect the girls. That's when it suddenly hit me—angels! I picked up my cell phone and called Mike. I excitedly told him I knew where the little girls were hiding and asked him to meet me there. I got into the car and drove over the speed limit to arrive in time to see Mike and Coyote pull into an empty parking spot. I hopped out of my car and raced to them.

"They're inside. I know they are."

"How do you know that?" Coyote asked as Mike lifted his brows.

"When we visited the Loretto Chapel, Isabella was mesmerized by the staircase. She remarked how close it was to heaven, so I know she'd feel safe there."

Mike checked his watch. "The chapel won't be open for another 15 minutes."

"Well, we're in luck. Look who's just arrived—the man in charge of the chapel." Coyote said.

We raced over, and I explained why we needed to enter the chapel immediately. I'm not sure the man believed me, but he finally agreed once he looked to Coyote for reassurance.

"Okay, let's go inside and see if we have visitors."

I stood behind him as he opened the door and pushed past him. "Isabella?" I called out as I ran inside the chapel. I heard shuffling sounds above my head. "Girls?"

I heard more shuffling. "You can come out. You're safe—we're here now."

I peered up at the top of the winding stairs and saw three pairs of eyes staring down at us. "Mama, I knew you'd find us!" cried Isabella, her relief evident.

"Please, c'mon down so you can tell us why you're here," I encouraged them.

They scrambled down the stairs, making noise in their haste, much to the dismay of the executive director, who bit his lip so he wouldn't snap at them for their carelessness on the stairs.

I gathered all three girls in my arms and kissed the tops of their heads. "What happened?" I asked. Three pairs of eyes peered up at me, then looked at each other. Nica pulled away from the others and walked to face her uncle.

"What is it, Nica?" he asked gently.

"It … it … was …" She looked at the girls, who nodded their approval. "It was Cou … Cousin Redmond. It was Stalking Deer, Uncle Coyote."

"What do you mean, Nica? What does Redmond have to do with this?"

Nica hung her head. "I'm sorry, Uncle Coyote. I lied to Grandmother," she said in a tiny voice. "This is all my fault," she sobbed and began to cry in earnest.

Coyote knelt and took her in his arms. "Why don't you tell me the whole story from the beginning?"

"Okay …" She looked at Isabella, who nodded her encouragement. "I surprised Isabella and Angela by showing up, and when I told them what I'd done, Isabella said we had to walk back to Grandmother to tell her the truth. She said it was bad to lie."

"I agree. That's not a good thing to do because it always causes trouble in the long run, doesn't it?" Coyote said.

"I know," she whispered. Isabella and Angela put their arms around Nica.

Isabella spoke up. "On the way, we saw Redmond, and when he saw me, he grabbed me. I got away when Sweet Pea jumped on him and tried to bite him." Tears began to flow. "That's when Sweet Pea ran away. Is she all right?" Isabella asked, dread in her voice.

"Yes, Isabella, she ran back to Maria's house. Sweet Pea's the one who alerted us there was trouble."

"Why did Redmond grab you?" Mike asked as he stepped forward and pulled Isabella to him. Isabella began to cry harder and couldn't speak.

Angela broke in, "He said she belonged to my father…."

I held Angela tight in my arms. She broke down then and sobbed as hard as the other girls. The three adults looked at each other with worry.

125

"I think he was drunk, Mama!" Isabella spat out in anger.

Coyote bent forward and held his hands over his eyes. He gave a long sigh. "I'll call Maria now and let her know we found the girls, and they're safe. I'll take Angela to Maria and Nica back to Grandmother. Why don't you take Isabella home, and we'll talk later. I have to find Redmond and see what's going on."

The girls ran to each other and hugged. I kissed them, put my arm around Isabella, and led her back to the car. Mike drove us home, and we were three silent people as we mulled over what'd happened. I knew why this had occurred, but I wasn't willing to share it.

CHAPTER 19

I n the early afternoon, Coyote called and asked us to meet at Maria's house. When we arrived, a sorrowful Maria opened the door and motioned us inside without a warm greeting or eye contact. Sensing the gravity of the situation, Isabella immediately went to Angela's bedroom, head down. Mike turned to me to see whether I knew what was going on. I lifted my shoulders in a shrug, not sure whether my thoughts were correct.

Coyote spoke to Miguel in Spanish in the living room, and they looked up as we entered. When Miguel looked at me, it was with shame, and he wouldn't meet my eyes. Coyote got up from the couch. "Why don't you two sit here?" he directed.

We did as asked, and then Mike questioned, "So, what's happening?" He looked first at Coyote and then at

Miguel, who began to move toward Maria as she stood in the doorway.

"I think I'll let Miguel answer that question," said Coyote sternly.

Miguel lifted his head to look at me. "I'm sorry ..."

"Sorry for what, Miguel?" I jumped in. "Sorry for trying to scare me away? Sorry for paying Redmond to put the dead crows on our door?"

"How do ...?" he asked, surprised.

"You didn't see me at Albertson's when you paid him off. That was you, wasn't it?" I demanded.

He slowly nodded and looked at the floor while Maria viewed him with such sadness that I felt sorry for her. It must not have been easy for her to learn of his betrayal. As he stood there in silence, I couldn't contain myself. My anger escalated, and I stood up to face him.

"So let's get down to the nitty-gritty, shall we, Miguel? Let's talk about the elephant in the room. Ever since we met, you've been surly and rude to me. I need to clear something up once and for all. The agency sent me here to help Isabella assimilate into your family, but only if this will be the best place for her." I caught my breath. "She's not a package to simply be left at your doorstep," I sputtered, "and this shouldn't be a struggle between *us*. This isn't about ownership either—whether you *own* her or I do. It's about a little girl who has experienced things that left her feeling unwanted and unloved. This is about what's best for *her*."

Miguel's demeanor was defensive and defiant when I first spoke, but I saw his stance soften by the end of my outrage. I continued, "I want to repeat that this isn't about you or me, Miguel. I want what's best for Isabella. I truly do, and I know Maria feels the same." I drew in a deep breath and, in a determined voice, added, "So, considering what you have done to interfere with this process, I'm proposing that moving forward, any decision made for Isabella will be best made between Maria and me. That way, I know whatever we decide will be the right choice for her, agreed?"

There was dead silence in the room. All eyes became glued on Miguel. He must have known I wasn't about to be talked out of this because he looked down and slowly nodded. I knew he was unhappy about it, but I saw he was beginning to realize what he'd created. I turned to Mike, grabbed his hand, and pulled him from the couch. I looked at Coyote, "Have you found Redmond yet?"

"Not yet," he murmured.

I gave a brisk nod in response. "Mike, get Isabella. It's time for us to leave."

"Okay," he said and headed out of the room.

I went forward and wrapped my arms around Maria. At first, she held herself stiffly, and I knew she was embarrassed. Then she relaxed, and I held her tighter and spoke solemnly, "We'll work things out, Maria. Don't worry."

When Mike came around the corner with Isabella, she sensed the turmoil and rushed to me, asking, "Are you okay, Mama?"

Miguel watched the exchange between us as I bent and kissed the top of Isabella's head. "Yes, sweetheart, everything is fine. Let's go home, shall we?"

For the rest of the day, we decided to hunker down. We watched movies, played games, and ordered takeout. I took time to send a story to the magazine for my spiritual column. I hadn't received a response yet to my new column about some of the best ways to enjoy the glitzy side of Las Vegas.

I went to my bedroom and lay on the bed to rest. I heard a light knock on the door. "Mama? Can I come in?"

"What's going on?"

"Can Sweet Pea sleep with me tonight?" she asked worriedly.

"Come here, sweetheart," I said and opened my arms to her. "Are you afraid?"

"Just a little bit." She paused. "Mama? Redmond said that I belonged to Miguel … that he owned me. He can't own me, can he? Grandmother told Nica that we're the only ones who can own us. Is that right?"

I was floored. What a question to ask. I tried to put it in simple terms. "Legally, children are the responsibility of their parents until they are 18 years of age. But I think Grandmother meant everyone's life is a chain of choices made by each person. You and I always make choices, and we can't blame anyone else for our choices. In other words, you own your choices." I looked at her as she stood there, taking in what I'd said. I added, "It simply boils down to how you choose to live. Does that make any sense to you?"

"Yes, now I understand, Mama." She bent down and kissed my cheek. "Then I choose to live with you," she said with a smile before she danced out of the room.

"But…" I called to her disappearing form.

CHAPTER 20

A fter I tucked Isabella and Sweet Pea into bed, I looked for Mike, who was making us a nightcap of Sambuca over ice in the kitchen. "Hmm, how nice!" I exclaimed as I took a sip and felt my stomach soothed by the licorice liqueur. I looked at Mike with a smile. "Alone at last."

He reached for me, and I set my glass down and entered his waiting arms. Several long, passionate kisses later, he said, "Grab your drink and let's go outside. We need to talk."

My heart began to thump. I prayed that whatever Mike wanted to discuss was something we could work out together. I sat down next to him. "What is it?"

"I know you're worried about your responsibility to Isabella and want to do the right thing. I love you, Rosie, and I want our relationship to work, but I'm not willing to sleep on the couch or in the spare bedroom. I came here to see …."

"Shhh," I said, placing my finger across his lips. "I agree," I answered with an intimate look, pulling him from the chair.

After another deep, romantic kiss, he picked me up, carried me into my bedroom, and placed me gently on the bed. "Don't move. I'll be right back after I close up for the night."

As I waited for Mike to return, I thought about our situation. I believed it was better not to hide our growing relationship from Isabella because that would only confuse her and create an unnecessary sense of falsity. I felt there was merit in modeling a loving relationship with someone who hasn't always experienced that. Any further thoughts were disrupted by Mike coming into the room.

Our lovemaking was tender and more relaxed as we became comfortable knowing how to please each other. Later, I woke up with a nagging sense that something unpleasant would happen. As I tossed about, I felt Mike's arm come around me, pulling me close. I relaxed into him and was asleep in no time.

The following day, I heard a soft tap, tap, tap at the door. "C'mon in, Isabella."

When she saw us in bed together, she smiled, pleased. "Good morning, Mama and Mike."

Mike sat up and patted the bed for Isabella and Sweet Pea to sit there. "What's going on?"

"Are you and Mama going to get married, Mike?"

I was curious to see what Mike would say. I was surprised when he answered, "Well, I'm not sure. Why?"

"Is Mama seeing if this is the best place for you like she is with me?'

Mike laughed, and soon we all were laughing. Sweet Pea joined in by barking. After Mike caught his breath, he said, "I believe she is."

I punched him lightly on his arm. "You never know."

Mike's cell phone rang, and he got up to answer it. When he came back, he said, "That was Coyote. He asked if I would come to the office because he wanted me to look at something. I said I'd meet him in an hour."

"Time to get up then," I said, throwing back the covers.

"I'll start the coffee," Mike offered. "Anybody for scrambled eggs?"

"Yes!" Isabella and I said in unison.

After Mike left to meet Coyote, Isabella and I got dressed for the day. Then, I went back into the kitchen to clean up the dishes. When Isabella and Sweet Pea came to me, I held her close and patted Sweet Pea. I said, "I'll do these dishes now, and you can help me with them tonight, okay?"

I was trying to share some of the household responsibilities to prepare her for what might be expected of her at Maria's house.

"Sure, Mama," she answered happily.

Sweet Pea was making little whimpering sounds. "Isabella, I think Sweet Pea needs to go out."

"Should I take her for a walk?" she asked.

"No, take her out back, and don't wander. I don't want you out of my sight, understand?"

After cleaning up the kitchen, I noticed the TV remote lying on the living room floor, but my phone rang before I could pick it up. It was Nancy from the real estate office. "Hello, Nancy. How are you?"

"Fine, just fine, Rosie. How are things there at the house? Are you enjoying being there?

"Yes, very much so. It's a delightful house, and I'm so glad you found this for us."

"Well, if you're interested, I have good news. The owner's vacation was a trip to France to check on his mother, who still lives there in the town where he grew up. He called to say that he's planning on moving there for good. His mother is not well, and he handles her affairs as the eldest. He wanted to know if you'd like to buy his house."

As Nancy talked, I'd been going into the living room to pick up the remote and place it on the table. As I got closer, I looked out the front window and saw a truck parked down the street. It looked like Maria's neighbor's truck. I hollered into the phone, "I'll call you later!" as I dropped the phone and ran to the back deck to see Sweet Pea running toward me, barking furiously.

I leaned over Sweet Pea and frantically asked, "Where's Isabella, Sweet Pea? Where is she?"

I heard a faint rustle behind me. Then everything went black. I awoke to wet kisses from Sweet Pea, nudging me with her wet nose. "What happened, Sweet Pea?"

As my thinking cleared, I scrambled to my feet and raced to the front of the house. The neighbor's truck was gone. I ran next door and pounded on the door. There was no answer. I raced to the next place and did the same, yelling, "Open up!"

The door cracked open, and I could see the woman who answered was frightened by my yelling. "Did you see a man with a little girl? Did you see a man drive away in a truck?" She shook her head no. "Did you see anything?"

The woman began to speak in Spanish and shut the door in my face.

"Stop it, Rosie. Stop acting crazy and get your wits about you now," I snapped at myself. I reached for my phone and remembered dropping it at the house. I ran back, found it, and called Mike. No answer. I hurriedly left a message. Then I put Sweet Pea in the house, grabbed my purse, and headed out the door. I jumped in the car and headed for Maria's.

In a frenzy, I would see whether the neighbor's truck was there. Mike called while I was on the way, and I told him what had happened and asked him and Coyote to meet me at Maria's house.

"Don't do anything until we get there. Do you hear me?"

"You better hurry then."

When I reached Maria's house, the neighbor's truck wasn't in his yard. Panic began to build in me. This can't be happening! Where had he taken her? Oh, my God! I felt a weakness come over me, and I barely had enough strength to climb out of the car. It was as if my legs were made of rubber—my body was completely drained of energy. Mike and Coyote pulled into the driveway. When Mike came to me, I collapsed in his arms. "He's not here," I moaned.

"Why don't you begin at the beginning?" he asked calmly.

Haltingly, I told them everything. Then, we heard the rumbling of an approaching truck, and we watched as it pulled into the driveway where we stood. It was the neighbor, and I began to pull away from Mike, who held me tighter.

"Let Coyote handle this, Rosie."

"Where have you been?" Coyote demanded as he stepped toward the truck's driver's side.

"Wouldn't you like to know?"

"Get the hell out of the truck now!" Coyote ordered.

"Why? I didn't do nuthin'!"

"If you didn't, why didn't you answer my question?"

"You and your kind rub me the wrong way. You act so high and mighty as sheriff, but I'm not afraid of you."

"Let me ask you again. Where have you been?"

"Nowhere!" he hollered. When he saw the look on Coyote's face, he added, "Honest."

"Get out now!" demanded Coyote. "Rosie, is this the truck you saw?"

When the neighbor looked at me, his upper lip rose in a sneer. He snarled, "You? You're nothing but trouble! Stay away from me."

Mike stepped toward him. "Watch it!" he warned.

Walking around the neighbor's truck, I noticed a dent in the tailgate. And this dent was old. I closed my eyes to recall what I'd seen when talking to Nancy, and I realized it couldn't have been this truck because the tailgate I'd seen had no dent. I swallowed hard and shook my head. "No, Coyote, I'm sorry. It wasn't him."

My denial didn't seem to lessen Coyote's stance toward the neighbor. "Watch your step, mister. Don't forget I'm keeping an eye on you."

The neighbor mumbled something and slunk away. Coyote walked over to Mike and me. My head began to pound, and I felt sick to my stomach. "Where is Isabella?" I mumbled.

Mike suggested, "Let's go back to the house. You rushed over here without checking everything in the house, right? Maybe Isabella returned to the house while you were outside, and you missed her. She might even be wondering where you are," he said, trying to appease me.

Death Returns

Perhaps I'd foolishly overreacted, but I remembered calling out for Isabella and getting no answer—but then everything had gone dark. After I'd come to, I hadn't looked further for Isabella. Maybe Mike was correct that I'd been so worried about Isabella that I'd raced from the house without any thought other than finding the neighbor. I rushed forward as Mike headed to my car and touched his arm.

"No, I can drive myself. You go with Coyote, and I'll call you when I get home. I'll let you know if she's there, and if she isn't, we may also need to use your car to search her out."

"Are you sure you're okay to drive?"

"Yes, I'm sure." I turned to Coyote. "Thanks for helping."

"I want to help. Let me know what's going on too. Come on, Mike, let's get your car."

I sensed I'd missed something on my way back to the house. As soon as I got there, I hurried to the shed and felt prickles along my arms. I silently crept up to the door. I drew in a deep breath, and then, with all my strength, I slammed the door open. When I looked inside, it was empty. Disappointment washed over me. As I took a second look, I saw Isabella's bracelet with the bear on it. It was the proof I needed to know she'd been there. Now, I knew exactly what'd happened.

I raced up the hill, grabbed Sweet Pea, and settled her in the car. I backed out of the driveway and headed to the Palace of the Governors. It was unnerving to find Grandmother waiting for me as I neared. As soon as she saw me, she began walking toward the car and steadied herself as she climbed in.

"The time has come, my daughter."

I called Mike and told him to meet us at the Pueblo and let Coyote know where Grandmother and I were headed. "Redmond has Isabella."

I parked the car and helped Grandmother exit when we got to the Pueblo. She grabbed my hand, and without saying a word, I knew she would lead me to the area that had been the scene of my little sister's death lifetimes ago. We did the slow climb up the hill and into the forest, where so many delectable plants lay as gifts from Mother Earth. It was dark and damp compared to the desert area, and its smell was intoxicating. When we reached a pathway familiar to Grandmother, she pushed me forward.

"You go first and hurry. I'll follow."

I handed her Sweet Pea's leash. As I hurried along, I became overcome with the oddest sensation that I was once again nine years old. My feet and stride seemed shorter, the forest thicker, and the daylight darker. I felt light-headed, and my heart pounded to the fast beat of fear of what lay ahead. I didn't know whether I could survive if Redmond had hurt Isabella in any way.

As I raced along, I began to recognize where I was—or had been in the past. I saw the bend in the path and instinctively knew whatever was to come was just around the corner. I continued, barely able to breathe. When I rounded the turn, I half-expected to see Little One on the ground with the deadly snake at her side. Instead, Isabella was sitting against a tree, a cloth covering her mouth, hands tied behind her. Redmond stood swaying over her. I picked up a rock and held it in my hand.

I could see he was drunk. "Hey there, Redmond."

"What are you doing here?" he asked, slurring his words, surprised to see me.

"I came to thank you for taking such good care of Isabella. I'll take over now."

"She's not for sale. She's mine."

"What do you mean, Redmond, not for sale? Are you into selling girls?"

"None of your business ...."

I was outraged at the thought he might be involved in child trafficking. "Redmond, stand back," I commanded. "I'm coming to get Isabella."

"No way," he said as he stumbled forward and sprang toward me. He grabbed me by my hair and forced me onto my knees, where I spotted a large stone. He bent down closer and threatened me. "You bitch ...."

I raised the rock and hit him as hard as I could alongside his temple. Down he went—out cold.

Grandmother had seen the whole incident and nodded in approval. I raced to Isabella and struggled to untie her while Sweet Pea rushed forward. She jumped on top of us and tried to lick me first, then Isabella. Tears streamed down both our faces. As soon as she was freed, Isabella clung to me. I pulled her into my lap, and we cried with relief at being safe. Then we nervously laughed at Sweet Pea's antics before more unbidden tears came.

I looked up at Grandmother, who smiled with relief to see us together and safe. I glanced at Redmond lying on the ground. He wasn't moving, and I couldn't see him breathing. My god, had I killed him? Was I going to save Isabella only to have killed Redmond? I abruptly got up and moved closer to his body while Nica raced toward us and threw herself at Isabella.

I heard Mike and Coyote behind her. My heart pounded with fear, and as they neared Redmond, I asked tremulously, "Is he dead?"

Coyote kicked him, and I burst into tears of gratitude when I heard him groan. I heard Nica crying and asked, "Sweetheart, why are you crying?"

"Because she's my sister-friend," she said.

The two of them were holding onto each other. Those simple words clarified everything, and I knew precisely what I needed to do about Isabella's situation ... if only Maria would agree.

CHAPTER 21

As the men stood over Redmond, Coyote looked at me, curious. "How did you know it was Redmond who had Isabella and that he'd be here?"

"What Mike had said about Isabella being at the house made me wonder—had I missed something? When I looked inside the shed and saw Isabella's bracelet, I knew what had happened. Isabella had promised to wear it for protection, so I knew she'd left it as a clue. Only two men had been in that shed—Redmond and the neighbor. We already knew it wasn't the neighbor, so it must be Redmond."

"Why at the Pueblo? Why here?"

"It's where he'd feel comfortable and most protected."

Coyote nodded in agreement and didn't need me to explain why it was this particular spot. I breathed a sigh of relief.

Mike came forward and crushed me to him. "Rosie, will I ever be able to not worry about you?"

I had to admit that was an interesting question I'd have to ponder later. I whispered back, "I love you too."

Grandmother was exhausted and ready to go home. I gathered the girls in my arms and kissed each little face enough times to make them giggle. Then I tilted Isabella's head up and looked deep into her eyes. "Have I told you lately how much I love you?"

Her eyes held mine. "In so many ways, Mama."

Isabella's wisdom and her choice of words continued to surprise me. Who was this precious soul? I thought of how strangely amazing it was for her to have come from her family in Mexico and endured what she had to find me in Las Vegas so that we could clear up old karma. How powerful the universe was with all its synchronicities!

I smelled my grandmother's perfume all around me and felt her love. "I love you too, Gram," I whispered.

I took hold of Grandmother's arm and helped her back down the hill as she leaned against me. We left Coyote and Mike to deal with Redmond, and this time he was in serious trouble—more than stealing food and camping out in my shed. I felt he would be instrumental in solving much of the mystery behind some child trafficking in Santa Fe.

When we got to Grandmother's house, I helped Grandmother into the oversized comfortable chair in the living room and went into the kitchen to put the kettle on. We all were going to have a special tea that Grandmother had waiting for us. It was a mixture of lavender and other herbs that would calm and relax us after such a difficult time. I got some of Grandmother's homemade cookies and put them on a plate in the center of the kitchen table.

When the tea had steeped, I called the others into the kitchen. I smiled as I watched Nica hover over Isabella, not wanting her out of her sight. When Isabella asked whether Nica could spend the night, I knew she was on the mend.

The girls excused themselves and left Grandmother and me so we could talk. Sensing something on my mind, she asked. "So what are you thinking, my daughter?"

I began to explain what I was planning to do with Isabella. By the end, she seemed pleased and nodded in satisfaction.

"Are you going to be okay, Grandmother, if we leave now?" I asked, concerned.

"Go, my daughter. You have much to do," she urged. I kissed her. "I love you, my dear mother."

"And I, you, Little Bird."

I called the girls to come. Nica had her overnight bag in one hand; her other hand clutched Isabella's. I'd have to talk to them about what happened so they could move forward. Isabella seemed ahead of Nica about that— probably because of all she'd endured in earlier times.

When we got home, the girls raced into Isabella's room with Sweet Pea at their heels. I immediately went into the kitchen to make my calls. I made an appointment with Nancy. I'd rudely hung up on her and wanted to give her at least the opportunity to tell me about the house. Then I called Maria, and we agreed to meet the next afternoon when her sister could babysit the kids. I would pick her up, and we'd return to the rental house, where we'd have the space to talk privately. I'd ask Mike if he'd be willing to entertain the girls, and I was pretty sure he'd agree.

Mike arrived home a while later. He held me close. "I love you, Rosie."

"I love you too, Mike."

Mike handed me an Amaretto and soda and pushed me forward. "Let's go out on the deck, Rosie, and relax. We have a lot to discuss."

"Not tonight, please. It's going to have to wait until morning." There was so much I wanted to tell Mike, but I was in no shape to do it then.

"I see how tired you are, baby. We'll relax tonight and then talk in the morning, alright?"

I smiled at him. "Thanks."

We sat back in our chairs, and soon the girls wandered out with Sweet Pea, who immediately slid under my chair for a nap. I think she was as tired as the rest of us. Isabella sat at the foot of Mike's lounge chair while Nica sat on mine. "What's up, girls?" I asked.

Isabella said, "Can we order pizza tonight, Mama?"

I chuckled. "You're a girl after my heart. Yes, we'll order pizza. Bring paper and pen so we can all choose what we want."

Isabella raced from her seat and hollered, "See, I told you so, Nica."

Nica looked at me. "Isabella said you'd be okay with our asking."

"You can always ask, but that doesn't mean the answer will always be yes."

Nica smiled. "I know."

After I tucked the girls into bed, I stayed with them until they fell asleep. When I left them, I could hardly keep my eyes open. I wanted to ensure they were settled enough to sleep and not toss and turn all night.

Mike followed me into the bedroom, and I thought of Brian for some reason. "Have you heard from Brian lately?" I asked.

Mike looked surprised. "I just got off the phone with him."

"Really? How is he?"

"He's good. He called to tell me he's heard from our mystery man."

"And?" I asked, curious.

"He's away on personal business but wants to discuss a new request. He said he'd call next week."

"Hmm, I wonder where he'll send you," I said, my heart falling at the thought of his leaving—again.

"I expect we'll find out soon enough."

I slept like the dead with Mike's arms around me that night.

CHAPTER 22

T he following day, I awoke and turned to see Mike snoring lightly beside me. As I studied him, I felt a rush of love. Worry filled me as I thought about our circumstances. It wasn't easy to see how this would work out between us. Many factors were unresolved, and I didn't know if he'd be ready for what I had in mind. I sighed. Hearing me, Mike stirred and opened his eyes. He reached out for me and pulled me against him. I relaxed and fell back against him to enjoy what was meant to be between two people who loved each other. It was everything I could have imagined—and more.

Afterward, we held each other, deeply satisfied. I got up my courage and told Mike what I had in mind. I waited to hear what he'd say.

"Rosie, whatever you do, I've said it's your choice, and I'll support you the best I can. But I have to be honest with you. A part of me wonders if all the people involved will agree." As I frowned, he raised his hands and added, "I'm just saying …."

"I know," I said sadly. Even so, I'd already made up my mind to forge ahead.

That morning, I went to meet with Nancy. When she emerged to greet me, she wore a huge smile. "Nancy, I apologize …" I began.

She immediately held her hand up, "Please, no apologies necessary. How is Isabella doing? Is she all right?"

"Fortunately, she seems fine despite all she's been through."

"I'm glad to hear it. Come on in, and I'll tell you what your landlord has in mind."

Once she explained that he wanted to sell his house "as is," except for a few things he'd have Nancy pack for him, she told me his asking price. I was surprised because it seemed more than reasonable, especially since it included all the furniture and accessories.

"May I have 48 hours to think about it?" I asked, becoming intrigued by the idea.

"Of course, Rosie. That'll be fine. I told him it wouldn't officially go on the market for another couple of weeks because I'd need time to gather the things he wanted me to send him. Besides, you still have time on your lease."

Although I saw how this could be an extraordinary gift, I wasn't interested in purchasing the house unless Maria agreed with my plan. That was the only way it would work.

"Gram? I hope you can hear me. Help me make this happen if it is the right thing for all of us."

I felt a puff of air move some of my hair, and her fragrance floated through the air. I closed my eyes and saw red roses, a sign of her love for me. That was all I needed to help ease my tight shoulders and release my tension and worry.

It was time to meet with Maria. As I arrived at her house, Angela answered the door. "Hi, sweetheart, how are you?" I asked as I wrapped my arms around her and kissed the top of her head.

"Is Isabella okay?" she asked, worry showing on her brow.

"She's fine, and she was asking about you too. We'll have a little girls' get-together soon."

"Cool." She turned and called out, "Mama, Rosie's here." She looked at me. "Want to see Rosa? She smiles all the time now."

"Yes, I'd love to see her," I responded.

"C'mon." Maria entered the room, and Angela said, "Rosie wants to see Rosa."

Maria smiled proudly. "She's become quite the entertainer."

When I poked my head into her bassinet, her beautiful little face split into a smile, and she began to coo.

I waited while Maria kissed the kids goodbye and waved to her sister. Then we headed out. When we got to the house, Mike's car was gone, which meant he had the girls with him, and the place was empty for our conversation. Bless that man!

I'd stopped at the bakery on my way to Maria's house so we'd have something sweet with the cups of tea I'd planned to serve. Maria still acted shy after all that happened, and I hoped she could relax away from her house. She was strong-minded about the things important to her, which was good because nothing would be resolved regarding Isabella unless we were open and honest. Whatever happened, I knew this meeting would be life-changing for both of us.

When we entered the house, Maria raised her brows in surprise. I'd seen the same expression on Mike's face when he'd first entered the house. When eyed from the road, the house's exterior didn't reflect the true magnificence of the interior.

I prepared our tea, and we sat at the kitchen table. We soon settled in and became at ease in each other's company. After a few sips of tea, I asked, "Maria, what are your thoughts about Isabella?"

Maria blushed. "I'm so ashamed of Miguel and what he's done, scaring you and Isabella the way he did." Tears filled her eyes and overflowed. "Then to learn the Indian he'd hired had kidnapped her yesterday is more than I can bear. Isabella has been through so much, and to think it was because of my husband—her uncle!"

I regarded Maria with sympathy. "Coyote told us that Miguel is now required to take a course in anger management and to see a therapist for the next six months as part of his agreement to avoid arrest and jail time. Is that right?"

Maria nodded. "I know he never meant to hurt you and Isabella; he just wanted to scare you so you'd leave us alone. He's a good man, but this will do him good. He needs to get rid of that chip on his shoulder."

"He may not have wanted to hurt us, but I'm glad he isn't getting off the hook for what he did. I think it's good he's going to counseling."

We both were silent for a few minutes. I sighed and studied Maria. "So what should we do with this beautiful little girl?"

Maria was quiet before she spoke. "Rosie, it is obvious how much Isabella loves you. She calls you Mama, thinks of you as her mother, and wants you to be her mother." She paused before looking intently into my eyes. "Honestly, I don't believe she'll be happy in any place that doesn't include you."

"I'm not sure how that's going to work," I responded.

Maria's hand covered mine. "If it were my Angela, I'd want her to be happy—whatever it took."

"What do you think her mother would want?"

Maria snorted. "There's no life for Isabella back in Mexico. Her mother would want Isabella to have all the world has to offer. We can't give her that." She looked embarrassed. "I don't mean it all boils down to money because if Isabella lived with us, we would love and care for her. But the truth is that right now, we hardly have room for another. We've had to squeeze Angela and Rosa together in that small bedroom."

"I understand. Isabella would make six children for you to tend to."

"It's not only that. The truth is that Isabella's been with you long enough to have a taste of a better life than we can offer her. I'm sure she'd want no less, and I can't blame her."

I was quiet for several minutes, collecting my thoughts. "Maria, the thing that's become so important to me is the relationship developing between Isabella and Angela, an exceptional relationship. And even further, the relationship between all three girls—Isabella, Angela, and Nica. It's unique and worth holding onto, don't you agree?"

With eyes filling, Maria nodded. "Sister-friends is what Angela calls them."

"I believe there's great value in being a family. Don't you?"

"Family has always been important; it's part of our culture. That's why this is so difficult for all of us."

"I have an idea of how this could work out. Let me ask you how you'd feel if we became family."

"What do you mean?"

"Maria, you have been an inspiration to me. I watched you and saw how you acted at the time of Rosa's birth and all you've gone through since then. You're a strong, loving woman—someone I intuitively trust. I feel we are good friends already."

Maria studied me. "I feel the same way about you. I know in my heart that you, too, want the best for Isabella. No one can ask for anything more than that."

We looked at each other with tenderness. "Have you heard the expression 'it takes a village to raise a child'?"

Maria smiled. "Yes."

"So why don't we become that village for Isabella and Angela? And Nica too?" I added.

This time Maria's smile was as wide as her face. "How would that work?" she asked, curious.

I chuckled. "Here, I've asked for us to become family, and now I'm going to ask you to look at it like we're divorced."

Maria laughed. "You mean we're going to share Isabella?"

"Exactly. If we can work out the logistics, we can make it work. I have an opportunity to buy this place, which means Isabella would have a home here in Santa Fe and one in Las Vegas." I let that sink in, then added, "Isabella loves you. I know she does. Given enough time and shared holidays, Isabella would come around and truly appreciate Miguel as her uncle. Who knows? Maybe he'd even get used to me."

Maria laughed, then became serious. "Do you think it's possible to work it out legally?"

"I think so. I'll need to work it out with the agency. If you, Miguel, and Isabella's mother agree, I can become Isabella's foster mother. We can see the options down the road, but the most important thing is for her to become a United States citizen, don't you agree? That way, she'll have the greatest opportunities."

"I agree that her greatest opportunities are here in the United States."

"I know this won't be easy, but if you agree with my proposal, we can convince the agency that this is a good plan and that I'd make a good foster mother for Isabella. There is also an excellent therapist in Las Vegas whom both Isabella and I can use to work out potential or existing problems."

Maria studied me. "Are you sure you want to do this? Kids aren't easy, and this is a lot to ask you to handle …."

"I love her and believe we're meant to be together in this lifetime. We have lost time to make up for."

I knew Maria wouldn't understand what I meant, but she nodded in agreement and seemed pleased with my response.

"This would also mean that we'd head back to Las Vegas in the next few days so I could get Isabella placed in school. Then we'll return for family time for Columbus Day break, Thanksgiving, and Christmas." I sighed. "There's a lot to think about, isn't there?"

We talked more about arranging things to make this happen. When I returned Maria to her house, she clung to me as we parted. "I think it will be wonderful for us to be family. We can do this; I know we can. I'll talk about it with Miguel." She hesitated, then with a smile, she amended, "No, I'll tell him our plan. I think he'll agree, knowing he's consented to follow what we come up with."

As I drove home, I laughed, "What I wouldn't give to be a fly on the wall when Maria tells Miguel that he and I are going to be family!"

CHAPTER 23

When I returned, Mike was there. "How did it go?" he asked as he pulled me into his arms.

"Better than I hoped it would," I said, smiling. "There's still much to do to make it all legal."

"Yes, you have your hands full for sure."

"Mike, where does that leave us if this all goes through? We've barely had any private time to explore our relationship. How do you feel about all this?"

"To be honest, it's a lot to take on."

My heart dropped. "I understand."

He raised my chin with his fist, forcing our eyes to meet. "All I'm saying is that we should take it one day at a time. Are you going to be okay with that?"

I nodded as his lips covered mine. Mike was right. A good solid relationship takes time to develop from a friendship into the kind of love that endures raising a preteen girl and any after her. I loved Mike and hoped with all my heart that I'd never have to choose between him and Isabella. I wanted them both to always be in my life.

The next few days were filled with love, laughter, and telephone calls to my sister-friends and the agency. Maria told me Miguel was willing to follow our plan, probably because he had no recourse. At the same time, I knew that Maria would have handled it so he'd accept it.

I'd met with Coyote to tell him about seeing the neighbor in the alley at the time of the first murder at Albertson's—something I hadn't intentionally hidden from him. Mike had agreed that the timing was right to expose him. Coyote could convince the neighbor it wasn't me but another person who'd stepped forward and identified him. I didn't want that man near Maria's family—my family now. I'd have to return for a deposition later for both murders. So things were far from over.

Coyote mentioned that when I returned in October, he wanted me to meet with him to discuss the child trafficking situation in Santa Fe.

Maria and I had the three girls spend as much as possible together. They were becoming so used to being in each other's company that I worried they would have a problem with Isabella's leaving. True to form, they handled it well, knowing she'd been back in a few weeks. Isabella was ecstatic to be coming home with me and kept hugging me, calling me Mama every chance she had. Several times she stopped me, looked deep into my eyes, and said, "Thank you, Mama." I choked back my tears and hugged her tight each time she did.

Mike had agreed to accompany us to Las Vegas. I knew he wanted to test whether we could grow our new relationship while dealing with a little girl—one we were becoming increasingly attached to. I also knew he wanted to support me when I dealt with the agency about becoming Isabella's foster mother since we had to smooth over what had happened in Santa Fe. It was going to be a huge adjustment for all of us.

We began to sort through the things we wanted to store in the shed and what furniture we would leave outside. Nancy had a key to the house, and whatever the owner wanted to remove from there was fine with me. Because of his generosity, I ended up with a great deal that included much in the house. Just as we were about to finish packing, Mike's phone rang. He looked at me and mouthed, "Brian."

My heart dropped. I felt sure Brian was calling to tell Mike the mystery man had a job for them. To my surprise, Mike said, "Here, I'll put her on speaker." He turned and held the phone aloft, waving me toward him.

"Hi, Rosie girl, how's Mike treating you? I hear things are pretty crazy there," said Brian.

"I'm fine, Cowboy," I said, using the nickname I'd given him. "How are you?"

"Not bad at all. We have a little business to discuss with you."

"Okaaay …" I said hesitantly.

"You know about our largest client, the mystery man, right?"

"Yes," I answered, puzzled.

"He wants to know if you'd be willing to meet with him privately sometime next week."

"Why me? What's it all about?"

"He wants to know if you can meet him in Utah. That's all I know. It's the only detail I have. If you agree to meet with him, he'll call you himself to discuss it further. Then it'll be between you and him from now on."

"Well, I guess I can at least hear what he says, right?"

I returned the phone to Mike so he and Brian could talk longer. Utah? Why would he want to meet me in Utah? I felt a flutter in my stomach. Something interesting was going to happen. I could feel it. Goosebumps covered my body and confirmed it.

That night, I dreamed again of the vision I'd previously had of calling for Isabella from a high elevation at the pueblo. Although it woke me, I shoved it aside and fell asleep.

On the last day in Santa Fe, Mike, Isabella, and I drove to the pueblo to say goodbye to Grandmother. She had decided to take some time off from selling her wares at the Palace of the Governors. She greeted us with enthusiasm. "Come, my daughters," she ordered, holding her arms wide as she stood in the doorway. Then she turned to Mike with a smile. "Hello, handsome." We all laughed as Mike's cheeks reddened.

Nica rushed from behind Grandmother, grabbed Isabella's hand, and pulled her inside. They ran off, Sweet Pea following.

"Let them go," Grandmother said. "C'mon in. I've made a special tea for us."

I raised my eyebrows, and she quickly amended, "Regular peppermint tea."

Mike was intrigued by all the artwork inside and kept getting up to look at piece after piece. Grandmother and I watched him and smiled. When it was time to go, we stepped outside and heard Sweet Pea barking and the girls' voices from afar. Mike reached for my hand, and we climbed the ridge beyond the house to look for them.

I searched the landscape at the top of the hill and called out to Isabella. She answered from a distance, "Coming."

Standing together, we watched Isabella, Nica, and Sweet Pea run toward us. I suddenly realized we were standing in the same spot as the vision I'd first seen the day I agreed to go to Santa Fe with Isabella. This time I was calling Isabella not out of fear but in love. This time, Mike was beside me.

I felt my grandmother's love and heard her whisper, *"You must keep in mind that all your visions don't always have to stand for something negative, lovey."* I smiled, knowing her words were a good reminder for me.

As Isabella came closer, she called, "Is it time to go?"

"Yes," answered Mike, "It's time for us to head home."

He looked at me tenderly and squeezed my hand. "That has a nice ring to it, don't you think?"

I could barely answer because I was filled with so much joy. The three of us returning to Las Vegas together was such a nice thought … yet there were unsettled things in Las Vegas. And Utah was looming. I wondered whether death was waiting for me there too. I heard my inner voice taunting me with, "What do you think?"

DEATH
RETURNS

Part 2

Las Vegas

CHAPTER 1

T here was no turning back now. I'd arrived home in Las Vegas with a little girl who wanted me to be her mother and a new man in my life who wondered where our relationship was headed.

I was unpacking from our trip to Santa Fe when I noticed my carry-on bag on the bed. It held my tarot cards, and I was reluctant to remove them from my bag. I didn't want any opportunity for the Death card to fall from the deck. It would signal another imminent death, and there had been too many of those lately. When I reached for the bag, it was as if it had been pushed, and out flew the cards. I bent down to pick them up, and the Death card stared me in the face. I sighed with foreboding.

"Mama? Where are you?" called Isabella as she pounded her way upstairs.

Isabella was settling into the townhouse and viewed it as her permanent home. I only hoped that I'd be able to make that possible.

The sad part was it would take time to become her foster mother legally. That was just one complication. The more pressing matter was the growing romantic relationship between Mike and me. I wasn't sure that was going to help my case.

Isabella raced into my bedroom, barely able to catch her breath. Worry marked her brow. "There's a policeman at the door asking for you!"

"Where's Mike? Go tell him to meet me at the front door. Hurry."

Isabella raced back down the stairs, Sweet Pea at her heels.

Mike joined me there. He'd been a police detective before he'd partnered with Brian to form their investigative agency in Boston. "What can we do for you, officer?" asked Mike authoritatively.

"I'm here to speak with Rosalie Bennett. Is that you, Miss?" he asked, looking my way.

"Yes. What's the problem?"

"Are you in charge of the construction site on Industrial Road? The one that's being excavated?"

"I'm one of the two in charge of that site. Why?"

"I think you'd better come and see for yourself."

"What do you mean? What is it?"

The policeman eyed me. "We found a body on-site there."

"Oh, my God! When did that happen?"

The policeman looked embarrassed. "Well, it's more of a skeleton … but we'd still like you to view it before it gets moved."

"Okay, officer, we'll follow you there," said Mike, taking charge. "Rosie, will your neighbor be willing to watch Isabella while we're gone?"

My neighbor Irene had already taken to Isabella on our first day back. I made the call, and Irene came rushing to the door. She put her arm around Isabella and led her to warm cookies from the oven.

Mike and I climbed into my SUV and closely followed the policeman's patrol car. It was drawing attention with its flashing lights and blaring siren, and I looked at Mike and shook my head in dismay at the policeman's display. I wasn't impressed.

We pulled onto the property, got out of the car, and started toward the yellow tape that closed off the far corner of the construction site. Had we not reconfigured the layout to remain within our property line, the body would never have been discovered.

Mike took my hand, and we gingerly crossed to where people were gathered. They opened a pathway for us to reach the edge of a large hole. When I looked down into the hole, there were only bones. It was indeed a skeleton and, unfortunately, just that. Unless anyone had found something else, there appeared to be no clues. Yet as I looked at it, I felt a strange feeling come over me. I thought it was a female who somehow was connected to me. I had no idea why.

I assured several police officers that I had no clue about the skeleton's identity, and we left. As we pulled into the driveway, my neighbor, Ron, was outside, and when he saw us, he headed our way. "Welcome back to the hood!"

Ever since Ron had unwittingly taken part in the shootout with the two people responsible for the deaths of my fiancé and my client, he had developed greater

self-confidence. Unfortunately, that meant Ron had
become a rooster ready to crow his newfound manhood.
Sometimes, I had to remind myself how much I cared for
him. This was one of those times. "Hey, Ron, how goes it?"
"Not too bad, not too bad. You've got a lovely girl there,
Rosalie. What's the story?"

"Too long a story to get into now, Ron," I said as I
followed Mike into the house. "Sorry."

I turned to Mike. "I can't believe this has happened! Do
you know what this means?"

"I think I do because ...."

"Exactly," I interrupted. "The construction company
will blame me if they go beyond the completion date. The
way the contract is written, they're fined every day after
that date if their work isn't complete. If that happens, they'll
say it's my fault for the delay and won't pay the fines. As it
is, we'll have to adjust for this delay. How can we get the
police to move faster to remove the bones and let us get
back to work?"

Mike deliberated. "I think the best way to handle this
is for me to visit the police station. I need to make the
acquaintance of the new Chief of Police anyway."

"Would you? That'd be great," I said, smiling.

"When I talked to Brian this morning, the new chief
had called him and asked if we were available since the
department is still cleaning up some of what went on while
B.B. was police chief."

"Does that mean you'll be here for a while then?"

He placed his arms around my waist and picked me up
off the floor. He swirled me around. "You can't get rid of
me now, baby."

I chuckled. Getting our relationship off the ground was
becoming more and more delightful. Who would have

thought that when working with me to find the murderers of my client and others, Mike would turn into the great love of my life?

Mike headed into the kitchen, and I called after him, "I ought to check in with Romano." I tapped his number and waited for him to answer. He didn't, leaving me no choice but to leave a voicemail.

"Hey, Mike, I will pick up Isabella next door. I'll be back in a few minutes."

Irene looked worried when she let me in. "Are you okay?"

"When excavating for the new office building, they dug up a skeleton. They wanted to know whether I knew anything about it, if you can believe that." Trying to make light of the situation, I added, "You know how the history of Las Vegas has always had people talking about dead bodies in the desert? Well, they're in the city too."

"Well, my dear, as long as *you're* okay, I guess that's all that matters."

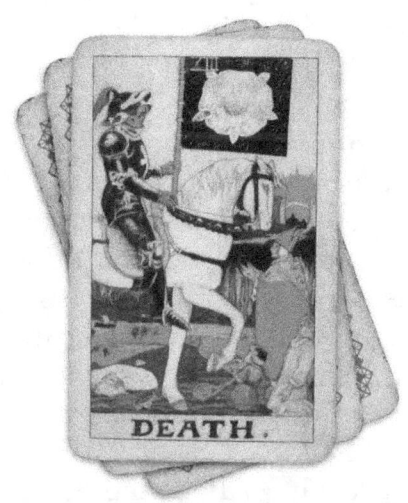

DEATH.

CHAPTER 2

T he next afternoon, I arranged for Isabella to stay with Irene while Mike and I met with the agency handling her case. Since the agency had veered from their strict procedures by having me accompany Isabella to Santa Fe, where her aunt and uncle lived, her case had been a bit unorthodox. Before I left Santa Fe, I had paperwork signed and notarized with her uncle's signature for himself and his sister, requesting that I become Isabella's foster mother.

We entered the building and were greeted by Jacklyn, the head of the agency. "C'mon in. Let's go back to my office where we can talk privately."

Mike gently guided me down the hallway, his hand on the small of my back. I was uneasy about how this would work out, but I was determined.

"Sit here," Mike said as he pulled a chair for me to face Jacklyn.

"Have you had time to review my proposal?" I asked.

"Yes, I have. I think it's fascinating how you and Maria intend to work this out between the two of you. I have to be honest with you, though; I'm not sure you'll receive approval from the state to move forward with this."

Mike put his hand over mine and bent forward, closer to Jacklyn. "Is there anything you can do to encourage them to approve of this situation? It seems like a win/win case to me—you have a little girl who needs a loving mother figure, and Rosie is all that."

I jumped in. "Jacklyn, I hope the state's Social Services representatives won't decide without first talking to Isabella and me. Can I request that?"

"Perhaps I can write that recommendation as an addendum to the report I must send in."

"I would appreciate it."

"Mike?" Jacklyn asked. "What is your part in all this?"

Mike's cheeks redden. "I'm here to support Rosie in her request. I've spent time with both of them and have seen firsthand how Rosie and Isabella interact with each other. I stand behind Rosie and what she's trying to do. I believe she'll be a great mother for Isabella."

The way Jacklyn observed Mike as he spoke, I believed she thought there was more to it than that, but she remained quiet.

"Jacklyn, if I'm going to get Isabella enrolled in school in time for the fall session, I'll need paperwork from you so I can."

"What school are you looking at?"

"I'd like her to attend the private Wilson Charter School in town … you probably know of it."

"Well, I'm not sure that's such a good idea. If you aren't approved to become Isabella's foster mother, and she needs to go into the system, she'd have to attend public school. The change could be difficult for her."

Mike looked as frustrated as I was, and Jacklyn noted it. "Unfortunately, when working with the state, a lot of paperwork is involved, and it will take some time to figure this all out."

"How much time?" asked Mike as he tightened his grip on my forearm. He didn't want me to lose my temper and say something I might regret later.

"I promise I'll do whatever I can to hurry this along. You have my word," Jacklyn spoke with conviction.

I was upset. I stared at Jacklyn, then spoke. "It's against all good sense not to allow a child the best instead of lowering standards by fitting her into a lesser package assigned by the state."

Jacklyn listened intently, and her cheeks grew pink at what I'd said. "I agree, Rosie, but sometimes, we must follow the rules."

Sensing my annoyance, Mike rose and extended his hand. "Thank you, Jacklyn, for your time. Anything that you can do to move this forward is much appreciated."

Filled with resignation, I rose from my chair and grasped Jacklyn's hand. "I know you'll do your best for us."

"I will, Rosie. Trust me; I will." She reached behind her and grabbed a printed paper from her desk. "This signed form states that you are Isabella's temporary foster mother. I want you to know I've gone way out on a limb by doing this. Otherwise, she'd be returned to the safe house where she was before. However, I believe it's in Isabella's best interest to be with you now. She's been through so much already."

This time I smiled gratefully and grabbed her to me. It surprised her, but we hugged with fondness.

"We'll be in touch, I promise," she said.

Settled back into the car, Mike asked, "Where to now, my queen?"

"Let's get Isabella registered in school."

"Which one?"

I cocked my eyebrows. "What do you think?"

"The one we were advised against—the private school, right?"

"But of course."

CHAPTER 3

T he Wilson Charter School was located in the residential section of an older neighborhood in Las Vegas. It was a pretty school with pink bricks and white trim, but it lacked some of the charms the older buildings had with more elaborate trim work.

We were guided into the waiting area, where we sat for nearly 30 minutes before the headmistress stepped out of her office and called us inside. Dorothy Brookside was an attractive woman appearing to be in her early 50s and had an air of no-nonsense. Despite her strict approach, she had a softness and twinkling blue eyes that gave away her sense of humor.

We'd just seated ourselves when there was a knock on the door that separated the two offices situated next to each other. A slightly younger black woman peered in. "You wanted to see me?"

Dorothy smiled. "Yes, come join us. This is the second headmistress, Alicia Johnson."

She looked to be in her 40s, tall and beautiful, with sparkly black eyes. It was easy to see the two of them were friends, comfortable with each other.

At our surprised expressions, Dorothy laughed. "You're probably wondering why we have two headmistresses here. Alicia and I have been friends since college when I was lucky enough to have Alicia as my roommate." She lifted her eyes from us to Alicia and smiled.

"After graduation, we wanted to see whether we could work at the same school and become a package of two. We proposed that, by having two headmistresses, there would be better coverage for whatever was needed. It's like job-sharing that goes on all the time at more progressive businesses today. I guess we can thank Tony Hsieh for that."

At Mike's confused expression, she continued. "Tony Hsieh was CEO of Zappos and is known as the one to initiate an enlightening blend of work and fun into the workplace. He also teaches dedication to the community and has invested $350,000 to improve old downtown Las Vegas. He's done a fabulous job there. Have you been downtown lately, Rosalie?"

"Not in a while. We'll need to put that on our list of things to do."

Alicia jumped in. "This school is quite different from many public schools here or anywhere. We teach here instead of gearing up children to pass national tests. I don't mean to disparage general education, for public schooling has many positive aspects. Our bent here aims to address the more needed education to not only exist in today's society but thrive in it. We do this by teaching the basics while at the same time, we help them *create* their life by making wise choices."

"That's right. Alicia and I believe it's never too early for them to evaluate the consequences of their decisions," agreed Dorothy.

"One of the most important factors here is that every student has to be involved in a sport and a creative activity, as well as some community involvement," Alicia added. "Is this something you're comfortable with for your child? A daughter, I believe you said on the phone, right?"

"Yes, it sounds fabulous, don't you think so, Mike?"

"Yes, I'm just wondering whether I'm too old to attend?" he asked. We all laughed.

"So then, let's hear your story. Something tells me you have quite the one," Dorothy ventured.

When Mike and I'd previously discussed Isabella's and our situation, we both had readily agreed that it made no sense to try and hide anything except for Isabella's and my past life history. "Well, it's an interesting story," I began.

After I explained what I was doing to become Isabella's foster mother and what had led me to do that, I looked at the women who studied me intently, caught up in my story. Both women were pleased when I explained the pact Maria and I'd made to raise Isabella.

Dorothy was the first to speak after a nod from Alicia. "That sounds like Alicia and me sharing the responsibility of this school."

Alicia rose from her seat and hugged me. At the same time, Dorothy came around her desk and shook Mike's hand. "Welcome to the Wilson Charter School!"

"Thank you so much. I barely know what to say." I was so relieved that I plopped back down in my seat.

Alicia said, "Well, there's more. We need her to be tested to determine where to place her. We want to make sure she will be comfortable here and will be able to excel."

"Oh, of course. When would you like Isabella to come in for the testing?"

"We want her to complete the tests at home in a more relaxed atmosphere. You can upload them onto your computer; she can type the answers through our system. She can answer in either Spanish or English; we don't care. You'll need to be available to time her. We don't want the testing to be filled with undue pressure if you know what I mean. This testing is to get an idea of how her brain works. We're not necessarily interested in accuracy now, especially since English is her second language."

"That sounds perfect. When will you send me the information?"

Dorothy answered, "Fill out this form right now, and you should receive all the information no later than tomorrow. Hopefully, you'll work with Isabella to complete it in a day or two." She handed me the form. "I'll wait for you to sign the form, and then let's take a tour, shall we?"

Alicia stood up. "It's so nice to meet you both. I am going to leave you now. I have another family coming in for an interview." She turned to Dorothy, "Just pop into my office after your tour."

The school had a relaxed, comfortable atmosphere, evident in how the classrooms were set up. Extensive equipment was available for science projects and incredible, colorful artwork was displayed everywhere. As we walked through the building, Mike squeezed my hand because he was as impressed as me.

After the tour, we thanked Dorothy, and I said, "This is a great place for any little girl to attend, isn't it?"

She smiled. "Yes, I agree."

Driving home, I couldn't stop smiling. "What a fabulous school!" Mike agreed with a nod.

"I want to provide this for Isabella ... I only hope that nothing gets in the way."

"I hope so, too," Mike said.

CHAPTER 4

As we headed into traffic, I suggested, "Since we're close to where Romano lives, let's pop in and make sure he's up to date on what's happened at the construction site. He never responded to my call, which is not like him."

"Sure, why not?"

"Let me call him first to make sure he's home."

Romano answered on the first ring. "Hey, Rosebud! What's going on?"

"Well, something exciting. Would you mind if Mike and I stopped in for a minute to catch you up on what's happened?"

"Of course not. Randy and I just returned from a short trip to California. We'd love to see you."

"We're right around the corner, so we'll be there in just a few minutes."

***

Randy opened the door. "C'mon in, you two."

Then, Romano trotted into the foyer, where we stood. "C'mon in. Randy, what do you think? Time for a glass of champagne?"

"Celebrating our good news with Rosie and Mike would be wonderful. I'll go get it from the refrigerator."

"Good news?" I asked as we stepped into the living room. "You're smiling, Romano; what have you two been up to?"

Romano puffed his chest out. "Randy and I got married."

"Married? How exciting!" Then realizing what that meant, I asked, "And why wasn't I invited?"

Randy stepped up with champagne in hand and chuckled. "Mister Romano didn't want to wait, so on the spur of the moment, we decided to tie the knot. It was just the two of us."

"I told Randy I didn't need a big wedding. Instead, we're going to have a celebration party as soon as I can organize it."

"And, Rosie dear, of course, you and Mike will be included," assured Randy.

We held our glasses high and tapped them together. Romano and Randy had teary eyes. Sniffling, Romano asked, "What is it you wanted to discuss?"

"I think you'd better sit down for this, Romano," I suggested.

"My little Rosebud, I learned quite a while ago that when you have something on your mind, it's always a good idea to sit down."

I told him about the skeleton found on site and the possible consequences. Romano shook his head.

"I'm going to visit the new Chief of Police tomorrow to see what can be done to get the contractor back to work," Mike said.

"Romano, I'll give Mimi a call and let her know what's happened since she's the one who owns the land at the construction site."

"Yes, she'll want to know about this new twist for sure," he agreed.

The grandfather clock began to sound. "We need to get home, Mike. I have to pick up Isabella at Irene and Ron's house."

"How is Isabella doing, Rosie?" asked Romano.

"She's had a tough summer, as you know, but seems to be doing fine. Mike and I just checked out the new private Wilson Charter School, hoping she can attend. We were very impressed with it and the two headmistresses we met there."

"It's quite a school," added Mike.

"Well, keep us informed about what's going on with her, okay?" asked Randy. He leaned forward to kiss me on the cheek.

Romano stepped forward to do the same, and I smiled— no more air kisses.

I thought about Romano and Randy's upcoming celebration. "I wonder whether Cindy will be invited. I'm sure she will, don't you think?" I asked Mike.

"If so, it'll be good to see her again."

"I think I'll give Cindy a call later. I've missed her too."

I never did call her that night or the next because after we returned home, Mike and Brian's largest client called, throwing everything out of kilter.

CHAPTER 5

I t wasn't as if the mystery man's calling me was a surprise. Yet, I wasn't ready to meet with him so soon. Isabella still needed to be tested for the Wilson Charter School, and I had not yet made any arrangements for hiring a housekeeper who'd be able to serve as a babysitter for Isabella when needed. I also had to schedule an appointment for Isabella and me with the therapist to deal with all that'd happened in Santa Fe. So when I answered the phone, and he asked me when I'd like to meet, I answered honestly, "How does next month sound?"

He laughed.

I began to explain. "It's just that I have …."

He interrupted. "Yes, I understand. Let me look at my calendar and see what fits our busy schedules." He paused. "How do two weeks from today look like for you?"

"I think that'll be okay. May I ask why you want to meet with me?"

"It's not really with me. It's actually for my mother. Many years ago, she had a tarot card reading with a woman who profoundly affected her life. When I heard you were working with Brian and Mike, I naturally did some background research on you. I discovered the woman my mother always talked about was your grandmother."

"Ohh … does she want a reading? If so, I can do it over the phone if that helps."

"No, it's a little more complicated than that."

"Can you at least tell me where we're going to meet? And what time?"

We set the day, and he said, "My chauffeur will pick you up at your place at 9 o'clock and drive you to Utah. I'll join you at the place where my mother is staying. Does that work for you?"

"Do I need to bring anything special besides my tarot cards?"

"No, everything else will be provided. Thank you, Rosalie. I'll see you in two weeks," he ended with a lilt in his voice.

I collected my thoughts. I smelled my grandmother's unique scent and felt her love surrounding me. "Gram, this is going to be interesting, isn't it?"

I heard the smile in her voice. *"Very …"*

I sought out Mike, who was in the garage, bent under the hood of my car, checking the oil. "Well, I heard from the mystery man. We're meeting two weeks from today. Tell me honestly, Mike, what am I getting into? What do you know about this man?"

"Not much. Brian was the first to do some work for him before we set up the agency. We have never met the man, only his chauffeur—a really nice guy. We usually work through him."

"Hmm. The mystery man sounded nice enough, but …. Have you scheduled an appointment with the police chief yet?"

"No, I think it's best just to stop and surprise him. I can learn a lot more that way."

I reached for him, turning him away from the car. His hands were dirty and oily, so he raised them but didn't touch me. Instead, he leaned toward me and kissed me tenderly on the lips.

"Hmm. Nice …" I sighed.

Mike smiled. "I love you, Rosie."

"I love you too, handsome." He was handsome, indeed, with dark curling hair, sparkling white teeth, and smoldering dark eyes. I tore myself from my thoughts. "I better get over to Irene's before she wonders why I haven't picked up Isabella and Sweet Pea yet."

He playfully knocked his hip against mine. "Git then…."

I laughed and headed to my neighbor's.

Ron opened the door. "C'mon in, Rosalie. You're right on time to save Irene. Your girl is giving her a hard time."

"What do you mean?" I asked, alarmed.

"She's beating the pants off Irene in checkers," he laughed.

It was evident by the way laughter floated toward us that Isabella had perked up the playfulness in their house by being there. Sweet Pea heard me and came running. I swooped down and gathered her in my arms.

I walked into the den, and Isabella looked up from where she was seated on the floor. "Mama, I love this game! I've won three times already," she fumbled in English.

I laughed. "Good for you." I turned to look at my neighbor, who smiled. "Irene, you're a sweetheart. I can't thank you enough for watching Isabella for me."

"My dear girl, it was my pleasure. You know how much I've missed my grandchildren since they moved away. I've told Isabella she is welcome here anytime—with your permission, of course."

"How sweet of you. Thank you so much. Isabella, it's time to head home."

"Do I have to?"

"Yup" is all I needed to say for her to jump up.

Irene said, "You go, I'll pick up the checkers this time, and you can next time."

Walking home, Isabella pulled on my hand. "Did you find a school for me, Mama?"

"A really great one. However, before you can attend, there are some questions you need to answer. We can do that tomorrow."

Isabella was silent for a few seconds. "What kind of questions?"

"Ones that will help them know more about you is all."

She lagged behind me, but I was sure I heard her say, "I don't see how that's going to help me …."

CHAPTER 6

As wonderful as it was, waking up with Mike beside me felt strange. I looked at where he lay, still asleep. I was happy he was with me and beyond grateful he supported me in becoming Isabella's foster mother.

For several days now, Isabella knocked on our bedroom door in the morning and plopped herself on top of the bed to ask what the day's plans were. It was interesting to see how easily she accepted our togetherness. On a more intimate level, we'd decided if we were to have our relationship grow in a healthy way, we had to be honest and open with Isabella and not try to hide our growing love.

I observed Isabella as she developed her relationship with Mike. She was starting to bond with him, but she still had a wall around her regarding men. After all she'd been through, I couldn't blame her—kidnapped for sex trafficking at the Purple Passion Lounge and seized again in Santa Fe.

When Mike got up to fix the coffee, she stayed behind with me. Her brow creased with worry. "Mama? What does the school want to know about me? Do I have to tell them everything?"

"What do you mean, Isabella?"

"You know … everything."

"Oh, sweetheart …" I hugged her. "The questions they want you to answer are about how much you have learned: math, language, science, etc. That's how they'll know where to place you in school— what grade to put you in or whether you'll need special help to catch up. That's all."

"Oh, good," she quickly said.

I studied Isabella. Her relief was evident not to have to share some of her personal experiences, which I understood. "Isabella, we need to talk. Move closer," I said as I patted the spot next to me. We leaned into the pillows piled behind us.

"What, Mama?"

"You'll have a chance to talk to someone—a professional—about all that's happened in your life, which will be good for you to do. Meantime, I want you to know how important it is for us to accept whatever happens in our life as part of experiencing all life offers. Sometimes, what happens in our life can be wonderful; at other times, maybe not. It doesn't mean you have to like the experience, but it's important not to bury it or pretend it never happened. Do you understand?"

"I guess so. Do I have to tell everyone about it?"

"Absolutely not. Let me try to explain what I mean, okay?"

"Okay," she agreed reluctantly.

"Not everyone is interested in what goes on in my or your life either. So why tell them? And I keep some things to myself because sharing them doesn't serve any purpose. Do you understand what I'm saying? In other words, it doesn't do anyone any good to know about it—it doesn't benefit anyone."

I knew she'd need to mull over what I'd said. "I share some things only with my sister-friends because I trust them not to share what we've talked about with others, especially if I've asked them not to. Expressing your thoughts and ideas is important, especially if you know you can with those who won't judge you. And in your case, Isabella, I think your sister-friends in Santa Fe might be ones you can trust."

Isabella smiled at the thought. "And you, too, Mama. You're my best sister-friend."

After breakfast, Mike left. "Why don't we get dressed for the day before we sit down to answer the questions for the school, shall we, Isabella?"

"Okay, Mama," she agreed with excitement.

I still had a sip or two of coffee left in my mug, so I remained at the kitchen table to finish it. Sweet Pea came to where I sat and placed her paws on my lap, wanting up. I looked into her eyes and saw such love and trust there that I was humbled. I picked her up and placed her on my lap. As much as she needed my care and love, Isabella required more. I only hoped I could do my part to raise her to be all she desired to be. Thank God I had Maria in my corner. I picked up the phone and called to tell her what we were considering for Isabella's schooling.

After speaking with her, I smiled. I was so lucky to have that woman in my life. I couldn't have found a more perfect partner to help raise Isabella. In addition to having Angela, Maria's little girl, and Nica in our group, I wanted to include Maria's three little boys: Armando, Ricardo, and little Miguel. It'd be fun to discover what little boys were all about, for I knew so little about them. We'd be there soon enough in October—only two months away—for me to find out.

"I'm ready. Are you coming, Mama?"

"Why don't you take Sweet Pea out back, and I'll be with you in a few minutes."

Isabella was perched in my desk chair, waiting for me. I moved another chair close to her, opened my e-mail, and downloaded the forms the Wilson Charter School had forwarded.

After setting her up with the questionnaire, I worked on my *Women Living Well* magazine column about Expectations. I heard Isabella grunt several times, and on one occasion, she slapped her hand down on the desk with frustration.

"Mama? I can't figure this out. Will you please help me?"

I looked at where she was stuck and realized how difficult this must be for her—trying to understand the meanings of some of the English words. "Isabella, why don't you use Spanish for this part of the questionnaire?"

"No, Mama! If I don't know the words in English, they'll think I'm not smart."

"I can speak for the two headmistresses when I tell you they wouldn't think that at all." I had an idea where she was coming from, and I wasn't having any of it. "Isabella, I want you to look at me and tell me whether I'm wrong. I'm sensing that you want to step back from your Mexican heritage. Am I right?"

Isabella bowed her head. She looked up at me with watering eyes. "Mexicans aren't treated as nice as white people, and you know that's true Mama!" she said, raising her voice.

"So, let me ask you this," I said softly. "If you pretend to be white and get away with it, does that make you better than Angela or Nica?"

She was silent for a minute or two. "Noooo ..."

"Then it doesn't make sense for you to try to be anything other than yourself! Do you know how much effort it takes to be someone other than who you are?" I'd gotten her attention now. "It takes so much energy to be someone you're not that it's EXHAUSTING!" I said, playacting it out. I looked up from dragging myself around the room to see a twinkle in Isabella's eyes and heard a small giggle escape.

"Mama, you look so funny! I think you shouldn't try to be someone else either!" Then she laughed out loud.

We laughed together. Sweet Pea barked, and soon Mike stepped into the office. "Glad to see you two having so much fun," he smiled. "When you have a minute, Rosie, can we talk?"

"Sure. Let me help Isabella switch this over to Spanish, and I'll be right there."

When I entered the kitchen, Mike stood at the sliding glass door, looking out. He was lost in thought and jumped when I touched his shoulder. "What's up, handsome?"

"Hey, my beautiful queen," he answered, pulling me close. "I thought I'd fill you in on my meeting with the new Chief of Police. He seems to be a nice enough guy—reasonably young and sticks pretty close to procedures. He's convinced there's still more going on with Johnny and Tony, but he hasn't been able to pin enough on them to put them away. I couldn't say much since we'd gotten involved because of the mystery man and the FBI. He said he hopes we can continue working together, for he wants to take Tony and Johnny down."

"Wow, that's interesting."

"I've already talked to Brian, and he said he'd take it up with the mystery man. Brian thinks he'll be all in, meaning he'll hire us … especially since those two are likely up to no good and most likely still involved in human trafficking. That's something the mystery man strongly opposes."

"What about the contractor and our construction site? Did the chief approve for them to get back to work?"

"He said they'd be finished by late tomorrow, so call the contractor to come in the day after tomorrow."

"That's great!"

"Rosie, there's something else I want to talk to you about. Both Brian and I want to know your thoughts on it."

"Me? What is it?"

"It's about our opening another office here in Las Vegas. It'd become our West Coast office. We'll be coast to coast then. What do you think?"

I let out a tiny whoop. "That would be wonderful!"

He chuckled. He grabbed my hand and led me to the kitchen table. "Let's sit for a minute. We have a few more things to discuss. Do you understand that if Brian and I do this, even though I'll be based in Las Vegas, it means long hours on my part to put this thing together and to get it up and running?"

"What are you saying, Mike?"

"Brian called me because he needs me to help him with an assignment back in Boston. With this new expansion, we'll both be looking to hire another person for the Boston office and now one for Las Vegas. Until that happens, it's going to be a rough few months. Are you up for it?"

"It's going to be a good way to test our relationship, that's for sure ...."

"You've got that right," he readily agreed.

I looked Mike in the eye. "This is such a crazy time to begin to build our relationship. We now have a little girl involved, as well as her other family members, to consider. It seems daunting knowing your time will be split between being away on business and building the business here in Las Vegas." Lost in worry, I said, "Do you realize we don't know each other well? I've never met your family, and you haven't shared that much with me ...."

Mike interrupted me. "I know I love you, Rosie. Isn't that enough?"

I studied him. "I love you, too. However, I'm not sure that's enough to build a lasting relationship. I think it takes more than that." I held my hand up. "No, I'm not asking for your commitment right now. It's too soon for one, anyway. If you're truly interested in growing our relationship, you must share more of yourself and your past with me."

"I can do that," he stated as he reached for my hand.

I looked deep into his eyes. "You have shown Isabella and me great kindness, and I adore you for that. The least I can do is help you get your business up and running. I'll have to trust we can work out the rest together."

Mike's eyes softened. He was touched and lifted my hand to his lips. "My queen and her princesses ...."

I leaned forward so we could kiss. When we finally parted, I looked at the clock. "Gotta run. Isabella's test time is up."

CHAPTER 7

T he next day, I called the Wilson Charter School for an appointment. They'd sent me an email saying they'd received Isabella's completed questionnaire and suggested she come in for a visit. Isabella was excited to see her new school, and I couldn't blame her. From what she'd said, I'd gathered that the school she'd attended in Mexico was pretty rundown. She said there weren't enough books, and they had to share them with one or two other students.

When we pulled into the Wilson Charter School, Isabella was awestruck. "Mama, is this it? Is this where I'll be going to school?"

"Yes, Isabella, it is."

"It's so pretty!"

"Wait until you see inside...."

"Hurry, Mama. Let's go inside."

We sat in the waiting room, and a short while later, Dorothy came to where we were seated. She smiled at Isabella. "So this is where you'd like to attend school, is it, Isabella?"

"Yes, please," she responded in an awed voice.

"I think we are fortunate to have you here, then. Let's go into my office to discuss details, shall we?" She held out her hand to Isabella, who eagerly grasped it. I smiled as I watched them walk together, Isabella with an extra little step.

Dorothy explained that she and Alicia had reviewed Isabella's questionnaire and thought it wise for me to hire a tutor for the next few months. "It's obvious Isabella is a quick learner. It was evident in her ability to answer many questions in English."

Isabella turned and looked at me knowingly.

"Do you have anyone in mind?"

"I do. She's a friend of mine and Alicia's—a retired school teacher, fluent in many languages. With her help, I think Isabella can be at the top of the 5th-grade level by the end of the year. Rather than throw her into the 6th grade, we'd rather see her excel in the lower level. She'll still have much to catch up on as it is."

"That sounds wonderful. What do you think, Isabella?"

"Am I going to be too old for the 5th grade?" she asked, worried.

"In this school, our classes don't go by age. However, two other girls from Afghanistan are older than you in your group. Many of the children in our school come from different countries around the world, which makes it interesting, don't you think so, Isabella?" Dorothy asked.

"I guess."

Dorothy looked at me and winked. "Well then, here is the name and contact information for Ruth Rutledge. I think you'll both like her. If you hire her, she'll bring all the books and paperwork necessary. Any questions, Isabella?"

"When does school start?" she asked, excited.

"In three weeks. You'll be here before you know it."

We left happy to have things settled. I'd send in a check to the school once I got home. We'd just gotten into the car when my cell phone rang. I looked at the name and was mortified—Mimi was calling from New Jersey, and I'd forgotten to call her. I was beginning to understand what it might mean to be so involved with a family that I'd let this, and perhaps other things, slip by.

"Hello, Mimi. I'm so sorry not to have called you before this. I certainly had every intention of doing so. Have you talked to Romano?"

"Yes, that's why I'm calling you. I'm going to catch a plane and be there tomorrow afternoon. I understand from Romano that Mike would contact the new Chief of Police to see what could be done to get the contractor back to work at the site. Did he have any luck?"

"Yes, he did. I've already called the contractor, and he'll bring his equipment to the site tomorrow night and be back on the job the following day."

"Good. How is everything else with you? I understand there's a little girl in your life now—one of the four you saved. Is that right?"

"Yes, it is. I can't wait for you to meet her."

"I'm looking forward to it. Shall we plan to meet for dinner?"

"Why don't you come to my house for dinner? I'll invite Romano and Randy, and we'll make it a party."

197

"Dinner at your house would be lovely. What can I bring?"

"Yourself is more than enough, Mimi." As soon as the words left my mouth, I realized I sounded rude.

"My father thinks I'm more than enough to handle, too," she laughed. "And no worries, I know what you meant."

"I'm looking forward to seeing you, Mimi."

"Thanks for everything you're doing to help with this project. I'm looking forward to seeing you and meeting your little girl."

"See you soon, Mimi,"

Once home, I permitted Isabella to use her phone to call her sister-friends. Before we left Santa Fe, I'd purchased cell phones for her, Angela, and Nica with strict orders for them to follow. They were forbidden to make calls without permission, and they were to use WhatsApp so I wouldn't have high phone costs.

When Mike entered the kitchen, I checked my freezer to see what I could prepare for our dinner party. "What are you doing?"

"Planning a dinner party for tomorrow night."

"Seriously?" he asked, brows raised.

Mike looked so disbelieving I laughed. "Mimi is coming to town, and I invited her to dinner. I think it'd be nice to have Romano and Randy too. What do you think?"

"Sure. That'd be nice," he smiled.

As I snuggled next to Mike that night, I was reminded of how easy it'd been to have him join Isabella and me in everyday life. It had given each of us a false sense of being a proper family. Proper family? I admonished myself. That was far from the truth. Nothing was established. Not Isabella becoming my foster child, and if I were honest, not Mike's and my relationship. And what about all the other things still unsettled? Isabella's tutor, therapy appointments, a housekeeper to be hired, my mysterious upcoming trip to Utah, and a skeleton to identify. What else?

I smelled red roses and knew Gram had sent me a message. What did she always say? *"The only way to eat an elephant is to take one bite at a time."* With that happy thought, I rolled over. I felt Mike's arm tighten around my waist as he pulled me closer to him. I immediately relaxed and was soon asleep.

CHAPTER 8

I woke up excited about having a dinner party. I hadn't formally entertained in a long time. After my grandmother died, I always spent the significant holidays with one of my sister-friends, mostly Karen and Susannah, in Boston. Nancy and her boyfriend often joined us there as well. Sweet Pea and I spent many of the lesser holidays alone. Now that Mike and Isabella were in my life, I was ready to entertain and show them off to my new friends.

"Isabella?"

"Yes, Mama?"

"We've got work to do. We're having a dinner party!"

She came running into the kitchen. "Who's coming?"

"Do you remember Romano, the chef from the Purple Passion Lounge?"

"Yes, he's the one who gave us cookies and hid us in the refrigerator."

"He sure did. He saved your life by doing that. His partner Randy is coming, and so is Mimi, the lady responsible for building the agency's new office and the restaurant for Romano. You haven't met Randy or Mimi yet, but we will celebrate Romano's and Randy's marriage."

"Ohh," she said, pondering that information.

I'd forgotten how much fun it was to fuss over setting the table with my best china and matching antique water and wine glasses. I folded and shaped cloth napkins into a flower and placed them in the center of the entrée plate at each place. It looked festive, and the aroma of baking brownies made it more so.

"Everything is so pretty," Isabella said, picking up a wine glass to peer at it. "This is heavy."

"Want to see something fun? Here, let me show you."

I held the glass by the stem and flicked my finger against the glass to produce a pinging sound.

Isabella's eyes got big, and she began to laugh. "Do it again, Mama."

Mike heard us. "What are you two up to now?"

I showed him what I'd done, and he picked up another wine glass and made his own noise. That made Isabella laugh even harder. We looked at each other and grinned. It was a moment I'd remember forever.

Later, Isabella came to my bedroom. "Mama, what'll I wear?"

"How about the outfit you got in Santa Fe? The pants with the matching top?"

She studied the dress I was holding in my hand. "I guess ..." she said without enthusiasm.

I tried not to smile. I saw where this was headed. Isabella wasn't happy she didn't have a dress to wear. "Or, we could make a quick run to Dillard's?"

Her face brightened. "Oh, Mama, can we?"

Shopping with Isabella was a new experience from the last time we'd shopped together at Neiman Marcus. There she'd been shy and had taken more time picking through things. This time, she whirled in and around the store, pulling out one dress and then another and piling them over her arm. We went into the dressing room area as soon as she finished perusing the racks of clothes her size. I sat outside the door on a chair provided for viewing. Two dresses stood out, and we bought them ... both classic styles.

Next, we purchased simple ballet shoes. I didn't want Isabella to wear any of the high heels many young girls wore, along with lipstick and makeup meant for someone older. There was enough time for all of that later. Luckily, Isabella wasn't interested in all that either.

After we dressed and waited for our company to arrive, Mike poured us an early glass of wine. When Isabella entered the kitchen, dressed in her new clothes, I exclaimed, "Isabella, you look beautiful."

She smiled shyly at both of us. "I know. Come on, Sweet Pea, let's go into the living room and wait."

Mike and I looked at each other, thinking the same thought. Mike spoke first. "We have a lot to learn from her, don't we?"

Isabella became the center of attention as she answered questions from Randy and Mimi, who were curious to hear about her new school.

Then, we heard the pop from Mike opening the champagne we'd bought to celebrate Romano and Randy's marriage. He poured each of us adults enough in a glass to give a simple toast.

"Here's to Romano and Randy. May good health and happiness be yours. Hear, hear!"

When Romano and Randy kissed, Isabella watched them closely. "Do you love each other?"

"Yes, why do you ask, Isabella?" asked Randy, curious.

"I think it's nice, is all," she answered.

Randy's eyes filled. "I think so too."

Mike poured a little more champagne into everyone's glass. "Now, it's time to toast Mimi and all she's doing for Romano and Rosie. Hear, hear!"

Mimi was touched. She patted the seat next to her for Isabella to join her. She pulled Isabella against her and hugged her. "You're the impetus for all that, little one."

"What does impetus mean?" Isabella asked.

"The reason for it all," Mimi answered with a smile.

We had finished our main meal, and Isabella excused herself to call her sister-friends in Santa Fe. "Let's talk about what's going on at the site. Did you find out anything more from the police, Mimi?" I asked her.

"I spoke with them this afternoon and asked whether they had identified the skeleton. They warned me they'd indefinitely shut down the whole project if another body or skeleton were found on site. The coroner said the bones were female, and he thought she'd died of strangulation because of a broken bone in her neck area.

Romano became exasperated. "How can they do that? It's not our fault a skeleton was found there."

A thought came to me. "Romano, who was that girl you liked—the one that was like a runaway freight train?"

"Oh, you mean Susan?" he asked, puzzled. "Yes, that's the one. What happened to her?"

"All I know is she disappeared while I was on vacation." He paused. "I wasn't surprised, though. No one was. We all thought she'd end up dead sooner or later."

"How did she die?"

"I was fairly new at the lounge, so when I asked about her, I was told she'd died. I think maybe an overdose, someone said. There never was a service or anything. I liked her, though."

"Hmm," I muttered.

"I see that look on your face, Rosie. What's going on?" asked Mike.

"I think that skeleton may be Susan."

"Why do you say that?" asked Romano.

"Just a feeling I have," I said, goosebumps traveling along my body, confirming it.

"What was her name?" asked Mike.

"Susan … I don't remember her last name," Romano said.

Mimi looked sad. "Whatever was going on at the Purple Passion Lounge was more than my father realized. Ever since his stroke five years ago, he's not been on top of things as he should have been—that's for sure."

We were silent. Mimi continued, "The only reason I became involved here was to do my father a favor and straighten things out. Nothing more."

Romano and I knew what she'd said was true.

"Romano, who worked at the lounge when you were there?" asked Mike.

"You mean those still left alive? Well, let's see. There is Tony, Johnny, and the bookkeeper. What's her name, Mimi?"

"You mean Sylvia?"

"Yeah, that's the one," replied Romano.

We sat lost in thought until Sweet Pea came bounding into the room with Isabella close behind. It was getting late, and instead of talking more, Romano, Randy, and Mimi rose and bid us good night.

We agreed to meet at 3 o'clock the next afternoon at the site, giving the contractor plenty of time to set up and return to his excavating.

Mike kissed Isabella goodnight, and I went upstairs to tuck her into bed with Sweet Pea. Then, Mike and I worked together to clean up the dishes. As we trudged up the stairs for the night, Mike grabbed me from behind and whispered in my ear. My face grew hot, and my body weakened with pleasure as I listened to what he said. I leaned down and pulled him toward me. I murmured, "Yes, please, all over."

He chuckled. "Then come, my queen, let's not delay."

CHAPTER 9

Memories of our lovemaking kept popping into my mind and flooded me with pleasure. It was Mike's last day before he flew back to Boston to work with Brian, and it would be busy. Isabella's tutor was coming that morning, and Mike and I would meet with the contractor on-site in the afternoon. I wanted our last night together to be special, although I didn't see how anything could top what we'd experienced after our guests had left the night before.

I called Irene to get her housekeeper's telephone number. Irene told me she was a lovely widow in her early 50s and a good cook. I called Virginia, who agreed to babysit that night.

I found Mike in the office. He was seated at the small make-shift area we'd made so he could have his own space to work. I kissed the top of his head. "I have a surprise for you."

"You do, huh?"

"Yup. How do a gourmet dinner and romantic dancing to big band music sound?"

"Where? Here in Las Vegas?"

I laughed. "Yup, it's not all strip teasing here in Vegas. We're attending one of the events at 7 o'clock at the Country Club. I thought it'd be fun." He hesitated. "I know you don't like to dress up, but …."

"No worries. Once in a while, it's good for the soul."

"Okay then, I'll call in our reservation," I said, happy he'd agreed.

I sought out Isabella to tell her my plans for the evening. "What's the sitter's name, Mama?"

"Her name is Virginia Grove. She's Irene's housekeeper, and she's going to be ours as well. She'll stay with you and Sweet Pea tonight while Mike and I go out. You'll like her … Irene says she's wonderful."

"Okay, I guess."

"You have your phone and can always call me if you need to," I reminded her.

Isabella studied me, absorbing my words, then nodded in approval. "When is my tutor going to be here?"

I looked at my watch. "Golly! In just a few minutes."

"I better get my paper and pencils ready," Isabella announced, eager to start.

I felt a tremendous peace when I opened the door and saw Mrs. Rutledge. She was beautiful for her age, and her clothes were colorful and flowing— almost like an older hippie but with more style. Her eyes sparkled with intelligence and humor.

"C'mon in, Ruth," I said, putting my arm around Isabella, who had just joined us. "We're so glad you're here. Isabella, why don't you take Mrs. Rutledge into the kitchen so we can have a cup of tea and talk before the two of you get started?"

"Okay, Mama. Here, I'll take that," she said to Ruth, taking the pile of things from her and leading the way into the kitchen.

We sat at the table, sipped tea, and nibbled on brownies until it became evident I was nothing more than a third wheel. The two of them excitedly questioned each other, enthusiastic about getting acquainted. I excused myself, and they never acknowledged my leaving.

I'd called Sarah, the *Living Well Magazine* editor, who asked if I'd write about perspective. We'd laughed together because it was such an individual thing that the article could be about anything. I became utterly engrossed in it, knowing that we can change our perspective simply by changing our lives.

Finished, I went into the kitchen to see Isabella and Ruth huddled, still working. "Are you almost finished?"

Ruth turned to me, smiling. "Just about."

We agreed that Ruth would come for two hours every weekday for two weeks, and I'd pay her an hourly wage. Afterward, we'd work out two or more sessions per week, depending on Isabella's needs.

I called upon Irene again to keep Isabella for the hour or so that Mike and I'd be on-site with the contractor. I didn't want Isabella connected to the job site in any way; I didn't want her to get hurt. I heard the lilt in Irene's voice as she said, "I'd be happy to have her here."

On-site, Mike and I headed straight to the hole where the skeleton had been. It was obvious the police had enlarged it. There was no way of knowing whether they'd found any evidence. I closed my eyes and stood still. My psychic thoughts confirmed it was Susan who had been buried there. Why had she been killed?

Mike stood beside me. "It doesn't make sense. Why here?" He picked up some of the loose dirt. "I'll be right back."

"Where are you going?"

"I want to talk to the men who found the skeleton. Something isn't right."

Mike left, and I greeted Romano and Mimi, who'd just arrived. We walked to where the contractor had put in posts and tied a string to connect them so that the building for the agency was outlined. Now Mimi could get an idea of the change in the building's location on the lot. It would work out okay, just tucked further back on the lot.

Mike came our way, frowning. "Did you find out anything?" I asked.

"Just like I expected. The two men who discovered the skeleton found it because it looked like fresh dirt and were curious to see what was there." He shook his head in dismay. "The hole was dug there so it'd be found, and you know what that means, don't you?"

Finally, I spoke. "You mean the skeleton was recently placed there even though she's been dead for years?"

"Yup. That's exactly what happened. We must determine who wants to stop you from building on this land. Mimi, what do you know about this property and how your father came to own it?"

"My father has owned it for as long as I can remember. My lawyer is researching the land for my agreement with Romano and Rosie. We'll have to see what he comes up with."

"Do the cops know about this? If so, how come they didn't mention it?" I asked.

"That's an excellent question, and I will take it up with the new chief. This doesn't bode well for these building projects or for you. I'm very concerned because this could be dangerous for you all."

We stood in silence, unnerved by this new information. Was whoever was responsible for this trying to frame Mimi? Or her family? I didn't see how it had anything to do with Romano or me. Having a nice restaurant there wouldn't threaten anyone, would it? Or building an office for human trafficking victims? Not likely. Both Romano and I looked at Mimi at the same time.

"I know what you're thinking," she said sadly. "It's got to have something to do with my father. You're probably right, but I have no idea why."

"Maybe it has something to do with Tony or Johnny," I said as I patted Mimi's arm. "We'll work this out. Don't worry."

"Do you both want to continue with the construction?" she asked, worried.

"Of course," we answered in unison.

"I can't wait to open my restaurant, and nobody is going to stand in the way of that," announced Romano with bravado.

"I feel the same way about the new office building," I said. "I'm not going to let anyone get the upper hand because of this."

"Okay then, we'll keep our schedule unless something else arises. I'll ask my father what he can tell me about the property. I'll probably go home and speak to him directly in a few days. Ever since his stroke, it's hard to understand what he says, especially over the telephone."

We said goodbye and went our separate ways. Some of the joy of what we were doing had dimmed, but we were determined to proceed.

CHAPTER 10

I struggled as I put on the same dress that I'd worn when my girlfriends and I had attended the play *Idaho* at the Smith Center. Mike had only seen it when he'd served as our chauffeur driving us back to Lake Las Vegas, where we were staying. If he were like most guys, he probably wouldn't remember it.

As I leaned forward, ready to zip up the back of my dress, I felt a hand on my bare skin and let out an involuntary yelp. Mike had stepped behind me, and I hadn't heard him enter the room. He lifted my hair and nuzzled my neck. His warm breath sent shivers of pleasure down my body, and I sighed with desire. "You scared me!" I said as I tried to steady my impulse.

"Just checking on my queen," he said as he zipped up my dress with kisses along my spine. "Are you ready? It's getting late."

I turned and smiled at him. "So you like the idea of a romantic evening, do you?"

Mike laughed. "As long as it's with you."

We joined Isabella and Virginia, who sat talking in the living room on the couch. Sweet Pea was at Virginia's feet, seeking adoration and receiving long pats along her back. She smiled her doggy smile. Isabella looked my way and smiled. "Oh, Mama, you look beautiful!"

"Thank you, sweetie. How is everything going?"

"Fine," both answered in unison.

I kissed Isabella goodbye and whispered, "Have fun. Call me if you need to. Love you."

Isabella bounced back onto the couch and continued her conversation with Virginia. I heard the word "popcorn" and knew they'd have a good evening together. I liked Virginia and felt I could trust her, especially with Irene's favorable recommendation.

When we arrived at the club, there was a doorman dressed in black and white. He opened my door with a flourish, and I couldn't help but be reminded of the Purple Passion Lounge. I turned to Mike, grinning. He must have known what I thought because he said, "Not quite the same, is it?"

Inside, I waved to a few people I knew who were older— more acquaintances of my grandmother than me— from established families who had known my parents in their heyday. Only in the past few years did I become involved in any of their events. Mostly fundraising. Since my parents were founding members of this club, the president often reminded me of my responsibility to represent them. This was one of those times.

Each table was beautifully set with colored linens and stunning centerpieces of assorted flowers in artistic hand-blown glass vases—each a different color. We found our place cards and sat with people we didn't know. I appreciated that at this event, the committee always made sure there was formal seating with the idea of making the club more of a community by having us mingle with people outside our circle of friends.

I thought we'd be left alone, but people were curious about Mike. Several women popped around to say hello and be introduced to him. He played his part, despite all that attention making him uncomfortable. We ordered cocktails and chatted with others at our table. The band began to play softer, dreamy music as dessert was served. Mike reached for my hand and said, "My queen." I blushed and placed my napkin in my seat before I rose. The older lady across the table smiled and winked at me, impressed with Mike's romantic gesture.

As I floated into Mike's arms, I whispered, "I love you, Mike."

He squeezed me tight, bent his head low, and whispered, "I love you, too, Rosie. I'm just sorry I have to leave so soon. But we'll work everything out … that is, my queen if you can stay out of trouble and not get involved with any more murders."

"What do you mean?" I whispered back, "*If* I can stay out of trouble?"

"You know what I meant, sweetheart…" he said, choosing not to discuss it further.

After the dance ended, Mike clutched me tight so I wouldn't escape. The big band orchestra had begun to play the next song, and he wanted to continue dancing. My heart melted when I listened to the music. It was one of my favorite romantic songs, and tears threatened as I recalled the words, "I'll never stop loving you whatever else I may do. My love for you will live 'till time itself is through …."

When the song ended, I lifted my head from Mike's shoulder and looked around. I stopped still. Mike stood away from me. "What's the matter?"

"You're not going to believe it! Do you see who I see?"

Mike looked around. "I don't see anyone I know. Who is it?"

"Sylvia. The bookkeeper at the lounge," I whispered.

"You've got to be kidding," exclaimed Mike as he tugged me back to our table.

Sylvia stared directly at me, and when our eyes met, she blanched. She hadn't been expecting to see me there. Instead of being seated at our table, I turned to Mike and said, "I'll be right back."

I followed Sylvia to the ladies' room and waited in the rest area to allow her private time. When she came to wash her hands, I stepped forward. "Hi, Sylvia. Do you remember me? Rosalie Bennett?"

"Oh, yes," she said unhappily.

"I was hoping you could answer a question for me. Susan was a girl that used to work at the lounge …" As soon as Susan's name was mentioned, Sylvia's face lost more color. "I was wondering whether you could tell me Susan's last name."

"I have no idea who you're talking about. Many girls rename themselves that," she said in a dismissive tone.

"I think you'd remember this Susan. She's the one who was wild and out of control. She died a few years back."

"I'm sorry. I'm afraid I have *no* idea who you're talking about."

I knew she was lying. "Oh, that's too bad. Maybe I can call in a few days to see if you …."

"Please don't get me involved in anything," she pleaded with slurred words. She wavered on her feet and turned away. She'd had too much to drink, and I let her leave without following her out. Walking back to our table, I saw Sylvia reach for her wrap, and she and her dinner partner left.

Mike asked. "What happened?"

"I asked Sylvia whether she knew Susan's last name, and she said she didn't. She wasn't telling the truth."

"Rosie, I'm asking you to leave it alone. Let the new Chief of Police handle it, hear?"

"Okay," I said, knowing things would work out as they were supposed to—whatever that was. I certainly wasn't going to argue about it in front of strangers.

When we returned home, Isabella was already in bed, asleep. Sweet Pea heard us and came down to greet us. Virginia was in the living room watching TV and knitting. Everything was peaceful, and I was grateful. I knew I was lucky to have Virginia there. She was a warm person with loving energy and hugged us both goodnight.

"Come, my sweet," Mike said with smoldering eyes. We tucked Sweet Pea back in bed with Isabella and went to get ready for our last night together for a while.

At first, I wouldn't be bothered to put on my nightgown. Then I quickly changed my mind. Is there anything more luscious than having your lover begin lovemaking by removing your clothes with kisses? I sure didn't think so.

CHAPTER 11

S aying goodbye to Mike was difficult for me. What I hadn't realized was how difficult it would be for Isabella.

"How come Mike had to *leave us*, Mama?" she whined.

Isabella had grown to accept Mike as part of our "family" and assumed he'd always be with us. Now it was being disrupted. Maybe everyone felt that way when someone we loved and relied on left for an undetermined time. I reflected on what I knew to be true for me. Ever since my parents' sudden deaths, my first fleeting thought when saying goodbye to someone I loved was a niggling fear that it would be the last time I'd see them. So goodbyes unsettled me until I gave others space in my mind to let them leave without worry. Maybe Isabella felt the same—as if her new security and sense of peace were threatened.

"Isabella, do you remember what Grandmother told you in Santa Fe about how no one can own us?"

"Yes, I remember," she answered, looking at me in expectation.

"We also talked about life as a chain of choices and making our own choices, remember? Now we must add to that—allowing *others* the *freedom* to make *their* choices. Understand?"

"I think so…" she said, slowly nodding in agreement.

"In other words, we need to give Mike the *freedom* to choose to work in Boston for a while. We must *trust* that he'll return to us when he can."

I watched Isabella as she sat silent and mulled over what I'd said. She looked at me and smiled. "Yes, Mama, but you said before, I don't have to *like* it, right?"

I laughed. "No, you don't, my dear, sweet girl. And neither do I!"

We began to settle in without Mike. The construction work continued without delay, and the two buildings' footings would soon begin. Isabella enjoyed her time with Ruth and loved all she was learning. Virginia and I reviewed what she'd do each time she came to do housework. I slowly developed a workable schedule by juggling time for everything happening. I missed Mike each day, as did Isabella and Sweet Pea, who kept searching the house for him. Mike called each morning, making his absence less obvious. All in all, we developed a routine that seemed to work for all of us.

I heard my phone beep in the kitchen where I'd left it. My heart raced when I read the text from the mystery man, reminding me that his chauffeur would be there the next day at 9 o'clock. I'd forgotten that tomorrow was my day to go to Utah. It was hard to imagine what I'd do with his mother or what was expected of me. I had no clue.

The following day I dressed more carefully and slipped on black, non-wrinkle capris and a white cotton shirt. I removed my Indian bead necklace from my jewelry case and slid on the beautiful pendant Mike had bought me in Santa Fe. It felt good to be more dressed up, not so sloppy.

Sweet Pea barked. I kissed Isabella goodbye and grabbed my satchel. My ride had arrived. When I opened the door, I saw an average-sized man in uniform standing next to the extended rear door of the limo. His hat was pulled low and covered most of his face. Remembering the wild limo ride I'd had with my girlfriends and the chauffeur who turned out to be an imposter, I hesitated for a few seconds. I shook off my discomfort and started down the stairs.

The chauffeur was in his 50s and looked in excellent physical health. When he looked up, his smile was broad, displaying white teeth against his sun-tanned skin. His eyes were sparkling sky blue, and his mostly hidden hair seemed dirty blond.

"Welcome, Miss Rosalie. My name is Cal. I'm your driver today." He held one arm open and bowed from the waist, welcoming me to the back seat.

"Cal, would you mind if I sat up front with you? I'd be much more comfortable sitting beside you than behind you. It'll be easier to talk as well."

"No, miss, that'll be fine. Come this way so I can open the front door for you."

Once settled, Cal asked, "Are you all set?"

"Yes, I'm fine. I have no idea what to expect. Can you fill me in?"

Cal was silent as he pulled the limo from the complex onto the highway. Then he asked, "What do you want to know?"

"How well do you know this mystery man?"

"Quite well, I'd say. Why?"

"I have no idea what he expects me to do. I understand he wants me to meet his mother, but then what? Do you know?"

"I know he loves his mother very much and wants to please her in any way possible." He drew in a deep breath. "She's not well; he just wants her to be happy in her final days."

We followed Route 15, and I remarked about the stark and slightly dull beauty of this part of Nevada. We passed Nevada's State Park —the Valley of Fire—and I asked, "Have you ever been there?"

"No, miss, I never have."

"It's an area where you can drive through the valley and view wonderful rock formations in reddish tones that make what you view seem like the valley is on fire with all its bright color. I think you'd love it."

We came to St. George and skirted the city, traveling along a winding road. We finally arrived at a spot with a tiny wooden sign at the end of a narrow paved road, small enough that I would have missed it if I'd been the one driving. The gold lettering without any splashy signage on the sign announced the retreat, and I knew then this was an exclusive place.

As we drove closer to the main building, my stomach became queasy with worry. "Cal, how will I recognize the mystery man?"

"Oh, miss, I'm so sorry I didn't tell you; he can't make it today. But he still wants you to go ahead and meet with his mother." He patted my hand. "You'll be fine. I'll come back for you in a few hours. Let's make it three o'clock, okay? I'll meet you right out front here."

"What will you do all that time?" I asked, curious.

"I'll be fine. I've got things to do in St. George," he smiled.

Cal helped me out of the limo and smiled at me tenderly. "Have a nice time."

A valet approached the front and guided me to the main entrance. I announced myself at the front desk, and the woman sitting there rose and greeted me with a smile. "We're so glad you're here. Elizabeth has been looking forward to your coming."

I followed her down a wide, plush hallway and marveled at a high-end facility with its antiques, artwork, and special touches. When we reached what looked like a separate apartment, the door was opened by a nurse who greeted me with courtesy. "Miss Elizabeth is on the patio. She's waiting for you there." She reached for my bag and took it from me.

I walked through the formal living/dining room onto the patio. A slight breeze ruffled the wisps of thin, white hair on the woman's head sitting there. As I approached, she turned, and a smile spread across her face. "Come, my child," she said as her smile broadened. "I'd recognize you anywhere—you look like your grandmother."

I leaned down and kissed her soft cheek. Her eyes were bright, alert, and the lightest blue I'd ever seen—like Paul Newman's, I thought as I studied her. I was unaccountably drawn to her. I pulled up my chair to sit closer to her.

"You're probably wondering why I asked you here."

"Yes, I am, Mrs …"

"Call me Lizzie, my dear."

"Okay, Lizzie."

She reached for my hand and held hers and mine together in her lap. She smiled as she began her story. "I met your grandmother many years ago at the coffee shop around the corner from where you used to live. She was there on a rare visit from Ireland, taking a break from your mother...."

At my expression, she said without embarrassment or thought of offending me, "I'm sure you were aware your mother and grandmother needed a break from each other occasionally."

I nodded, and she continued, "It's only natural sometimes between mothers and daughters ...."

She closed her eyes, lost in long-ago memory. "I was so lost that day. I didn't know what I was going to do. I was so angry to be in the situation I was in. I didn't feel fit to be a mother. I was debating whether to give the baby away or not. I was so confused and upset," she said, squeezing my hand tighter.

"I'm so sorry ...."

"No, no, my dear," she interrupted. "Thanks to your grandmother's abilities and loving spirit, she showed me that if I kept the baby, I'd have the most glorious life with him ... and I have." She brightened, her thoughts happy.

"I'm so glad for you. What can I do for you?"

Instead of answering, she looked at me with twinkling eyes. "I think as we age, we feel we've paid our dues just by living as long as we have. We've survived the ups and downs—the rollercoaster of life. But the fact is, whether life is supposed to be easy or not, we tend to mess it up just by being human."

I chuckled because I heard the truth in what she'd said.

"I look at you in all your beauty and all the years ahead of you, and I have to be honest … I'm a bit envious. It's hard to age. Even my 92 years feel like several too many to carry around." She chuckled, shaking her head. "Here we are born as a beautiful baby, all fresh and new. As we age, we become like an old, worn-out car—still running, but barely. And our looks! Oh my! We look so unappealing! And this is how we are to be remembered?" She laughed. "Life has an odd sense of humor. I guess all we can do is laugh at it."

I laughed with her. My grandmother had felt the same way. "So, how can I help you?"

She looked at me with sadness. "I'm not well. I'm dying. I don't want to die with regrets about what happened in the past. Do you understand?" I waited for her to continue. "This is about my daughter. I want to ask her forgiveness before I cross over."

"Why don't you ask her to come here and meet with you?"

Tears filled the older woman's eyes. "I wish I could …."

Suddenly, I understood that her daughter was no longer alive, and she was hoping I could contact her and help set things right between them. However, it didn't always work that way. "Shall we see what the tarot cards say?"

I returned to the kitchen area, where the nurse sipped coffee at the small kitchen table. She retrieved my satchel, and I walked back to the patio. I pulled out the cards and began to shuffle them. Although I'd offered to take the cards to her, Lizzie waved away that idea and painstakingly made her way to the table and sat down. She was out of breath, and her face turned pale from getting to me. I continued shuffling the cards until I placed them in the center of the table. I asked Lizzie to cut the cards twice and make three separate piles so I could gather them in the correct order. Her eyes brightened.

I double-laid them out with two cards in each of the five spots so that the second card was the one to influence the first. It was always an exciting way of reading the cards in the layout of "the way of desires." As we looked at the 5th pile and the last two cards, Lizzie and I gasped when we saw the Death card with the Sun card, the influencer. The Death card and the change it would bring meant a new beginning for Lizzie and confirmed her actual death. The Sun card showed the development of a more open attitude and a promising sign for partnership. That boded well for Lizzie and her daughter to restore their love.

"Lizzie, these cards show you the possibility of you and your daughter resolving the difficulties you both experienced in the past. You do know, don't you, that the cards aren't the magic? They are to be used for guidance. The magic happens when you take the necessary steps to create forgiveness between your daughter and yourself. It's not as difficult as you may think. Send loving thoughts and spoken words to her. Ask for her forgiveness. I'm sure she's ready to hear those words and return her love to you."

Lizzie reached for my hand and squeezed it as tears rolled down her cheeks. "Thank you so much, Rosalie. I believe you might be right."

The nurse stepped into the doorway. "Are you ready for me to serve lunch?"

"Yes. Your timing is perfect. And don't forget the champagne! You will join me, Rosalie, won't you? I think we have several people to toast."

Lunch was delightful. We lifted our glasses of champagne and toasted Lizzie's daughter and my grandmother. I saw Lizzie's heart lightened with the hope of what she intended to do to rectify the past. After a bit, I noticed she was beginning to fade.

When I rose, Lizzie reached for my hand. "Wait, I have something for you. Can you please ask the nurse to bring it in?"

The nurse must have known about this because she was already heading our way, holding a velvet box. She handed it to Lizzie, who smiled and held the box out to me. "Thanks to your grandmother, this helped me from making a huge mistake. I'd look at this periodically to remind me I'd made the best, most loving choice. It now belongs to you … I'm simply returning it," she said as she handed me the box.

When I opened it and looked inside, I saw a silver necklace I'd picked out as a little girl for my mother to give to my grandmother as a gift. I gasped and felt off balance, as though someone had shoved me. I could barely breathe as I became mesmerized at seeing it again. It brought forth a miserable memory. "How did you …?"

"Oh my! I didn't mean to upset you," Lizzie said in a distressed voice. "Did you not know I had it?"

All I could do was shake my head.

It was close to 3 o'clock, and Cal would be outside, waiting for me. I stood up, wanting to escape. "Lizzie, it's been such a pleasure to meet you. I'm so glad we had this time together."

As I bent to kiss her, she grabbed my hand. "Rosalie, I'm going to be selfish and ask whether you would consider visiting me again. Maybe next week?"

I gave her a feeble smile. "Of course. I'll have to check my schedule to see what I can work out." I planted a kiss on each of her wrinkled cheeks. "Many blessings, dear one." I gave her an extra hug and left.

Saying goodbye to Lizzie wasn't a simple thing for me to do because she reminded me of my grandmother when she had been close to death. I saw the same look about her and had the same feeling for Lizzie that I'd had just before my grandmother passed. I knew she didn't have much time. Hopefully, she would be able to release her fears about not being forgiven for whatever she'd done and would be able to rest in peace when her time came.

I hurried out front, where Cal stood waiting for me with the front passenger door opened. This time, I surprised him by saying, "Cal, would you mind if I sat in the back?"

"Certainly, miss, not at all."

Once on our way, I pulled out the jewelry box from my pouch and looked again at the necklace. It was a large silver rounded heart strung on a silver link chain that, in its simplicity, was magnificent. Memories drifted from my mind. As a small child, I was aware of the rift between my mother and grandmother, making some of our times together awkward. One day while shopping with my mother, I insisted on her buying this necklace for my grandmother, hoping it would symbolize a renewed connection between them. My mother had been rewarded for her efforts when she saw the pleasure on my grandmother's face as she opened the box and saw what was inside. I closed my eyes, lost in thought. Looking back, I remember going to the coffee shop that day with my grandmother. I vaguely remembered my grandmother reading the cards for a lady there, which I now knew must have been Lizzie. Several days later, my mother asked my grandmother where her necklace was. My grandmother said she'd given it away, and upon hearing that, my mother became furious and hurt, not allowing my grandmother to explain. The two began to argue as I stood back, watched, and listened to them until I couldn't stand it anymore. I screamed at them to stop. I'd shouted, "I hate you both!" and marched away.

My grandmother's visit ended abruptly, with all three of us harboring bad feelings. A day later, my parents readied themselves for a performance in Italy. At the time of their departure, I'd remained stiff and aloof, unaware that their plane would crash and I would never see them again. Even today, that memory filled me with such regret that it still causes me pain.

I sensed Cal watching me, and I looked to see his worried expression in the rearview mirror. "Are you okay, miss?"

"Oh, Cal. Regrets are such a curse, aren't they?"

"Yes, miss, for sure … until you set them free."

I closed my eyes and leaned back, thinking I must do everything possible to ensure Isabella wouldn't regret her relationship with her mother. Cal coughed to awaken me gently when the limo pulled up to the front of the house. He stood next to the opened door waiting for me to collect myself and my belongings.

"Thank you, Cal, for letting me rest."

"Of course, Miss," he said, worried.

"Please call me Rosie." I paused. "Cal, can I give you a hug?"

He looked surprised for a second, then opened his arms. I hugged him goodbye. I walked away and turned back, "Oh, Cal, I almost forgot. Lizzie would like me to return for another visit next week. I'll have to check my schedule first, though. Please convey her wishes to your boss and let me know what he wants me to do."

"Yes, miss … Rosie. I think he'd be very pleased you'd consider doing that."

"But of course. Lizzie reminds me of my grandmother, which makes her special to me."

"Yes," said Cal solemnly. "Grandmothers are special, all right."

A thought flittered through my mind and left me before I could grasp it. Sweet Pea came running toward us, barking a welcome. Cal bent down to greet her and looked up with a smile. "She's cute."

Sweet Pea's tail flew back and forth. Then Isabella joined us. "Hi, Mama! Who's this?"

I introduced Isabella and Cal. They smiled as each took time to study the other. Finally, Cal said, "Well, I better be going. I'll be in touch."

Isabella stood by my side as we watched him leave. "He's nice, isn't it, Mama? Will we see him again?"

I nodded. "I'm sure we will."

CHAPTER 12

I was beaten... completely exhausted. I went through the motions of fixing dinner while my mind remained stuck on the necklace. Later, Isabella went upstairs to her bedroom to call Santa Fe while I stayed at the kitchen table. The phone rang, and I was pleased it was Mike. "Hi, sweetheart! Is everything okay?"

"Just checking on my queen and her entourage now. Wasn't today your trip to Utah? How did it go?"

"It was okay," I answered with heaviness. "I didn't get to meet the mystery man... he couldn't make it. You're right about Cal, though. He's a very nice man."

"What did the mystery man's mother want?"

"Lizzie? Unfortunately, she's ill and is dying. She wanted to clear up issues with her daughter and asked for a reading. I think it helped her. She would like me to visit again. I need to check my calendar first. What about you? What's going on there?"

"Brian and I hired a new guy who worked in the field with us today. Brian thinks he will work out just fine, which means I should be able to return home in a few days."

"That's great!"

"Yes, baby, it sure is."

Mike and I needed to talk soon about our relationship. I wanted our relationship to strengthen. I didn't wish Isabella and me to fall so much in love with him that it'd be devastating for us if the relationship fell apart. A niggling worry overcame me, for he still hadn't shared that much about himself. I felt I needed to learn more about Mike and his past. Maybe I'd do a background search on him.

Our call ended, and the phone rang again. This time, it was Mimi. "Hi, Rosie! I thought you should know Tony is headed your way—supposedly on vacation—but I don't trust him. He has no business being on the construction site or having anything to do with it. Just to be on the safe side, I'm going to be there in the next day or two."

"Tony being here sounds like trouble for sure. Let me know if you need me to pick you up."

"I'll take a taxi to my newly rented apartment just off the strip. How is that darling little girl of yours doing, Rosie?"

"She talks about you all the time and all you're doing because of *her*."

Mimi chuckled. "See you soon."

It was time to head to bed. As I climbed the stairs, I heard Isabella laughing, swelling my heart. I knocked on her door. "Hi, Sweetheart. How are the girls?"

"Here, Mama, do you want to say hi?"

I reached for her phone. "Hi there, Nica and Angela! How are you girls doing?"

It was fun to talk with them for a bit. "Well, give my love to Grandmother and Maria," I ended.

I handed the phone back to Isabella. "Just a few more minutes, Isabella, then it's time for bed. I'll be back to tuck you in."

I smiled when she mouthed, "Okay."

I was curious to know what tomorrow would bring. At that thought, I remembered the saying, "Curiosity killed the cat ...."

CHAPTER 13

T his would be Isabella's last time with her tutor before school started in a few days. Today was big for them since Ruth would test Isabella on what they'd been working on.

After Ruth arrived, I fixed her a cup of the special tea I knew she liked, and we sat at the table and waited for Isabella to join us. Ruth said, "I'm sure you know how bright Isabella is. You probably have realized by now she has a gift for languages. She speaks English as well as anyone who grew up with it. Let's get her involved in Asian languages because it will provide an opportunity for her in the future. How do you feel about that?".

"I couldn't agree more. Are there some things Isabella needs to work on?"

"She's a perfectionist, which we both know can be a drawback as much as an asset. Even though I push for

235

accuracy, I don't want anything less than perfect to be discarded as not worthy. That's unhealthy, so maybe we can help her with that between us."

"I want to ensure that Isabella doesn't feel she'll only be loved and accepted by me if she's perfect or the best at everything. Who needs that pressure? Besides, that's not the way I roll. I want Isabella to live the most wonderful life possible—whatever that is."

Ruth smiled and nodded in agreement.

A headache had formed, and worry about what was happening at the construction had grown. I felt the urge to get to the site right away.

"Will you be alright if I run a quick errand, Ruth? I need to check on the construction site."

"Isabella and I'll be busy anyway, so take your time."

Once at the site, I parked on the side street, walked in, and saw Tony talking to the construction foreman. The foreman looked up and saw me. He said something to Tony, who turned around, surprised to see me. "What are you doing here?"

"I might ask the same of you, Tony. What are you doing here?"

"I have a right to be here. I'm the owner of all this."

"No, you're not, Tony. Mimi told me that you're not even allowed on the property. Do you want me to call her right now and see what she has to say about that?" I challenged.

Tony flushed with anger, and instead of lashing out at me, he turned his back and ignored me. He began to talk to the foreman again, but I was having none of it. I caught the foreman's name embroidered on his shirt. "Butch, I need to speak to you right now."

Butch looked torn between Tony wanting his attention and my command. "That's okay, Butch; we'll catch up later,"

Tony said. He refused to acknowledge me as he passed by and headed to the car where his flunky, Lorenzo, was seated in the driver's seat.

The foreman and I watched Tony walk away. Then I turned back to Butch. "What did Tony want?"

"Nothing ..." Butch muttered.

"Butch, let me be clear that Tony is not allowed here on this site. He has no authorization for anything to do with these jobs. Do you understand? No one outside this construction company and the subs is allowed on this site except for Mimi, Romano, and me. Oh, and Mike too. And just so you know, I *will* report this to Mimi."

Butch held up his hand in defense. "Okay, I'll see that it doesn't happen again."

He walked away to one of the workers who had called out to him as I pulled out my cell phone and headed to my car.

I called Mimi and left a voice mail message "Hi, Mimi, I'm just leaving the construction site now. You had a right to worry about Tony; he was already on site when I arrived."

I had no sooner hung up with Mimi than the phone rang again. This time it was Jacklyn from the agency. "Hello, Rosie, how are you?"

"I'm fine, and you?" I asked nervously.

"I'm just going over some paperwork regarding Isabella. Thank you for letting me know she's registered at the Wilson Charter School. We'll need background checks on those in Isabella's immediate life. We'll keep it simple and make it just those in Las Vegas. I'll need you to complete a list and forward it to me. Please include Ruth, perhaps your close neighbors, and others who will positively influence her daily life. Oh, and don't forget to add Mike."

I said I'd get back to her in a day or two. I'd had an odd sensation wash over me when Jacklyn mentioned Mike, so I phoned him for details.

"Hey, Rosie, is everything all right?"

I told Mike about my conversation with Jacklyn. "So Mike, when and where were you born?"

"I was born on January 27, 1979, in Jackson Hole, Wyoming."

"You're an old man, Mike. You're seven years older than me!"

"You forgot wiser, didn't you? Older and wiser?" he teased.

I laughed. "What's your middle name?" There was silence. "Well, come on! What is it?"

"Shiye ..." he answered.

"Can you spell it? Is it a family name?"

"S-h-i-y-e. It's Navajo for a son. My mother was a Navajo."

"Well, it's a beautiful name. Is she still alive?"

"No, neither of my parents is," he answered, dismissing them. "I was going to call you anyway because I plan to leave tomorrow and head home. Sorry, baby, but Brian's calling me, and I've got to go."

"Can't wait to see you! I love you, Mike."

"Love you too, baby."

With the middle name of Shiye, it should be easy to find Mike's background search online. I wanted to do this before Jacklyn could do her background check on Mike ... I didn't want any surprises.

When I got home, Ruth said, "Isabella did well on her test."

"Do you want to know what I scored, Mama? I scored 96! At first, I was disappointed not to have them all correct, but Ruth said it's no fun if there's nothing new to learn."

Ruth smiled and winked at me.

"I agree," I said as I took Isabella in my arms and kissed the top of her head.

We said goodbye to Ruth, and Virginia showed up to do some fall housecleaning. Instead of helping her, I met Romano at the construction site. He called to say there was a problem and he needed my help.

Once there, I saw Romano talking to Butch, who stood there with a smug smile and his arms crossed over his chest in a bullying fashion. Randy stood back from them and frowned. Closer, I heard Butch say, "Here she is; you'll have to clear it with her."

"What's going on?" I asked, perplexed.

Romano's face was beet red, and sweat appeared on his brow. He was distressed and practically hurled his words at me. "He said Randy is not allowed on site with me to check out the restaurant."

I was furious. "Butch, you know better than that. I didn't think I'd have to spell it out for you. If we show up with someone, we approve them to be on site. So what's your game, Butch?"

"Just following your orders …" he said.

"Next time, why don't you try to follow your brain," I snapped. "C'mon, Romano and Randy, let's see what's happening at your site."

As we headed there, Butch tagged along behind. Looking at the poured cement, Romano and I shared the same thought. "It looks so big, doesn't it?" Romano exclaimed, pleased.

"It's going to be wonderful to have Romano's restaurant up and running, right?" I asked Randy.

"Yes, it is. Did you know that I'm going to be the maître d?"

"No, I didn't. How exciting is that!"

Romano paced around the hole, imagining the finished product. Randy and I smiled as we watched him. Butch left us, and we walked to our cars.

CHAPTER 14

T he next morning, Irene called and invited Isabella to spend the day with her to bake cookies and freeze them for her after-school snacks. I hesitated but realized I'd have to let go of having Isabella all to myself and allow her relationships outside myself. I kissed her goodbye and sat at the computer to research Mike's name.

As expected, there were many Michael Williamses. When I narrowed it down to Jackson Hole, Wyoming, there were five different ones. When I added Shiye, there were two Michael S. Williamses. I clicked on the first one, and it said he was married, so I clicked off that one and clicked on the next. This one said he was born on June 27, 1979, and I wondered whether I'd misunderstood the month Mike had told me he'd been born—January 27, 1979. This Michael had two siblings—sisters—and was divorced. My heart skipped a bit, and a flush of heat coursed through me.

I paid to download more information and searched for Mike's picture. A photo of the man flashed across my screen. It wasn't Mike. I had the wrong person! I immediately went back to the first Michael S. Williams, which stated he was married, and when I saw the photo of Mike, my heart fell. My mind screamed that this had to be a mistake. I couldn't allow anything more to tempt the state not to consider me fit to become Isabella's foster mother! I had enough to do to overcome Isabella's kidnapping in Santa Fe while I had been in charge of her.

As the severity of the situation hit me, I started to cry big gulping sobs. Had I reached the point where I'd have to choose between Mike and Isabella? There was no way I'd let Isabella down, and if that meant my relationship with Mike would bar me from being Isabella's foster mother, I had no choice. As tears trailed down my face, I made noises of distress as I tried to contain my anguish— so much so that Sweet Pea came to where I sat, put her paws on my lap, and whined.

"Oh, Sweet Pea, what has just happened?"

The longer I sat at my computer, the madder I got. I became enraged and let out my anguish because I knew I'd be a bigger mess when I confronted Mike if I didn't release some anger. I'd received a text message that he was on his way home and would arrive later tonight— he'd catch a cab to the house. I replied, "Good," because I'd be relieved to deal with this disaster sooner rather than later.

Isabella came running in the door, all excited. When she saw I was crying, she came close and studied me. "Are you okay, Mama?"

"Yes, sweetie. I just read something sad, which made me cry, but I'm okay."

She took me at my words and excitedly said, "Gramma Irene wants me to ask you whether I can sleep over because they have the Cinderella movie. And we're going to have pizza for dinner too!"

I love the Universe because things always seem to work out in mysterious ways. Isabella's being at Irene's was the perfect solution to provide Mike and me our private time to deal with this new situation. "I think that sounds wonderful, sweetheart. Go pack your overnight bag, and I'll call Irene."

"Thanks, Mama."

I closed my eyes and began to meditate. I felt my grandmother's hand as she smoothed my hair like she used to do when I was little, *"Listen to what is said and know obstacles are not there to stop you but are there for you to overcome, making the victory even sweeter. I love you, darling girl."* And she was off, leaving a whiff of her perfume behind.

When I heard the cab pull into the driveway later, my heart beat faster with a joy that I couldn't squelch. I needed to be strong and knew well enough that I'd need to control my temper. When Mike entered the door, he was excited to be home and expected me to be, too. I had to force myself to remain seated in the living room and not jump up and run to him. When he heard me say nothing more than "Hello, Mike," he looked puzzled.

"Hey, baby, what's up?" he asked, perplexed.

"Mike, we have a problem. Take time to settle in, and then we need to talk," I stated flatly.

"No, Rosie, let's talk now," he said as he bent forward and kissed me while I sat stiffly.

"Alright," I said in a heavy voice, "we might as well get this over with."

He sat beside me and placed his arm around me. It took all my resolve not to snuggle against him, but I needed to be strong and settle this predicament. "What's the problem, Rosie—so much so, you didn't even welcome me home?" he asked, worried.

His words stung. No one likes to be treated the way I'd acted toward Mike. "As you know, Jacklyn called to tell me she needed to do some background search on those who would have the greatest effect on Isabella. That's why I called you for your birth date and full name."

"Yes, so what's the problem?"

"I thought I'd do my own research since you haven't shared that much with me. I wasn't happy with what I found," I said sadly.

His face got red. "Listen, I was just a kid who was left to fend for myself most of the time. Yes, I got into trouble back then, but as you know, I straightened out. I served in the Marines, got into police work, and became a detective. They won't hold anything against me for things I did as a kid, are they?"

"Nooo… It's not that. What else can you tell me?" I asked in a soft voice.

"Nothing, really," he answered with certainty. "Why?"

"How about being married?" I snapped, annoyed that he hadn't been forthcoming.

"I'm not married! You must have me mixed up with someone else!"

"Mike, I want you to look me in the eye and tell me you've never been married," I demanded.

"Where does it say I'm married? Married to whom?" he challenged, looking around as if the answers were right before him. He sat with a faraway look until disbelief crossed his face. "Oh no, this can't be happening...."

I remained quiet and held back a nasty retort. "I'm going to kill Brian! Rosie, it was never a real marriage, honest. Several years back, Brian and some other guys came with me to Las Vegas to celebrate my joining the company as Brian's partner. The guys knew I didn't drink, so they got me so drunk that I remember very little about the trip. The next morning when I got up, the guys teased me and said, "Congratulations." For most of the day, they refused to tell me why they'd said that. They just laughed each time I asked. Finally, Brian filled me in on their little joke. We all were drunk, but since I was so out of it, they thought it'd be funny for me to get married to a dancer they had partied with that night. I guess I'd passed out, and nothing happened. Afterward, they paid her to sign the papers for an annulment and get it filed."

"You want me to believe something that stupid?" I asked, incredulous.

Mike's face fell. "I know it sounds ridiculous, but it's the truth. We were just crazy guys visiting Las Vegas— out on the town—doing all sorts of dumb-ass things. Call Brian. He knows more about it than I do," he urged.

"So, what was her name?" I demanded, furious. "Her real name, please, since it's listed as Martini Darling."

"I don't even know ... maybe Brian remembers. I don't," he ended in a small voice.

"Why are you listed as still being married? I need the truth, Mike. All this affects my chance of becoming Isabella's foster mother, and I can't allow anything to interfere with that," I pleaded, angry tears beginning to flow.

Mike was nearly as upset and angry as I was. "Let's call Brian right now. I'll put him on speakerphone, so you can hear what he has to say, and you can ask any questions you want."

I sat in dismay at this turn of events. Mike stood up and punched in Brian's number. We both held our breath as we waited for him to answer.

"Hey, Mike, how goes it?" asked Brian when he picked up.

"You're on speakerphone with Rosie and me. We have a problem, Brian. Do you remember when we guys came to Las Vegas to celebrate my becoming your business partner?"

Brian began to laugh. "Who could ever forget that time? You were so drunk—I can't believe we put you through all that mess. It's a good thing you finally forgave me. What's the issue?" he asked, chuckling.

"There's nothing funny about this, Brian. When Rosie did a background check on me, I'm still listed as married!" he roared angrily.

"What do you mean, still married? We paid off that dancer to take the signed annulment to the registry. You mean she didn't do it?" he asked in disbelief.

"Apparently not," said Mike in disgust.

I interrupted. "Brian, what was her name … her real name? Do you remember it?"

There was a long pause while Brian racked his mind for the answer. "I don't remember her full name or whether she even told us what it was. Everything was pretty hazy. I remember looking at the signed paper, but she didn't use her full name. It was supposed to be a joke. Listen, I'm really sorry …."

I interrupted. "We'll need you to help locate this Martini Darling as soon as possible. This is a priority, Brian. Do you understand? The agency that handles Isabella's case will be doing their background check on Mike, and what they find can ruin my chances of becoming Isabella's foster mother. I can't have that, do you understand?" I said as my voice rose louder and higher in pitch.

"I understand," said Brian in a small voice. "We'll start on this first thing in the morning, I promise. I'll contact the other guys to see whether they can remember more than me. We were pretty drunk ..."

"Any more questions to ask him, Rosie?" asked Mike tightly.

I stood next to Mike so that I could speak on the phone. "How will I stop killing you two if this doesn't work out?"

Mike pulled me toward him. I collapsed against him and began to sob. I heard Brian say, "I'm so sorry." at the same time, Mike said, "Talk to you later," and ended the call.

Mike gently pulled me back onto the couch, gathered me in his arms, and held me tight. His face twisted in sorrow, and I saw a tear of his own as he said in a thick voice, "We'll fix this, Rosie, I promise."

CHAPTER 15

I woke up the following day with Mike scanning my face, a worried expression on his. His hand reached out, and he traced my eyes with his thumb, wiping away little crusts of dried tears. He then leaned closer and kissed each eyelid. He said in a tender voice, "I hate to see you cry, especially if I'm the one who caused those tears."

I knew he didn't want to hurt me. "Mike, you have to straighten out this mess right away," I urged, trying not to cry.

"I will, I promise," he said with a kiss. He changed gears and asked, "You said something was happening at the construction site. What's the problem?"

"Believe it or not, Tony showed up there."

"I wonder what he's up to? I want to show you something I discovered while I was in Boston. I reviewed the photos

I'd taken of the skeleton on my cell phone, and I noticed something was way off. Look at this," Mike said, getting up to get his phone.

"What is it, Mike? What's wrong?"

"Look at the bones and see whether you see what I do." I reached for his phone and scrolled through the photos. Then it hit me. "Oh my god! There are too many bones, aren't there?"

"Yes, and look! The femurs are different sizes!" he said as he enlarged the photo and pointed them out. "I want to meet with the Chief of Police and see what's happening."

My mind raced, worried that this would pull Mike away from solving his circumstances.

As if he read my mind, he said, "And no, Rosie, I won't push aside what we need to do about my situation ..." he said with conviction. "But I must say, I don't like what's happening at the site."

"Nor do I. I'm worried there's more trouble to come. Mimi should be in Las Vegas by now. I'm supposed to meet with her today. Why don't you join us?"

"Yeah, I'd like to. I want to make sure all three of you— Romano, Mimi, and you—are safe."

"Do you think we can solve both murders soon?" I asked.

"I sure hope so. The odds are in our favor because 60% of murders get solved."

"You mean to say that 40% of all murders don't get solved?" I asked, astounded.

"According to statistics, that's right. Amazing, isn't it?"

"I'm shocked. I guess we were lucky to clear up the murders attached to the Purple Passion Lounge," I said with a shiver.

Mike turned to me with a glint in his eye. "Enough, my queen. Let me show you how much I've missed you," he said in a husky voice as he pulled me closer and nuzzled my neck.

Later, Mike kissed me goodbye and left to meet with the Chief of Police in the new SUV he'd bought. Soon Virginia would be here, and I'd head out to the construction site, leaving Isabella and Sweet Pea behind.

At the site, I stepped out of the car and felt chills. I recognized Lorenzo's car as it sped by as if in a hurry not to be seen. Tony was seated next to him, and as he turned his head my way, our eyes met—his in anger.

Mimi stood with Romano and Randy, and when they heard me approach, they looked up and smiled. Mike pulled in, and I waited for him to catch up to me. Together we walked toward the others. "How did it go with the Chief of Police?" I asked.

"We need to meet so I can tell you all what's happening."

Mimi approached us with a huge smile. "It's looking good. Instead of envisioning it, we can see how nicely the two buildings will coexist on the property."

I hugged Mimi, Romano, and Randy as Mike said, "Yes, quite a difference since you and I were here last, Mimi."

The foreman headed our way. "Do you have a moment?" asked Mike, taking Butch's elbow and leading him away.

I whispered to the others, "Mike's been to see the Chief of Police about what he discovered and wants to share what they discussed with us."

The condo Mimi had rented was just off the strip in a new building with six floors of living space, 12 condos on each floor. It was a small building between two taller ones and was exclusive, with a valet ready to serve its pampered clientele. All the amenities were on the ground floor—the swimming pool, exercise room, and offices. Before visitors were allowed beyond the relatively large, comfortable reception area, they had to sign in with the concierge. It was a very pleasing arrangement.

Mimi's space was furnished and tastefully decorated. She ordered delivery pizza before we gathered around the cherry dining room table, anxious to hear what Mike had to say. Mimi turned to Mike, "What are we dealing with here?"

He searched through the photos on his cell phone and then passed his phone around the table, asking the same question he'd asked me. "Look closely. Do you see anything out of order?"

Randy spotted the difference right away. Afterward, he pointed it out to Romano and Mimi, and we all sat silently.

"What did the Chief of Police say?" I asked Mike.

"Roberto is a pretty good guy. I'm going to enjoy working with him. He called the forensic lab where the skeleton was taken, and they agreed with my assessment."

We looked at each other, stunned by the confirmation. Two skeletons?

"That's not all, folks," added Mike. "Roberto agreed that there'd likely be more bones showing up on site since they've confirmed at least two victims so far."

"That's a real concern, isn't it?" I asked.

"Yes, Rosie, it's hazardous for you all. I want to be clear about that. Do you all understand?" Mike paused. "That's why I'm hiring several men to be on the property at all times. They will act as security guards above and beyond what the construction company provides. Before going on-site to view the progress of your building, you must call one of them to meet you at your car. I'll give you their names and numbers when I set that up. Until then, stay away from the site or call me should you need to go there, and I'll go with you. Do you understand?"

Mimi spoke up. "Do you think we should stop construction altogether, Mike?"

"Stop construction for what purpose, Mimi?" asked Mike bluntly.

Looking confused, she said, "Well, I don't want anything to happen to Rosie, Romano, or Randy ...."

"Of course, you don't. My apologies—that goes without saying, Mimi. What I meant is that our finding the skeleton there might not have anything to do with the construction of the buildings but have more to do about causing trouble for you, Romano, Rosie, or anyone else. By having some of my men on site, we'll have a better chance of capturing whoever is playing this game ... and learn why."

"I dunno, Mike," said Mimi, unconvinced. "Rosie and Romano, I'm setting you free of your obligations to see the buildings completed ...."

"Oh, no, you don't," I interrupted, Romano echoing me. "We're in this together, which means to the end."

"Right on, Rosie. No one will stop me from having my restaurant," Romano said.

We all jumped when the doorbell rang—the pizza was here. Mimi got up to answer the door, and I saw her eyes fill. Did we have a choice but to continue forward? Whether the skeleton or its intended revenge had anything to do with any of us, it didn't mean we'd necessarily be safe simply by staying away from the construction site.

As hungry as I was, especially with the tantalizing aroma emanating from the pizza, I could barely choke down a piece. All of us, except for Mike, picked at our food. It was apparent who was the most experienced in handling stressful situations like this.

CHAPTER 16

At home, Mike went into the office to make calls and line up the men serving as security at the construction site. My cell phone rang, and I answered it to hear the mystery man's voice, heavy with sorrow. "Hello, Rosie; I thought you'd like to know that my mother passed away early yesterday morning. Some of her last words were … well, somewhat strange. She mumbled that death had waited—but then she said you'd know what that meant." He paused. "She died at peace, and I think she'd want you to know that too."

My eyes watered. "Thank you so much for telling me that. No one can ask for more than to die peacefully."

"She left something for you, Rosie. Are you going to be around tomorrow? I thought I'd have Cal drop it off for you."

"I will be, yes. When do you think I may expect him?"

"Probably in the afternoon. I have some things to take care of here first," he replied vaguely.

A thought flickered in my mind and remained. "Please relay to Cal that we'd like him to stay for dinner and be our overnight guest if he'd like."

"How thoughtful of you. Just ask him if that's okay with you when Cal arrives."

"Of course. Thank you so much for your call. My condolences to you, for I know your mother meant a lot to you."

"The world."

"We'll look forward to seeing Cal tomorrow. Meantime, please take care of yourself, and if there is anything we can do for you, please don't hesitate to let us know."

I went to find Mike. "I just received a call from the mystery man who wanted me to know his mother passed away yesterday morning. He's pretty broken up about it. I know how much his mother meant to him."

"That's too bad," said Mike. "I'll let Brian know."

"We're going to have a dinner guest tomorrow. Can you guess who it is?"

Mike looked up, grinning. "Somebody interesting, I'm sure. Who?"

"His chauffeur, Cal. Lizzie left me a memento, which he will deliver tomorrow. I asked the mystery man to relay to Cal our invitation for dinner and to be our overnight guest as well."

"Well, that's different, huh? Cal is a nice man. Are you inviting the others for dinner too?"

"We might as well make it a party, don't you think?"

"Why not?" he answered as I kissed the top of his head.

His arm came around my waist and held me against him while he remained seated. "I've lined up a few guys to interview tomorrow, and Brian is working on it from the other end. He's using his contact at the police station here in Las Vegas to get them vetted."

"Great, when do they start?"

"The day after tomorrow if I can set up everything in time. I still have to buy their uniforms and walkie-talkies."

"Don't worry about barbequing tomorrow night, Mike. I'll fix a casserole—something simple."

I left him to invite Romano, Randy, and Mimi to join us for dinner and to meet Cal. I called Romano first.

Hello, my darling Rosebud," he greeted me. Once I explained why I was calling, he immediately said, "Don't worry about making dessert. I'll do it. I've got it covered, okay?"

"That sounds wonderful. Am I sensing that you're missing your daily baking?" I asked, amused.

"Honestly, I didn't realize how much I'd miss the challenge of creating all the wonderful things I did daily for the lounge." I heard him chuckle. "I think I've lost a few pounds."

"Oh, Romano," I laughed. "I'm glad that you and Randy can join us. I'm thinking around 6 o'clock. Does that work for you?"

"Perfecto, my darling girl," he answered as I pictured him kissing his fingers.

Mimi was just as enthusiastic about joining us for dinner too, and when I told Isabella we were having dinner guests the next day, I saw her glance at me meaningfully. I realized she wondered whether there might be another shopping trip in store for her, so I immediately squelched that.

"Now you'll get to wear the other new dress."

Isabella sighed. "Okay, Mama."

Before going into my bedroom to change, I tucked Isabella into her bed with Sweet Pea snuggled beside her. After tossing and turning the night before with no sleep, I was happy to end the day because I needed a good night's sleep.

I waited for Mike to join me. I certainly loved that man.

CHAPTER 17

The following day, Ruth Rutledge called and asked whether it would be a help if she took Isabella to shop for school supplies. I knew she wanted to be the one to do that. After they left, I grocery-shopped, completed the casserole, and finished the prep work for dinner. Mike was at the police station interviewing candidates for the security positions. He was using the spare office at the police station since he was working with Roberto to see whether they could trap whoever had left the bones at the job site.

I fixed a glass of iced tea and relaxed on the patio. Sweet Pea began to bark as I rested my head on the lounge chair. I headed to the front, and no one was there when I opened the door. At my feet was an 8.5 x 11 brown envelope with my name scrawled across it. I picked it up, and it was light as a feather, as if nothing was inside. I tore at it and pulled out a single sheet of paper with large printed letters that read, FOLLOW THE DOTS. I was perplexed, and chills raced down my body as anxiety built. What was it Steve Jobs said? "You don't connect the dots moving forward; you connect them moving backward."

Who would have sent me this? I put the envelope on my desk and returned to finish my iced tea. I didn't realize I'd fallen asleep until I heard Sweet Pea bark and felt her paws on my legs. She raced to the front door, and I followed her. I opened the door, and Cal stood there with red-rimmed eyes. My heart went out to him.

"C'mon in Cal. It's good to see you. I hope you will take us up on our invitation for dinner and stay overnight with us."

"Yes, that'd be very nice, Rosie," he said shyly.

"Good. How about a glass of iced tea? You must be parched in this heat."

"That would be perfect."

I poured the tea and handed him his glass. "Let's go out back, shall we?"

We sat at the high-top table at the far edge of the patio. Cal's shoulders slumped, and his sadness filled the air. "So, how's the mystery man?" I asked pointedly.

My eyes sought his. "Not so good, I'm afraid," he answered, looking away.

"Cal? I know who the mystery man is."

"You do?"

"Why are you keeping it a secret?" I added, "I will keep it a secret if that helps you."

"How long have you known that I was the mystery man?"

"I wasn't positive until yesterday. When you told me about your mother, you forgot to lower your voice to sound like the mystery man instead of sounding as Cal does."

He smiled shyly at me. "Don't tell the boys yet, okay? By acting as the chauffeur, I learn much more than I would otherwise."

I agreed despite not liking to keep things from Mike.

"Once people realize you have a lot of money, they treat you differently, and you can never be sure whether they're acting nice to you because of you or your money. At least, that has been an issue with me."

I studied him and saw how that could be a problem for him because he was a gentle soul and nice-looking, but not so much so that it'd caused women to fall all over him. Knowing he had money automatically made him more appealing to most women, sad to admit. "I'm sorry to hear that. If you don't mind my asking, how did you make your money?"

"I've invented several things that most people don't know anything about, but it has made me a very wealthy man."

"Mama?" called Isabella. "Where are you?"

Sweet Pea barked and raced forward, alerting Isabella to our whereabouts. Cal perked up at seeing Isabella again. He leaned forward in his chair. "Hi there, do you remember me?"

"Yes, you're Cal, the chauffeur."

"That's right, I'm Cal, the chauffeur," he repeated with a smile.

Ruth was standing in the doorway, and I turned to Cal. "I'll be right back." I'd asked her to bring me the receipts so that I could reimburse her for the items she'd paid for Isabella.

"Hi, Ruth. How did it go?"

Ruth chuckled. "She's quite the shopper, isn't she? I need to take a nap after this."

I laughed with her. "She likes to pick through everything, doesn't she? I know Isabella was excited to have you with her. Do you have the slips, including the one from the restaurant?"

"Here are the slips for all the items, but I'm going to pay for lunch. It was my treat," Ruth stated, not allowing any argument.

"Why don't you come out and meet a friend of ours, and you can say goodbye to Isabella out there too?"

"I'd love to."

I introduced Ruth to Cal, and then she turned to Isabella, "Have a good first day at school, and let me know how it went, okay?"

I returned to rescue Cal from Isabella's chattering and suggested, "It's getting late, Cal; why don't you bring your things in? Isabella and I will get you settled into the guest room so you can refresh yourself before the company arrives.

"Thank you, Rosie ... for everything," said Cal in a low voice as he walked beside me and rested his hand on my shoulder in a fatherly way.

CHAPTER 18

I finished in the kitchen and changed my clothes into something more appropriate. Mike came in as I headed upstairs, and when I saw him, I smiled and stopped to greet him with a kiss. After turning away from him to continue up, he pulled me back against him, and I lost my balance and nearly fell. He caught me in his arms and murmured, "That's not quite how I planned it."

"Wow, who knew kissing you could be that dangerous."

We laughed.

"Is Cal here yet?" asked Mike.

"Shhh. Listen …" I said, pointing upstairs.

We heard Isabella explaining something to Cal about the test she'd taken with Ruth. We looked at each other and smiled.

"That girl sure knows how to talk," said Mike, shaking his head.

"Amazingly, she seems so at ease with anyone she meets," I added.

When the doorbell rang, I sent Isabella to answer it, but Sweet Pea beat her to the door, barking and dancing around. As I joined them, I bent down and lifted the dog into my arms so our guests could enter. All three of them stood there—Romano with his arms full of treats for dessert, Randy with a bottle of wine in hand, and Mimi holding a bouquet of fresh flowers. Mimi and I locked eyes and smiled as we watched Isabella allow one person through the door at a time.

After we finished our entree, Isabella said she'd have dessert later and excused herself to call her sister-friends in Santa Fe. While we munched on the tasty peach tart, topped with homemade vanilla gelato Romano had made, talk turned to the construction site. It didn't seem to bother anyone to have Cal included in our conversation, and he paid close attention to what each of us had to say.

Mike asked, "So Cal, what do you think the mystery man would have to say to all this?"

Seeing Cal's expression, I choked on the wine to suppress my laughter. My face grew hot with embarrassment. Cal winked at me before he answered. "I think he'd be pleased with what you all are doing to resolve the murder of yet another young girl gone missing."

Randy spoke up. "The problem with all these young girls who come here to Las Vegas wanting the glorified position of "dancer" or "escort" is that after they become hooked on drugs, they can't see a way out of their proverbial rabbit hole and involvement with the men who control them. It's all very sad to me."

We all nodded in agreement except for Cal, who held his head low and avoided looking at anyone for several long seconds. When Cal looked up, our eyes locked, and our minds met with complete understanding. Now I understood how Lizzie had become his "mother" and why he was so attached to her. It was clear that it was because of his birth mother's situation that he'd become passionate about wanting to resolve the murders of young girls who had ended up like her. I envisioned a young woman in the same position that Randy had spoken about, and I instantly knew that was what had happened to Cal's mother.

After our guests left, Cal sat talking with Isabella at the kitchen table as she ate her dessert. When she finished, I said, "Isabella, why don't you get into your pajamas and come downstairs to say good night."

Mike fixed a nightcap for us and led Cal outside onto the patio. Soon Isabella came out to us to say good night. "Good night, Mike," she said, kissing him on the cheek. Then she turned to Cal and said, "Good night, Grandfather."

We looked at her in surprise, and she quickly explained, "He looks kind of like Grandmother, right Mama?"

Cal was perplexed. I repressed a smile, knowing Grandmother was more than 25 years older than Cal, but to Isabella, she must consider anyone old if they showed *any* signs of aging.

I explained, "Isabella was addressing you as a formality, as she learned to do with a wonderful Native American woman we met in Santa Fe."

Cal looked pleased. "Isabella, I'd be delighted to have you call me Grandfather anytime."

Isabella stepped closer, kissed him on the cheek, and looked at me with a happy face. I understood what she was doing— creating her own family with people she liked.

When I returned to them after tucking Isabella into bed, they were talking sports. The interplay between Mike and Cal was comforting, especially in light of Cal dealing with his grandmother's death.

"Cal? Why don't you spend a few more days with us? That way, you can check the construction site and see where the skeletons were found."

He remained thoughtful for a few seconds. "I think that'd be very nice. Thank you."

Later, when we were getting ready for bed, Mike said, "I think it's good you invited Cal to stay for a few days. He'll be able to give the mystery man a first-hand lowdown about what's going on here."

If you only knew how first-hand that would be, I thought, not liking to keep that from Mike. But a promise was a promise ....

CHAPTER 19

Mike had tossed and turned all night until I finally nudged him. "What's the matter?"

"I dunno, I can't get the construction site out of my mind. I should go check on it; what do you think?"

"Something feels off. I'll go with you. Just give me a minute to get dressed." We looked at each other. I couldn't leave Isabella alone, even with Cal in the house.

"No, you need to be here when Isabella wakes up," Mike agreed.

I followed Mike downstairs and made coffee for him to take. I hadn't had a chance to show him the note, and as I sat at the kitchen table and sipped my coffee, I wondered at the message—*follow the dots.* Who had sent it?

Cal stopped in the doorway. "Good morning!"

"How about a cup of coffee, Cal? It's nice to take it outside to enjoy the beautiful day."

"Ah, yes, that'd be nice."

As I poured his cup and refilled mine, I heard the pitter-patter of Isabella and Sweet Pea coming down the stairs. I added water to the Keurig and got out a cocoa cup for Isabella. We went outdoors and sat at the high-top table.

"What are we going to do today, Mama?" asked Isabella.

"What would you like to do?"

Isabella smiled shyly at Cal. "I'd like to go to Gramma Irene's and bake a special cake for Grandfather. She said she'd show me how."

"That sounds lovely, but we'll see if that fits into Irene's schedule today. She mentioned she wanted to cook with you again before school started, so I'll give her a call later."

Isabella turned to Cal and explained, "Gramma Irene lives next door. She's very nice and teaches me to bake all kinds of things."

"She sounds like an excellent neighbor." He winked at me.

Sweet Pea barked, raced forward, and jumped upon Mike as he entered the doorway. He was a mess! His pants were dirty, his hair awry, and I saw blood on his shirt.

"What happened to you?" I exclaimed.

He looked chagrinned. "Well, what I predicted came true." He looked to Isabella. "Why don't you take Sweet Pea inside and give her a treat?"

"So, how long do you need me to be gone? I know you want to discuss things privately with Mama and Grandfather."

Mike gave her an affectionate hug. "Why don't you get dressed for the day? I think that will give me enough time, smarty pants."

Isabella smiled. "C'mon, Sweet Pea, let's go."

"What do you mean, your prediction came true?"

"At the construction site, I heard a noise from the back building area, so I walked there. When I came to where the skeleton had been found, I saw the hole had been cleared out again. When I peered inside, I saw a bunch of bones just thrown in as if someone were hurrying to get rid of them. Then I felt someone behind me, and everything went black. I woke up with this goose egg." He rubbed his head.

"Are you alright? What about the skeleton? Did you let the police know about it?"

"I called Roberto, and he immediately called in the medical examiner. They met me within a few minutes. It was still dark out, so the medical examiner had time to remove the bones, and the forensics team had time to search for evidence before the workers arrived. There weren't enough bones to be another whole body. I need to talk to Butch about the fact there was no security guard on site. I want to find out why not?"

"I'm so sorry, Mike." I rose and kissed him. I checked his head to make sure it wasn't still bleeding.

He gently pushed me away. "I'm okay. Thanks, though."

"Would you like a fresh cup of coffee?"

"That'd be nice." Turning to Cal, he said, "I'd like to run something by you if you don't mind."

I decided to get showered and dressed for the day. I called Irene, who was delighted to have Isabella join her for a baking lesson.

Mike took Cal to pick up uniforms and get walkie-talkies for the new security guards. In the interim, Mike would continue to use my office as his until he found a place to rent.

Isabella came home with a beautifully decorated chocolate cake and a unique birthday candle set in the middle that, once lit, opened up like a flower. "I know it isn't Grandfather's birthday, Mama, but the candle is so beautiful, and Gramma Irene said I could keep it."

After dinner, Isabella called me into the kitchen, and I helped her light the candle to carry the cake to the table. My heart melted when I saw the expression of delight on Cal's face. His eyes filled as he viewed Isabella holding the cake too heavy for her. He rose from his chair and helped her set it before him. He smiled. "How beautiful, Isabella, thank you."

"Grandfather, look at the candle … it's opening … see? I know it's not your birthday, Grandfather, but this candle is so beautiful."

"It's the most beautiful cake and candle I've ever seen," he said hoarsely.

"Thank you, Grandfather," Isabella said and turned to me, glowing.

***

After Isabella was tucked into bed, I joined Mike and Cal at the high-top table on the patio to discover that Cal would be leaving the next day. I was unduly disappointed because he'd become part of our family even in this short time. Isabella would be crushed to have him leave as well.

"I hope you will return soon, Cal, for we will miss you very much."

"I was telling Mike I thought I'd look into buying a place here in Las Vegas. It'd be a good escape for me."

"You mean if the mystery man can spare you, don't you?" Mike chuckled.

Cal and I locked eyes. I waited for him to say something, but he didn't. Mike looked at me and said, "What? What's going on?"

"I think it would be fabulous if Cal moved here," I told Mike. "Meantime, Cal, you always have a room here with us while you're house hunting. And if you want, I'd love to help you find the right house."

"I could use your assistance."

"I'm glad you're considering a move here. I know Isabella will be happy to have you close by now that you're her grandfather."

Cal's eyes softened at what I'd said. He leaned forward and pulled a small box from his pocket. Emotionally, he said, "My mother wanted you to have this. She said to tell you her wish in giving this to you was that you'd be reminded of the heavenly love that comes about when you bring a lost child into your life."

As I reached for the box Cal handed me, I wondered whether he'd used the words—his mother—in error or if he wanted Mike to know his true identity. When I opened the box, I was stunned at what I saw—a magnificent gold ring with a heart-shaped diamond. I recognized it was the same ring Lizzie had worn when I'd visited her in Utah. Tears came at Lizzie's beautiful sentiment, and a sudden fear washed over me that Isabella, only temporarily in my life at this point, might never be mine.

Seeing my tears, Cal patted my hand.

"Oh, Cal, this is beautiful, but I can't accept it. When you marry, this should go to your wife."

"Rosie, Lizzie meant this ring for you and insisted it is yours. There are other rings for any woman I choose to marry. Please accept this with all the love intended," he urged.

I rose from my seat, hugged Cal tightly, and whispered, "Thank you, Cal, for this lovely reminder of your beautiful grandmother."

As I re-seated myself, Mike rose and faced us. "Okay, you two, is there anything you'd like to share with me?"

CHAPTER 20

At breakfast the following day, I watched Mike eye Cal with tremendous respect after learning who he was and why he had become obsessed with righting the wrong of any young girl mistreated and taken advantage of as his mother had been. Earlier, I'd overheard Mike on the phone with Brian explaining Cal's situation and chuckling over the embarrassment that they'd missed the mark as detectives.

Cal had left, and Mike went to meet with Butch. I went to my bedroom and slipped the new heart-shaped diamond ring, now mine, onto my finger. I admired it as I held out my bedecked finger and fluttered it. What do you think, Gram?"

"There's something to be said about diamonds being a girl's best friend, right? It's a beautiful reminder that love connects us all, so my darling girl, wear it knowing what I said was the truth."

273

"Thank you, Gram. I love you so much."

"And I love you, Rosie girl." Then her spirit floated away, leaving me with greater peace.

"Mama, did you hear me?" asked Isabella, breathless from running up the stairs.

"No, I didn't, sweetheart. What is it?"

"Virginia wants to know whether she should start cleaning upstairs or down."

"Oh my, I never heard her arrive. I'll go down now."

"Oh, Mama, what a beautiful ring," said Isabella as she held my hand in the air and admired it.

"It is, isn't it? Someday, it'll be yours," I said as I pulled her to me.

"Really?"

"Yes ... someday."

Virginia was a blessing to us as a housekeeper, babysitter, and someone becoming part of our family.

I was curious to see if the note referring to dots that'd been dropped off had come from Sylvia. I'd googled where she lived and, when I arrived, was surprised to see the house looked deserted, with all the shades pulled down and no welcoming signs of any kind by the front door. I pulled into the driveway, exited, and searched the house. As I reached the back area, I nearly screamed in fright as a landscaper hurried around the corner. He scowled. "What do you want?"

"Is Sylvia here?"

He shook his head and replied, "No."

"Do you know if she's due back soon?"

"She's on vacation and won't return for a long time."

"Do you know where she went?"

"No," he said and walked away from me and any further discussion.

I thought it odd she'd left on an undetermined vacation until I remembered what she'd said in the ladies' room the night of the dance at the club—"Please don't get me involved in anything."

Isabella was to start school the next day. I wanted to be sure she had everything she needed in addition to the required uniforms that we had ordered and now hung in her closet, ready for her to wear. She was excited but nervous about attending her first day at school. Mike and I would drive her there. I had received a notice from the school that all parents were required to drop off their children in the morning and pick them up at the end of the day for the first week. After that, the private bus schedule would be completed and ready for service.

At home, all was quiet. Isabella was reading a book Ruth had suggested, and she sat with a Spanish-to-English dictionary beside her. I kissed the top of her head and went into my office to work. When Mike joined me later, he was scowling.

"Well, the guy hired to watch the construction site that night has disappeared for good. Nobody can find him."

"Well, he's not the only one to disappear."

"What do you mean?"

"When I went to check on Sylvia, I ran into the gardener who said she was on vacation and wouldn't return for a long time ...."

"You mean you went there to see Sylvia and didn't let me know?" A frown deepened on his brow.

"Well, you were busy."

"Never too busy for you to let me know what you're up to since you know what happens when you get into the middle of things ...."

"Exactly what are you implying? You can't control my every move, and I can't control yours—it doesn't work that way. Besides, I'm trying to clear up things as fast as possible so that you'll spend more time finding *your wife*," I said in a low, frustrated voice.

Mike flushed. We glared at each other until he reached for his phone. "Hey, Brian, what have you learned about the wedding disaster?" He paused and said, "Dammit, Brian, you need to find her *now*! I don't remember that time, so it's up to you, do you understand? It's a big problem; my hands are tied to set things right at the construction site." He listened more and said, "I'll ask her and let you know, but why don't you plan on it."

Mike turned to me, troubled. "Brian said they are having trouble locating this girl, and he believes it makes more sense for him to come to Vegas to track her down. What do you think about having him stay with us since the apartment he used before is no longer available."

My heart raced with pleasure. "I think that makes a lot of sense. When is he planning on coming?"

"Within the next few days. Brian has to get the new guy settled in so he can leave Boston knowing things are in good hands." Mike studied me. "Come here, my queen," he commanded in a firm voice as he held his arms wide. "I know you're upset about this marriage thing, and I can't blame you, but we'll work it out. I promise," he whispered into my ear.

CHAPTER 21

T he following day turned into a circus when Irene and Ron came from next door with cameras ready, and then Virginia arrived, followed by Ruth, who apologized for interfering. All competed with Mike's commands of where Isabella should stand and when to turn. Sweet Pea was hoisted into Isabella's arms and then unceremoniously dumped repeatedly as Isabella tried to fill each order for a picture. After a few minutes, she said, "No more."

When it was time for her to leave, Isabella graciously accepted hugs and kisses before I ushered everyone out the door. Mike got into the driver's seat, and I sat next to him while Isabella and Sweet Pea climbed into the back. Isabella had insisted the dog come with her, and I realized Sweet Pea served as a type of security blanket for her, as many dogs did for their owners.

When we pulled up to the school, cars were double parked, and it looked like traffic at the airport with children and school bags being unloaded.

I turned toward Isabella and asked, "Are you ready?" I was surprised that her lower lip trembled and her eyes filled. "Oh, no. What's the matter, sweetheart?"

"I've always wanted to go to a school like this, and now I am," she answered tremulously.

"So you're happy, not sad?" I asked, worried.

"Yes, Mama, I'm sooo happy to be going to school here, and I'm going to learn everything I can."

"I'm sure you will, Isabella. After school, look for me outside … I'll be waiting," I smiled.

"Okay. Goodbye, Mama and Mike."

Mike reached for my hand and squeezed it tight as I tried not to cry when I watched Isabella walk toward the school. She looked tiny compared to others but marched with her head held high. A horn honked loudly close by, and I looked to see a black limo had pulled up beside us. A blond-haired older girl flung open the back door, rushed out, and raced up the walkway. She collided with Isabella and pushed her aside. The girl never stopped but continued without a backward glance. Isabella picked up the books knocked from her, looked our way, and gave a crooked smile. I held my thumb up, and Isabella waved before she turned to enter the school. My heart pounded with anger at the girl's rudeness, and I realized this must be how every mother feels when her child is mistreated, no matter how small the infraction.

"It's okay, Rosie. Isabella knows how to handle herself." Mike said with an encouraging smile.

I smiled and patted his arm. "You're right; I've got to let Isabella be."

Romano called as we pulled away from the school. He wanted to know if we'd meet him and Randy at the construction site so they could see what had been completed so far.

"Mike, do you have time?"

"Sure, why not? My guards don't start until tonight. By tomorrow, I'll have a list of their names and phone numbers for you."

"Mike says okay. We'll see you there in a few minutes," I said to Romano.

"I want to talk to Butch and see if he's located the missing worker," said Mike as we pulled to the curb across the street from the site. Romano pulled in behind us.

When Mike opened the car door, I waved him onward as I reached to pull my ringing cell phone from my pocket. I smiled when I saw it was Maria. I knew she was curious about Isabella's first day of school. I got out of the car and began to walk forward as I laughingly told Maria my reaction to Isabella being knocked into by the girl from the limo. Suddenly, I felt a blow to the center of my back, and I was shoved forward with so much force it took my breath away. I looked back at the same time I heard squealing tires as the speeding car threw me to the side and Randy into the air. Then all went black.

When I woke up, I didn't know where I was. Bright lights glared, and two faces I didn't recognize peered at me.

"She's awake, doctor."

"What happened?" I mumbled.

"You're a fortunate young lady. You were hit by a car and only have a concussion and a few broken ribs. Unfortunately, your friend wasn't so lucky, I'm sorry to say."

It all came back to me … Randy. I screamed, "What do you mean? Is he dead?"

The nurse took my hand and said, "Calm down."

"Please tell me, is Randy dead?" I pleaded.

"No, but he's not in good shape. We understand that he saved your life and took the full brunt of the hit."

I sobbed uncontrollably until I felt a prick in my arm, and all went dark.

The next time I awoke, Mike sat in a chair beside my hospital bed. "What time is it? I've got to pick up Isabella. I can't be late," I said as I rose.

Mike's hand gently pushed me back onto the bed. "Not to worry, Virginia picked her up," he soothed.

"And Randy? Is he going to be okay?" I began to cry.

Mike looked glum. "Things don't look so good, but they're doing all they can. He's in surgery right now, and we should know soon."

"Where's Romano? He must be devastated."

"He's outside waiting to see you. Are you up for it?"

I nodded, and Mike rose and went to the door. He waved Romano in, and I cried as soon as I saw him. "I'm so sorry, Romano. I'm so sorry."

Romano came to me. "My darling Rosebud, it's not your fault."

"But …"

"No!" Romano held up his hand. "None of that … no blaming yourself for anything. Randy certainly wouldn't hear of it, and I don't want to either. Understood?"

I numbly nodded. "How is Randy?"

"I just talked to the doctor before I came to see you. They've put him into an induced coma because his brain is swollen from the injury. We have to wait and see. He's pretty broken ..." he choked the words out before he fell back in the chair and sobbed.

Mike stood behind him and patted his shoulder. It was so surreal to think a few hours ago, all was well, and now it was such a mess.

"How soon can I see Randy?"

"You won't be able to because he's isolated in ICU," Romano answered.

"I *need* to see him, do you understand? Please let me know as soon as they let me. Promise?"

His eyes were wet. "Yes, Rosebud, you'll be the first to know."

"Mike, when can I leave?" I wanted to make sure Isabella was safe.

"The doctor wants you to spend the night because of your concussion, so maybe they'll let you go by tomorrow."

I dreaded asking the next question. "Mike, was the accident deliberate?"

Mike and Romano locked eyes. "Tell me," I demanded.

Mike said, "It was Lorenzo."

"Lorenzo? Mike, please tell me that isn't true!"

"Lorenzo admitted to the police that he had been speeding and had taken his eyes off the road for just a second to reach for something he'd dropped onto the car floor. He adamantly stated that he had no intention of hitting you or Randy, and Tony confirmed what he'd said was true. They both were pretty distraught and shaken up at what had happened. I believe they're telling the truth."

I remembered seeing Lorenzo as he sped by the construction site a few days earlier. Although I believed that things happened for a reason, I couldn't think of a single one that made any sense or felt right. I leaned back against the bed pillows and nearly screamed out in pain

281

but bit my lip, determined to be brave. Nothing more than a concussion and broken ribs were a blessing in their way, but damn, it hurt.

Romano's phone rang, and he immediately answered. He smiled sadly, "They're taking Randy into ICU now, and I can see him."

"Romano, can you please tell him that I love him and to please hang on?"

He nodded and left a broken man.

CHAPTER 22

T he following day I awoke with a heavy heart and a headache that wouldn't quit. Anyone who tried sleeping through the night while a patient in a hospital stood little chance of doing so. It was no different for me. I was exhausted and ached, but I was determined to leave the hospital that day and go home to heal.

I crawled out of bed, tightly wrapped my hospital gown around me, and headed down the hall to see if I could peep in on Randy. I hadn't gotten very far when I heard a nurse ask in a scolding tone, "Where do you think you're going, young lady?"

Tears came unbidden as I explained that I needed to see Randy. "I just need to know that he's still alive."

The nurse took my arm and led me back to my room. "You can't see him, but I'll call ICU to check on him, okay?"

I climbed back into bed and waited for the doctor to release me. Before I knew it, I was in a wild dream where everything about the accident returned to me. I remembered the scene from a higher level, able to look down on what was taking place—my out-of-body experience where I heard the thuds of Randy and me hitting the car and then the ground and the screams of distress from the onlookers. I quickly closed my eyes again and took in the shocked expressions of Lorenzo and Tony, and I knew without question they hadn't intended to hurt us. But why were they so interested in the construction site? What did they want? Why were they even in Las Vegas?

Mike and the doctor entered at the same time. "Hi, sweetheart, how are you feeling?" asked Mike, concerned.

"Pretty good, considering."

The doctor came and placed his hand on my forehead. "No fever. That's good. Let's check your eyes. Looks okay." He paused and studied me as if questioning himself. "Want to go home? You can as long as you follow my orders. You can take these pills for pain," he said as he wrote out a prescription, "and keep your ribs bandaged ... that will help with the pain. You need to stay in bed and rest for a few more days, though, understood?"

I agreed, and he left with a nod to Mike. I tried to silence the headache that pounded in my ears as I dressed. On our way out, we stopped at the nurses' station and learned that Randy was resting peacefully but not out of the woods. One look at my face, and Mike held me tight and whispered, "Have faith, Rosie."

My phone rang as we drove home, and I handed it to Mike to answer. I was in no shape to talk to anyone. Mike's expression changed from worry to relief as he listened to the caller. "Thank you, Jacklyn, and I'll be sure to relay your message to her."

"Oh, no, what did she want?"

"She said she heard about your accident, and she's delayed the foster care hearing until next month since you're under the weather. She said to send your listing of those with the greatest influence on Isabella to her when you get the chance."

Our eyes locked. "Thank God for the delay."

Virginia opened the door when we got home, and I gave her a teary smile. "Thank you so much for being here, Virginia. How is Isabella?"

"Very concerned about you," she answered honestly.

As we stood in the doorway, a florist truck pulled in and delivered a beautiful bouquet. Virginia took it from the delivery man, and I pulled the message card. It read, "Tony."

My face flushed with anger. "Just throw it out, Virginia."

Virginia and Mike looked at me in question. Mike gently pulled the card from my hand and read it. "Oh," he said. "Better do as she asks."

I crawled into bed and felt a black cloud surrounding me as my thoughts darkened and anger smoldered. If Randy should die, I would never be able to forgive myself for having unwittingly been the cause of it. "Gram, please don't let him die," I pleaded. There was only silence, and devoid of any encouragement, I fell into an exhausted sleep. I never stirred until I heard whispering. "Mama? Mama, are you awake?"

I opened my eyes and stared into worried dark ones. "Hi, Isabella; how was school?"

She held Sweet Pea, and when I spoke, she gently placed the dog by my side and gingerly sat on the edge of the bed. Then Isabella picked up my hand and held it while she relayed all that had happened in her first two days of school. She was excited, and her eyes glowed as she talked— fuzzy words to my addled mind.

"Rosie, it's time for your medicine," said Mike as he entered with a tender smile. I forced myself halfway up and obediently swallowed what he handed me. "Okay, I can see you're tired. Is there anything we can get you before we go?"

"No, thank you," I answered listlessly.

"Virginia is making some wonderful soup, and I'll be back with some for you later, okay?"

I nodded and immediately fell back on the pillows, stifling a moan of pain. I needed to change my attitude because I was lucky with only a concussion and a few broken ribs, not in the hospital banged up like Randy. But at the moment, I didn't care.

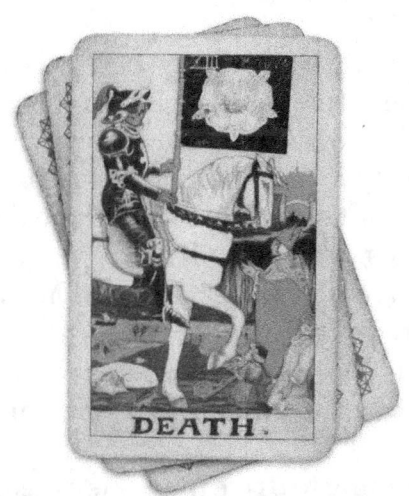

CHAPTER 23

I awoke in the morning alone—no Mike. I vaguely remembered he'd said he would sleep in the guest room so he wouldn't disturb me. I inched my way to the edge of the bed and felt the searing burn of pain along my right side, where my ribs were broken. Despite the pain, I was determined to get up and begin my research to find the identity of the skeletons.

As I moved slowly, Mike entered and smiled when he saw I was up. "Feeling a bit better, I see." He came to me and held me lightly in his arms. "I missed you last night. I don't like sleeping alone."

"I missed you too, handsome," I smiled.

"Are you sure you're ready to get up? Just don't overdo it, hear?"

"If I don't, I'll just sit with my dark thoughts and be useless to anyone. There's something I want to do."

"What, Rosie?"

"I want to research what I can here at home for what we know to be true – two young girls in their early 20s were killed here in Las Vegas. We don't know whether they were killed together or at different times and whether others were involved. I intend to find out. The warning note said to follow the dots, which I will do."

"Mama, you're up!" squealed Isabella, happy to see me when she entered my bedroom.

I gave her a loose hug and kissed the top of her head. "Let's eat breakfast together before Virginia drives you to school."

"Aren't you going to drive me?" she asked, disappointed.

"Not today, sweetheart. Maybe tomorrow. We'll see."

After Isabella and Virginia left, I took two pain pills and sat at my desk. My cell phone rang. I was surprised to hear Cindy's voice, my undercover investigative partner at the Purple Passion Lounge and part of Mike and Brian's team. "Why hello there, my friend. How are you?" I asked.

"More to the point, Rosie, how are *you*?"

"You heard about what happened then?" I asked with a heavy heart.

"Mike called me. He knew I'd want to know. So tell me, how are you … really?"

Unbidden tears came. "Poor Randy," I sniffled. "And poor Romano."

"I just talked to Romano, and he said Randy is comfortable, but we'll have to wait and see what happens," she said, worried.

"I feel like it's all my fault he was hit and not me. Before you say anything, I know intellectually that I'm not, but I still feel responsible."

"I called because I can't leave all of you there going through it all without me. Besides, I want to help you identify the skeletons."

"Did Mike ask whether you would help us?"

"That man loves you, Rosie, and he's concerned about you and his marriage situation. So, yes, he did, and I'm delighted to work with you again, Rosebud," she replied, using the nickname she had given me. "Besides, I would have come on my own after hearing what's going on."

Knowing Cindy was on her way felt like a weight had been lifted from my shoulders. I trusted her ... and she was brilliant. "We'll work out sleeping arrangements ...."

"Already taken care of," she interrupted. "I'll be staying at Mimi's place."

"When will you arrive? I can't wait for you to see how Isabella has grown."

"Late tomorrow night, and I'm looking forward to seeing both of you."

I smiled after I ended the call. I was relieved that Mike wanted Cindy to help clear his marital status. That alone gave me renewed energy to start Googling information on my computer.

My thoughts turned to Mimi and the turmoil she was left with after the accident caused by her cousin and his flunky. As if I'd conjured her up, I heard Mike say, "Good morning, Mimi; it's nice you could come." Had he invited her here?

"Oh, Rosie, I'm so sorry for everything. How are you doing?"

The doorbell rang, and Mike left to answer it. "Hi, Romano, how are you doing? I'm glad you could make it."

I painfully rose. "Let's go into the dining room to sit together."

Virginia had returned and must have known that Mike had arranged this meeting because she had coffee ready and assorted pastries on the table. My eyes flew to Mike, but he just gave a crooked smile.

"Okay, everyone, I called this meeting so that we can look at what we are dealing with."

All eyes turned to him. "As you know, Brian and I hope to have an office here in Las Vegas. We're still waiting for all the legal arrangements and state approval. During the interim, we've extended our services to work with the local police, whom we've found helpful and forthcoming. But with an average of 5 -7 people missing each day from the City of Las Vegas alone, they have their hands full."

"Five to seven people missing *each* day?" asked Mimi, incredulous.

"That right … that's more than 200 people missing each month. Amazing, isn't it?" asked Mike.

Shock registered on each of our faces. How were we ever going to find out the identity of the skeletons?

Mike continued. "I've called in Brian and Cindy to help us out, for we need to work on all three cases: the identity of the skeletons; who is involved in putting them on the construction site and why; and the identity of my false wife," he added with flushed cheeks.

Romano and Mimi looked perplexed. "What do you mean 'your wife'? What is going on?" Romano asked.

Mimi looked numb. "Yes, let's hear your story, Mike," she said disappointedly.

Mike painstakingly relayed what'd happened at his celebration in Las Vegas and the urgent need to clear his name before I went before the board about becoming Isabella's foster mother. Upon hearing this, the room became heavy with palpable despair.

I spoke up. "If we follow the dots as the written note said, we'll succeed. I think all three are linked together."

Mike said, "Cindy flies in sometime tonight, and Brian will be on the later Red Eye flight and arrive in the morning. Meanwhile, I have a list of security guards' names, telephone numbers, and work schedules. They will duplicate the same work schedule each week. Again, I'm advising you not to go onto the construction site without the permission of our security guard— day or night—understood?"

Numbly, we nodded. "In no way do we want the construction company to think they can slow down their pace and blame us for the slowdown. Mimi can't afford that, so continuing, as usual, is important. Any questions?"

"Romano, any update on Randy?" I asked.

Romano shook his head. "And I don't want you to worry; you have enough on your plate. Just get better."

"I'm glad that Cindy will be staying with you, Mimi. That's nice of you to offer," I said.

"It's the least I can do," she responded.

"Gotta run," announced Mike as he leaned down and kissed me. "I'm meeting with the police chief to set up things for Brian, Cindy, and me to work."

After everyone left, Virginia came to my side. "Time for you to nap, don't you think?"

I had barely enough strength to agree as she led me upstairs and tucked me back into bed.

CHAPTER 24

T he following day, I awoke feeling more like my old self despite the pain of my broken ribs. I felt hopeful that with Brian and Cindy here in Las Vegas, we'd be able to resolve our issues. Mike tenderly pulled me against him, and I knew no matter what came about, I wanted Mike in my life because he, like Isabella, had become part of my heart.

A light tap at the door signaled that Isabella was awake and wanted to join us. "C'mon in, sweetheart," I called out. I stifled a groan as Sweet Pea jumped on the bed.

Isabella cautiously came to my side of the bed and kissed me. "Are you driving me to school today?"

"Virginia will drive, but I'll ride with you."

"Okay," she said, satisfied.

"I guess we'd better get dressed then," I said as I rolled over and kissed Mike long enough to let him know I'd missed him and our lovemaking. He reluctantly climbed out of bed and hurriedly dressed to pick up Brian at the airport.

I had programmed the security guards' names and telephone numbers into my cell phone and coded in their schedules. I was surprised yet pleased that Thomas was listed as the security guard today. I liked him because he had worked undercover with us at the Purple Passion Lounge.

On the way to school, Isabella chattered away. When we neared the school, she became quiet. "You'll be here to pick me up this afternoon, won't you, Mama?"

"Of course, sweetheart. Virginia and I will be waiting for you right here."

"Okay, Mama," she said, relieved. "Goodbye, Virginia."

"Goodbye, Isabella," Virginia said.

Isabella climbed out of the back seat and stood outside the door. When she saw a few of the girls by the door, she stilled and drew in a deep breath. Determined, she marched forward. Watching her progress, I saw the same blond-haired girl who had pushed into her the first day of school standing by the door with her arms crossed, glaring at Isabella. My heart hammered.

"Don't drive out just yet, Virginia," I ordered. "Let's see what's going on here."

When Isabella reached the door, several girls opened a pathway for her, but not the blond-haired girl, who moved to block Isabella. She pushed Isabella, who looked back our way to see whether we were watching. Without hesitation, Isabella shoved the girl back hard enough for her to fall and marched through the double doors.

Virginia grabbed my arm as if reading my mind and said, "Let them work it out for now, Rosie."

I knew she was right. "It's going to take some time for me to become an experienced mother, right?"

"Not that long, Rosie. You have a natural mothering instinct when it comes to anyone hurting your baby," stated Virginia smiling.

I chuckled. Riding home, I was disturbed by the thought that most of the second skeleton was still missing. Would whoever had the bones dare to return and leave them for us to find?

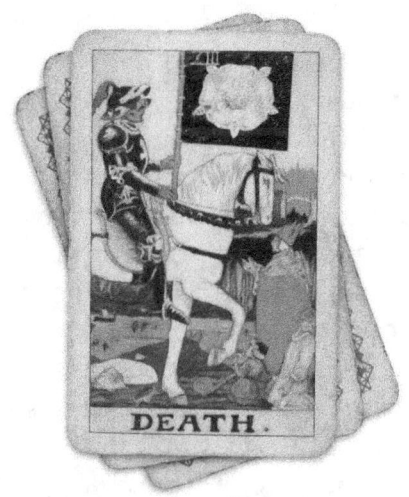

CHAPTER 25

Mimi, Romano, and I were sitting in the living room when Mike, Brian, and Cindy pushed through the door with an excited air.

Brian's blue eyes settled on me before he grabbed me in a bear hug, forgetting my broken ribs. I stifled a squeal. "Oh, Rosie, I'm so sorry for the mess I created for you and Mike."

"Oh, Cowboy," I sighed, "You have to find Martini Darling before it's too late. It means everything to me."

Cindy pushed Brian aside. "We will, Rosie, I promise you." She whispered in my ear, "We'll do it together."

Cindy turned away and approached Romano. He opened his arms wide while she stumbled forward and tried to hold back her tears. His eyes welled up, and they held onto each other without words.

Brian went to Mimi, wrapped his arm around her shoulders, and pulled her close. "How are you holding up, Mimi, with all that's going on?"

She flushed. "I've had better days."

Mike came and stood beside me. "Let's move into the dining room to sit and talk. I'll have Virginia order sandwiches. Is that okay with everyone?" I asked.

We munched on excellent BLT sandwiches with their own special sweet hot sauce—a specialty from the deli not far from the house. Talk turned to the time of Mike's fake wedding. Brian and Mike were embarrassed.

Brian said, "I know what you're thinking, and I can't blame you. I'm sorry to admit that I don't remember much of that weekend clearly, but I remember something different about Martini."

"What?" I asked, hopeful that maybe we were getting somewhere.

"Well, she had unusual light-colored eyes, not blue and not gray, almost colorless … sometimes like the sky gets in the early morning, if you know what I mean."

"Anything else?" I prodded.

Brian closed his eyes in memory. "Her hair was dyed blond, but I could tell it was dark brown and curly. I don't know much about how you girls do things, but I think it was naturally curly." Brian looked uncomfortable. "And she had large fake boobs. Does that sound right, Mike?"

"I guess," Mike answered with flushed cheeks.

Romano leaned forward in his seat. "Hmm," he muttered.

"What's the matter, Romano?" I asked.

"Her eyes …that sounds as if it could be …. "

In a flash, a thought came. "You mean Susan? The girl who was like a runaway freight train?"

"Brian described her eyes exactly," he answered, lost in memory. "Very light, very unusual."

"Do you know what this means?" I screeched with excitement.

"Now hold on, Rosie," Mike said as he grabbed my arm to calm me. "Let's not jump to conclusions without hearing more from Romano. For Susan to have been my fake wife is one chance in a million."

I held my chin high. "I, for one, believe in miracles, and that is what we need right now for me to become Isabella's foster mother."

No one said a word as they studied me and took in the ramification of what I'd said.

"Romano, what can you tell us about this girl?" urged Mike. "Anything will help."

He had dark circles under his eyes, and it was clear he had not slept well since Randy's accident, but he prevailed. "It was as if she didn't have a care in the world and wanted to experience everything life had to offer—no matter the consequences. She and her roommate were always getting in trouble...."

"What kind of trouble?" interjected Mike and Brian in one voice.

"They were arrested several times for soliciting."

"Was this at a time when B.B. was the Chief of Police?" I asked, excited.

"Yeah," confirmed Romano.

"Oh my, God! Are you thinking what I'm thinking? Is it possible he was mixed up in this? My mind traveled back to the two cops who had interviewed me at the Purple Passion Lounge. "Mimi, what about the cops interviewing me about Richard's death? Do you have their names?"

"Those two guys?" asked Mike. "They've been suspended until the new chief clears them regarding your former fiancé's murder."

"They are dirty cops," I said.

Brian turned to Mike. "We've got our work cut out for us."

Romano looked at his watch and said, "I need to get to the hospital and look in on Randy."

"I'll go with you, Romano," I said, not wanting him to sit there alone.

Then Cindy rose. "Mimi will take me to the construction site and show me where the skeletons were found."

When we got to the hospital, Romano slipped away from me for his time with Randy, and I sat in the waiting room and waited for him to return. I got up and went to the nurse's station. "I understand two family members are allowed in the ICU at a time; is that right?"

The nurse looked me up and down. "That's not always the case, but in this hospital, we allow that."

"Good," I said with the idea of talking to Romano about my becoming his 'sister.' He was already showing the wear and tear of trying to be the only one to check on Randy.

When Romano returned, I said, "Romano, I have an idea I'd like to discuss with you."

After listening to what I had to say, he grabbed my hand and pulled me toward the nursing station. "I'd like to introduce you to my sister, who will be changing off some of the visits with Randy," he stated in a firm, challenging voice I'd never heard before.

The nurse eyed me again with an expression that was hard to read. "All right, Romano, sign this sheet for our records, and you both can go in next time."

I continued to sit with Romano and tried to ignore the pain of my broken ribs. He picked up my hand and held it in his lap. "Rosie, what do you think is going to happen to Randy? Tell me honestly."

"I don't think Randy is out of the woods yet, Romano. That's why you and I need to take turns being here."

"I was afraid you'd say that. It's a feeling I have too."

When we entered the ICU and Randy's room, he was lying in bed with various machines surrounding him, ready if necessary. His right leg and arm were in casts, and he had an IV hooked up to his left arm. An oxygen mask was slung over his headboard but was not needed. I was stunned at how he looked—almost radiant with color in his cheeks and not a facial wrinkle or crease on his brow. He looked beautiful and peaceful, with his brain comatose and no apparent stress. Tears threatened at the thought of losing him. He was one of the good guys, and I was determined to do all I could not to let that happen.

I bent low to Randy, held his hand, and kissed his cheek. "Hi, Randy, it's me, Rosie. I'm here with Romano. I miss you and love you—we all do. I leaned closer and whispered, "So that you know, Romano is a hot mess without you. So hurry up and come back to us soon."

Romano took Randy's other hand in his. "Hello, sweetheart, Rosie's right. It's lonely without you, and I sure do miss you. Please wake up," he pleaded in an unsteady voice.

We sat, and each held one of Randy's hands without any response from him. The nurse came to check on Randy, and I said goodbye to Romano so I could join Virginia when she picked up Isabella at school.

When I walked to my car, goosebumps crawled along my body, and my heart fluttered. I looked around and expected to see whoever had caused that eerie feeling, but I saw no one. I walked faster, and as I hurried along, I couldn't shake off the sense that someone was watching me from behind. I rushed inside the car, ensuring the doors were locked, and rested my head against the steering wheel. Where I'd parked the car, it was devoid of people. I needed to get a grip and not create trouble where there was none. I started the car and headed home.

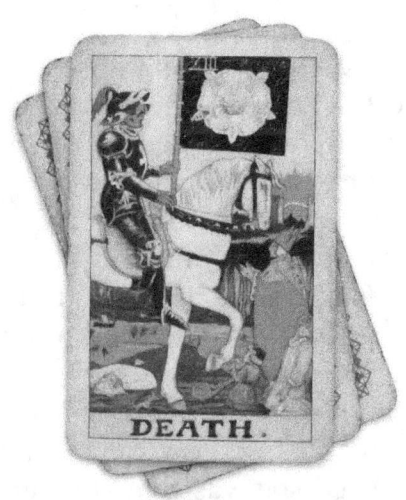

CHAPTER 26

While we waited for Isabella at the end of the school day, Virginia was as curious as I was to see what, if anything, would happen when the students exited the building. As soon as Isabella spotted us, she sprinted toward us. Once inside the car, she said, "Hi, Mama and Virginia."

"Did you have a good day at school, sweetie?" I asked.

Isabella remained silent, and when I looked back at her, I saw she was figuring out what to say. "Well …" I prodded.

"You saw me push that girl, didn't you, Mama?" she asked, worried.

"Yes, I did. Do you want to tell us what that was all about?"

Isabella let out a long sigh. "That was Tiffany. She's the one who knocked into me the first day of school, remember?"

"Yes, I do."

"She thinks she's so smart because she's the leader of some girls there. But I'm not afraid of her. My sister-friends, and I think the only way to get her to stop pushing me around is to fight her."

I smiled at her term 'sister-friends.' My mind flew back to when I was a young girl and had done just as Isabella had and fought back at the boy who'd bullied me. I had gotten in deep trouble with my grandmother, who'd been upset with me for doing so.

What was the best way to handle this situation with Isabella? A puff of air alerted me that my grandmother was around, and I sensed she was chuckling at my expense. A little bit of what goes around comes around, maybe? Then I heard my grandmother caution, *"Be loving but firm."*

I turned back to Isabella. "We can't change what's already been done. But I want to make it clear that this is not going to be allowed going forward. That behavior doesn't solve the issue anyway, does it?"

"No, but Mama …"

"What?" I snapped.

Isabella was quiet, shut down by my impatience. Then she defiantly lifted her head and spat, "I'm not going to let anyone push me around, Mama. I think she's afraid of me now, and I'm glad she is."

We stared at each other. Finally, I spoke, "Let's make a deal, okay? No more fighting. If she continues to harass you, we'll need to go to the principals to handle it. Agreed?"

Still looking defiant, Isabella said, "Okay, Mama."

"So, tell us about your day at school. What did you do?"

Isabella was excited to tell us about all she was learning. "Do you want to help me with my homework, Mama?"

Seeing how tired I was, Virginia jumped in, "May I be the one to help you with your homework today? I'd love to see what you're doing."

"Then I'll look it over with you once it's completed, Isabella," I added.

I sent Virginia a smile of gratitude. At home, the two of them went into my office to work, and I went upstairs to lie down for a nap. The next thing I knew, a small hand on my shoulder gently shook me.

"Mama, it's time to get up. Virginia has supper ready for us. She made soup, and I helped her."

When I entered the kitchen, Virginia was stirring the soup. She looked up and smiled.

"That soup smells so good!" I said. "What is it?"

"My special chicken and rice soup. It's my own recipe," she said as she held a full soup spoon toward me to taste. The three of us enjoyed our soup together, and I saw the significance of having Virginia in our lives. I didn't know what I'd do without her. We all helped clean up our mess. Virginia headed home, and Isabella and I headed upstairs to bed. I fell into a deep sleep, dreaming about a missing thought that floated above me like a balloon, and I could not reach it.

CHAPTER 27

I stirred when I smelled coffee brewing and heard Mike in the kitchen like old times. I heard him laugh at something Isabella said, and Brian joined in. I hadn't heard any of them get up. I sighed and crawled out of bed, feeling 100 years old. I grabbed my cashmere robe and threw it around me before I headed downstairs.

"Well, look who's up?" teased Brian when he saw me.

I leaned down and kissed Isabella's head. "I think you had better get dressed for school, sweetheart. It's late."

"Okay, Mama. If I hurry, can I come back for another cup of cocoa?"

"Sure." I headed to Mike for my morning kiss.

Brian watched us closely. "I can't believe you two. You're already like an old married couple – with a kid and everything."

I loved Brian because he said it as he saw it. "Did you talk to Lorenzo? Did you learn anything?" I asked, curious.

"Besides the fact that he's only rowing with one oar?" said Brian, shaking his head.

"Did he say why Tony's here?"

"He heard about the body," Mike answered.

"So?" I asked, confused. "That's it?"

"I think Tony wants to make sure that nothing falls back on him," Brian added. "We need to talk to Tony ourselves. What are you and Cindy up to today?"

"Researching those bones ..." I said despondently.

"Honey, just trust. Isn't that what you always tell me?" asked Mike.

I smiled, aware it was easier to say that when the shoe was on the other foot. "Yes, you're right, Mike."

I raced upstairs to shower before Virginia drove Isabella and me to her school. This would be the last day we'd be responsible for getting Isabella to school since the new bus schedule would begin next week. Laughter was coming from the kitchen when I entered.

Brian was teasing Isabella as an older brother would, and Mike winked at me. I smiled.

Isabella looked at me with twinkling eyes. "Uncle Brian is being silly, Mama!"

Brian was startled upon hearing his new name. Then he smiled broadly. "Does this mean you'll call me 'Uncle Brian' from now on, Rosie?"

"No, Cowboy. You'll always be Cowboy to me."

Brian winked at me. "Just checking."

I eyed Mike, and our thoughts meshed. Brian loved the nickname I had given him, and it was amusing to both of us that he now wore a cowboy hat.

Death Returns

Virginia arrived, and I turned to Isabella. "Grab your things, sweetheart. We'd better go."

No girls were gathered by the door when we dropped off Isabella, and she sailed inside without any interference. When we returned home, Cindy was there with Mimi, talking and laughing with the guys. When Mimi saw me, she lifted her coffee mug in greeting. "I hope three is not a crowd. Do you mind that I'm joining you and Cindy?"

"I'm glad you are. You're part of this crazy group now."

"Okay, Rosie, where do we start?" asked Cindy.

"Let's go to my office so I can show you how I've divvied things up for our research. Then we'll head to the library."

I showed them the note that read, "Follow the Dots," and again referred to Steve Jobs's definition. I knew he was right. It was the only way to discover the identity of the bones.

Before we left for the library, Mimi contacted the CPA that handled some of the tax consequences for the Purple Passion Lounge. She wanted him to send her the tax information for the past five years in the hopes of receiving a list of all the former employees. The accountant was not very encouraging since things had not been handled professionally, and he was worried he'd be in trouble. After Mimi threatened to turn him in, he reluctantly agreed to send her the information online.

It was amazing that there had been so few personnel records on hand when Mimi searched for them when closing the lounge. When she'd asked Tony about that, he pleaded innocent and was no help.

We decided to stick together in the library. Mimi would peruse the information sent to her by the CPA on her iPad while Cindy and I would search through the local newspapers for the past five years. Girls like Susan often appeared in photos taken at an event in the arms of a man who wanted a stunning woman by his side—often hired for a single event alone. Mike and Brian had promised to get a list of all the reported missing young girls from four and five years ago from the police chief. The problem, of course, was that not all those missing were reported missing—some had become lost in the shadows.

We went to the back of the library and spread our laptops and papers on a large mahogany table that could easily seat twelve. Next to the table were three cubicles that held a microfiche machine each, and Cindy and I each sat before one. The librarian's assistant came forward with a box of microfiche. The library had continued to do this for the local newspapers despite the easy access to obtain some but not all of the same information via the internet.

Searching through newspapers worldwide with *Google News Archive Search* was possible, but only for specific periods. The Library of Congress and the National Endowment for the Humanities teamed up to create the site *Chronicling America,* which provided two free searchable databases of digitized newspapers. Another site was *newspaperarchive.com,* where it was possible to find obituaries, marriage records, birth records, arrest records, and murder cases. However, until we had more concrete information, I believed it made more sense to see if we could hit upon something through our local newspapers' photos.

We sat in front of our machines and pointed out different photos to each other from newspapers that were four years ago and older and continued to work backward. It was amazing to see pictures of B.B., the former police chief, in many social photos as a prominent figure in Las Vegas. He was a huge man and dwarfed others in the pictures, usually wearing a smug smile that indicated he was used to being deferred to … a true bully.

"Wow!" muttered Mimi. "I don't believe this. Talk about underhanded. If I'm reading these reports right, I'd say that Tony and Johnny were skimming my father!"

"I can't imagine your father would be pleased to hear that," said Cindy.

"Absolutely," Mimi responded.

We went back to our task until our eyes became bleary. I shoved my chair back and stood up. "I need a break! Let's go to lunch."

CHAPTER 28

Munching sandwiches at the nearby café, we were quiet, each lost in our thoughts. "Now that we're finished scanning the newspapers from four years ago, maybe we'll be lucky and find something in those older than that. I have a strong feeling that B.B. was connected to both girls." I said.

"I wouldn't put it past him. Talk about a corrupt, vile person … his sister, too," said Cindy.

"I didn't realize all that was happening under Tony's handling of the Purple Passion Lounge. I've never wanted anything to do with my father's dealings, so I've steered clear of them. I can't believe my father was aware of all this, but again, maybe he was," sighed Mimi.

"It's not your fault, Mimi," I consoled.

"It's just maybe if I had been interested, those girls wouldn't have died," lamented Mimi.

313

"Mimi, don't go down the road of 'if only.' Let's see what we can do to find their identity and finally give these girls some peace." I snorted. "Or I should say, their parents some peace. I can't imagine being them, waiting for death to be finalized for their daughters. That state of limbo must be so wearing."

"I agree," commiserated Cindy.

"Alright then, let's get moving and see what we can get done."

We returned to the library and picked up where we'd left off. As I viewed the society section of the newspapers, I pointed out a picture of a group of men standing before the Purple Passion Lounge. "Hey, Mimi! Is this your father?" I asked as I pointed to an older gentleman.

"That must have been taken just before his stroke. And that other man next to him is my uncle … he passed away not too long ago," Mimi said, glued to the photograph.

The following photo was one with Richard and Sophia, the original owners of the Purple Passion Lounge, standing next to Tony and Johnny.

"What do you know about Johnny's involvement with the lounge? Brian told me there wasn't anything that legally connected him to the lounge," I asked.

"I honestly don't know. I guess that's maybe something for the boys to take up with Tony," replied Mimi, frowning at the figures in front of her.

"Eureka!" cried Cindy. "Look at this. It's the police chief with an attractive showgirl on his arm." She leaned forward to study it further. "I don't think it's Susan, though."

The three of us gathered around the machine to stare at the photo. Cindy spoke out loud about what we all were thinking. "Boobs are too small. I'll print it out anyhow, though."

"That's a good idea, Cindy. If we can identify some of the women in the photos, they may be able to tell us about Susan, her roommate, or Martini Darling."

We were dragging by the end of the day. We gathered our things, and Mimi asked, "Same place and time tomorrow?"

"Do you all want to come back to my place? We can order dinner in."

"I've got a splitting headache, and I'm going home," said Mimi. She looked at Cindy. "Why don't you drop me off at the condo, and you can take the car."

"Are you sure?"

"Yes, I'm going to grab a bite to eat and go to bed. Rosie, I'll see you here around 10 o'clock tomorrow, okay?"

"Wonderful. Thanks for all your help. Take care of yourself, hear?" I said as I hugged her.

On the way home, I called Romano. He said he'd gotten a good night's sleep the night before and for me not to come to the hospital. He was going to stay with Randy.

"How is he doing?" I asked.

"Pretty much the same."

"Any news regarding his bleeding?"

"They want to do another MRI in the morning to check it out," he answered with a sigh.

"Okay, then, if you're sure you don't need me to relieve you later, I'll check in with you in the morning. Take care and kiss Randy for me, okay?"

Back at the house, I thanked Virginia, and she left for home. Soon after, Cindy pulled into the driveway, announced by Sweet Pea. Isabella was pleased to have Cindy and me all to herself. With pride, she meticulously showed and explained each school paper to us. I gathered her in my arms and kissed the top of her head. "You are so special to me, Isabella. I love you."

"I love you too, Mama." She shyly looked at Cindy and smiled and didn't say a word. "Is it alright if I go next door and show my papers to Gramma Irene?"

"Of course, sweetheart, as long as it's okay with her. Let me call before you go over."

Cindy and I curled up in the living room with a glass of Pinot Noir and tried to relax. Despite spending as much time as we had, our research had not brought us anything concrete, and we both felt stressed. Patience, Rosie, patience, I kept telling myself.

Mike and Brian came through the door looking much as we did—exhausted.

"Hi guys," greeted Cindy, who perked up at seeing them. "How's it going?"

"It's going. That's about all I can say," answered Brian.

"We went down to check on the site. I wanted to introduce Brian to Butch, but he wasn't there. Have you been down there today?" Mike said.

"Not today. What's that in your hand?"

"Brian and I were working on this at the police station."

"What is it?" Cindy and I chorused.

"A partial list of arrests of women from 5 and 6 years ago, but we'll do more tomorrow," Brian answered.

"Where's Mimi? And where's Isabella?" Mike asked.

"Mimi had a headache and went back to her condo to rest. Isabella should be back any minute. She went next door to show Irene her school papers."

Mike turned to Brian, "Ready for a cold one?"

"I thought you'd never ask," teased Brian.

Cindy and I joined them in the kitchen. My phone rang just as I was ready to sit down, and when I saw who it was, my face blanched. Mike gave me a questioning look, and I mouthed, "It's Jacklyn from the agency."

He nodded and held a thumbs up in encouragement. I excused myself and answered, "Hi, Jacklyn; how are you?"

"More to the point, how are *you*?"

"Feeling better, thanks."

"I thought you'd like to know your hearing date has been set for three weeks from now."

"Three weeks? Is that when it will be decided whether I can become Isabella's foster mother? What do I need to do to prepare?" I asked, nearly frantic with the thought of Mike's situation unresolved.

"I still need you to send me your list of people who will be involved in Isabella's life so that I can show the court she will be surrounded by people in good standing who will positively influence her life."

Tears formed, and I swallowed a lump and squeaked out, "Anything else?"

"Normally, this process is usually straightforward and not difficult. It's because of the unusual circumstances of Isabella's blood family requesting you to be her foster mother that has drawn attention to this case."

"I understand. I'll get that list to you soon. Thank you, Jacklyn, for everything. I really appreciate it."

"I know you do. We both want the best for Isabella, so get me your list as soon as possible. You will receive a formal letter in the mail. Review it, and feel free to call me with any questions. Goodbye, Rosalie."

"Thanks again, Jacklyn."

I stumbled back toward the kitchen, and the conversation halted as I entered the room. Three pairs of worried eyes stared at me, demanding answers.

"We go to court in three weeks. Jacklyn is asking for the list of people who will influence Isabella, and that means you too, Mike." I tried to control my frustration with his situation.

Mike pushed his hand through his hair. "I know, I know," he sighed as he glared at Brian.

Brian had the grace to flush. He turned to Cindy, "Is there anything we're missing? Mike and I are looking through the arrests; you and Rosie are checking the photos in the newspaper, and Mimi is seeing if there is anything in the financials and company records."

I interjected, "I think it's all tied back to the person who is leaving the bones of those girls ..." Chills raced across my body, affirming that thought. "Maybe we should look into who might have a grudge against us building there or what we're building and see if anything is against any of us involved? Isn't that the real question?"

Brian agreed while scratching his head. "I think you might be onto something there, don't you?" he asked, looking at Mike and Cindy.

"That's a definite angle to look into," agreed Mike. "Rosie, while you were on the phone, we talked about our meeting with Tony, and I'd bet my last dollar that he has nothing to do with this. Since there doesn't seem to be any love lost between Mimi and him, I think he came here to watch his cousin squirm through this mess."

"I can't imagine anyone having a grudge against Romano, or even Mimi for that matter, because she hasn't been around until recently. Does it make any sense this has something to do with Mimi's father?"

Cindy looked at me. "What about you, Rosie? Would anyone have a grudge against you?"

"If so, I'd think it would've been B.B., but that's no longer an issue, so it can't be me."

"Well, if we keep working backward like the 'Follow the Dots' message says to do, we'll find our answer," Mike said.

My head began to whirl as I thought about my situation with Isabella, Randy's accident, and all that was happening at the site. A fleeting thought kept dancing away from me—out of my reach, much like the dream I'd had the other night. I shook my head to clear it, and, much to my disappointment, my mind remained cluttered with scattered worries.

Isabella came bursting through the door. "Are you getting hungry?" I asked.

"I'm starved," she said, patting her stomach. "Can we order pizza, Mama?"

"You are a girl after my heart, for sure. Everyone game?" I asked.

Mike pulled more beer from the refrigerator and handed another one to Brian.

"Want to see my papers, Mike and Uncle Brian?"

I pushed them toward the living room while I set the table, and Cindy threw together a salad. Cindy caught my eye. "We'll get to the bottom of this. I know we will. Keep the faith, my friend."

I agreed, knowing we'd do our best to make that happen.

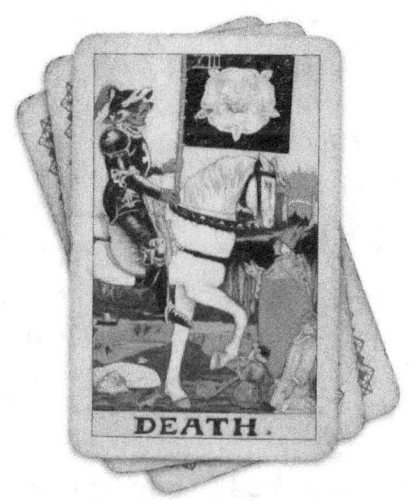

CHAPTER 29

T he following day, I rolled over and watched Mike snore softly. He must have felt me staring at him because he immediately jerked awake. "Caught Ya!" He grabbed me and pulled me roughly against him and began to place countless kisses on my neck and upward to my face until I couldn't help but giggle. We chuckled at our antics until his lips found mine. Then all became quiet with our need for each other.

As I stepped into the shower after our lovemaking, the warm water soothingly ran down my body, and I gave myself over to my special silent place where my inner thoughts could surface. It's so near, and yet I can't reach it. What am I missing?

I smelled my grandmother and heard her say, *"I can't help you any more than to remind you of the message left for you.*

Follow that and remember everything in its own time, my darling girl. You'll understand soon enough." And puff, she was gone.

I loved my grandmother for all the ways she was there for me. We were very close, able to read each other's minds, much like Isabella and I were growing to do. In time, I knew Isabella would far exceed my psychic abilities, but I was not willing to get her involved in any formal training in the different spiritual modalities yet. That would have to be down the road ... and only at Isabella's request.

I smelled the coffee Mike had brewed and hurried to get dressed. Brian laughed with Mike downstairs, and I raced down to join them. I smiled broadly as he held out a cup of coffee as soon as I entered the kitchen. Brian sat there with his hair matted, looking like he'd had a sleepless night.

"Hey, Cowboy, it looks like you had a rough night. Didn't you sleep?"

"Not much," he said with a groan. "I get this way whenever I'm on a murder case. Ask Mike, and he'll tell you."

Mike tipped his head and held open his hands, confirming what Brian had said.

"What are you two up to today?" I asked.

"We're returning to the police station to download more female arrest records from the past six or seven years. Would you scan over what we've already printed out and see if anything jumps out at you ... you know what I mean," said Brian.

"Sure, and I'll also have Cindy and Mimi take a look. We're returning to the library and hopefully finishing what we started yesterday. If we can recognize some of the people photographed with B.B. more than once, we might be able to interview them to see if they remember Susan with her remarkable light eyes. I think it will be those eyes that help us identify her." Mike agreed.

"Today is Saturday. What about Isabella?" he asked.

"Virginia is coming this morning, and then this afternoon, they're going to the movies to see the latest Cinderella movie, newer even than the one she saw at Irene's."

"Thank God for Virginia, huh?" Mike said.

"For sure. I want to check in with Romano too."

"I thought I'd grill some steaks tonight. Shall I get enough for everyone?" asked Mike.

I smiled to myself. After living alone with Sweet Pea these past years, thinking of so many wonderful people in my life now and in my home was wild. I loved it.

"Yes, and you might want to pick up some more wine and beer too."

"Right on. Brian, I'll run to the store while you get showered."

"Oh, will you please get some salad greens too?" I asked.

"Yes, sweetheart; anything else?"

"How about some gelato? You know ..."

"Coconut!" we said in unison and then laughed.

Brian just shook his head. "You two might as well be married already."

Isabella came in, rubbing her eyes and looking sleepy. "Morning, Mama, Mike, and Uncle Brian."

Sweet Pea greeted us and then headed for the sliding door to go out.

I held my arms wide, and Isabella snuggled in. I kissed the top of her head and said, "You are going to have a wonderful day with Virginia."

"Yesss, I am," she squealed.

After Mike and Brian left, I said goodbye to Isabella, Virginia, and Sweet Pea, who was fast getting used to my leaving her behind, which made my departure pleasant.

I pulled into the library parking lot and watched Mimi and Cindy climb out of their car. I parked beside them, and we all walked inside together. "How is your headache, Mimi?"

"Much better, thanks. I just had to get away from the accountant's numbers. They indicated that all that took place at the lounge was not good. The accountant and I have a lot to go over that he isn't going to like." She shook her head in disgust.

"Then today, why don't you join Cindy and me looking through the newspaper photos? That way, hopefully, we can finish up that part."

Mimi perked up. "Yes, let's find those girls."

We printed out pictures of the deplorable former Chief of Police from the society sections of several newspapers, showing him always with a different girl on his arm. It wasn't until I got closer to more than five years ago that I saw a photo of B.B. with a girl that caught my attention. The look on his face made me point out this photo to Mimi and Cindy … he looked smitten. The girl had turned away, so her face was in profile, but there was something about her stance that was fearless. The other couple in the photo seemed entranced with her as well. Goosebumps covered my body. Who was the girl, and who was the couple with them?

"Look here; I think this is her!" I exclaimed.

"Lemme see," cried Cindy. "Here, Mimi, you can look too." She scooted aside to make room for her.

"How do we find out who the couple is?" I asked.

"Maybe Tony or Johnny would know," suggested Mimi.

"Good idea," agreed Cindy.

"Let's keep going and see what else we find, okay?" I said.

We eagerly jumped back to our tasks. Another photo of this same girl and B.B. came up, and this time there was a full frontal shot of her. She was beautiful as she stood tall and boldly as if to defy anyone to act toward her in a less than hospitable manner. Even in this black and white photo, her eyes stood out, and I was drawn to them. They seemed to glow. In the following picture of them at the same fancy event, she was unaware of the camera as her eyes were steadfast on the man at the edge of the photo as she smiled at him. B.B. stood there, looking at her with a scowl. Trouble in paradise?

Cindy came across a photo of several people arrested in a drug raid, and there she was again, the girl with glowing eyes. This time, she looked disheveled as she and another girl wrapped their arms around each other as if to guarantee no one could separate them. The article underneath expressed B.B.'s anger, calling these girls lowly whores as they sold their bodies for drugs.

Another picture showed B.B. behind a podium speaking with one arm raised high as if making a point. The article below the photo quoted him as saying, "We will not tolerate drugs coming into our city, and we are doing everything possible to stop it. Anyone caught selling or distributing drugs will be thrown into jail without bail, and I will see to it that they receive the maximum sentence. Do I make myself clear?"

My former fiancé had been murdered by B.B. when he tried to expose the drug dealings within B.B.'s precinct, so I knew he'd been speaking falsely, and my heart pounded with anger at his lies despite his no longer being alive.

Mimi said, "That's it for me. I've gone through all my stack to review."

Cindy chimed in, "Me too. How about you, Rosie?"

"I have two more newspapers to review, and then I'll be done too. I think we have enough to work with, don't you?"

"Yes, I do. What do you say we show some of these to Tony and see what he can tell us?" Cindy said.

"We're going to have to just show up at his doorstep because if we call him, he will probably refuse to see us," said Mimi.

Cindy said, "Did you know that the new Chief of Police ordered Tony and Lorenzo not to leave town until they see if Randy makes it through? Otherwise, Lorenzo will be up for manslaughter, and Tony might be involved."

"Let's plan on talking to Tony tomorrow, then. When I spoke with Romano this morning, there have been no changes. He'll be joining us tonight, and we'll be able to find out more. It's time to call it a day. Why don't you come to the house at 5:30, and we'll be able to relax before Mike throws the steaks on the grill? Don't worry about bringing anything because Mike has it covered, okay?"

CHAPTER 30

I raced to the bakery to pick up a baked flan for dessert before Isabella and Virginia returned from the movies. I made it just in time. They both came through the door with smiles that broadened when they saw me.

"Oh, Mama, Cinderella was sooo beautiful. And you should have seen her dress when she danced with the Prince. I loved it!" exclaimed Isabella.

"We'll have to buy the video when it comes out," I said.

"Oh yes, Mama." With a dreamy expression and arms held wide, she twirled around as Cinderella had done at the ball.

Virginia smiled. "That movie certainly makes you believe there is such a thing as true love. No doubt about that."

I thanked Virginia for spending the day with Isabella and tucked a large tip in the envelope I handed her.

Tomorrow being Sunday, Virginia wouldn't be back again until Monday, which meant we'd stick to the rule I'd made about having Sunday be a family day. It was important for all of us to maintain a balance in our lives between work and family. Fortunately, Mike had readily agreed, but it would be interesting to see how Brian would handle it.

Irene called and asked if Isabella would like to join them for supper. When I handed Isabella the phone and she heard the invitation, her head bobbed up and down. I tried not to be jealous when it was apparent how important Irene was becoming to Isabella. I knew better. It was not a competition for Isabella's affection, and I needed to allow them to grow their relationship without my interference. There was plenty of love to go around, I scolded myself. I kissed Isabella goodbye, and she headed next door, Sweet Pea following because she had been invited too.

I set the table, placing crystal glasses and fancy silverware at each place. It felt so good to use the best of what I had, passed down from my mother and grandmother.

Romano looked flustered when he arrived. When I asked him how Randy was doing, he frowned. "I don't know. He seems uncomfortable and moves around a lot, although he is still not awake. I don't know what's going on."

"What about his bleeding? What was that all about?" I asked.

"His spleen got torn in the accident, and they missed a small section when they cauterized it. So they said if it didn't start healing in a day or two, they'd go back in and fix it. Maybe that's what was bothering Randy," he said.

"After dinner, I'd like to go with you to the hospital to see him. I haven't been there for a while," I said, feeling something was wrong.

Mike poured wine for everyone except Brian, who preferred beer. The tension of none of us finding what we were looking for dissipated, and we began to relax. We laughed at some of the stories Brian told. When Cindy asked him if he'd had any luck getting the girl in Boston to go out with him, we all burst into hysterical laughter as he relayed everything he was doing to get her attention to no avail. Nothing had worked so far.

"I haven't given up yet. I'm sure she's just playing hard to get," Brian said confidently, and we laughed harder. He was used to getting his way with girls, but this one might be the one who got away.

Romano received a telephone call from the hospital saying Randy was awake as we finished dessert.

"Wait, Romano; I'm coming with you!" I said as he was dashing out the door. Realizing I couldn't just leave, I said, "No, I'd better meet you there."

Mike came to my side. "Go, just go. Brian and I will clean up and be here when Isabella comes home."

"We'll help," said Cindy and Mimi together.

I grabbed my purse and headed out the door. When I arrived at the hospital, I quickly parked and raced down the hospital hallway with my heart pounding. Something was wrong; I could feel it.

I walked into the room where Romano stood by Randy's bedside. The nurses had propped him up in bed, and he looked at Romano with such love that it stopped my heart. Unaware, Romano bent down to kiss him. The nurse looked at me and tipped her head toward the door.

"I'll leave you alone now, and then I'll return in a few minutes to check on him."

Randy saw me and whispered, "Rosie."

I went to his side with tears falling and grabbed his hand. It was ice cold. I kissed him on the cheek and wondered why he was so chilled. I had a vision of him lying dead, and I frantically stepped back from him and asked, "What's wrong, Randy?"

"Can't breathe," he puffed out.

"Nurse!" I screamed. "Please help us!" I raced to the doorway, and immediately, two nurses headed our way. The heart monitor was showing distress. I looked into the back corner of the room and saw darkness there. The longer I stared at it, the darkness began to take shape into the form I knew as death with a black cloak and scythe. I began to scream, "You can't have him! Do you hear me? You cannot take him. I won't allow it!"

My face was red, and I had spit on my chin as I heard a commotion behind me. I'd startled everyone in the room, and one of the nurses began to come my way. I headed further into the corner and screamed again, "You can't have him! He's not yours to take. He belongs here with us!" As the nurse took hold of my arm, I pulled away. "Romano, say something! Over here. Do you see it?" I asked.

Romano looked past me. He stepped forward and shook his fist at the form. His face paled, and his eyes widened with disbelief. "He's not yours. He's MINE, and you can't have him!" he yelled, choking on his words.

A code-blue alert was in effect, and two doctors ran into the room. When they saw us there, one of them screamed at the nurses, "Get them the hell out of here, now!"

They had the defibrillator paddles out and placed on Randy's chest, and it was horrifying to watch Randy's body jerk as a result. We heard the heart monitor begin to beep again, and we wept silently in relief as we were pushed out into the hall and shoved aside to let the gurney pass to take Randy into the operating room. We stumbled down the hall and into the waiting room. We sat on the leather couch and clung to each other, numb to all that'd happened. Romano's arm was around me, and he pulled my head onto his chest. He held me close. "What was that, Rosie?" he asked fearfully. "Did you see what I saw? Is that why you were yelling?"

I nodded and sniffled. After a few minutes, I stirred and said, "I'm returning to the room. I want to see if it is still there."

"I'm coming with you," Romano said, rising from the couch.

We walked back down the hallway, and when we got to Randy's room and peeked in, a nurse was making up the bed with clean sheets. My heart fell, and Romano nearly collapsed against me. "What are you doing?" I demanded.

The nurse smiled and said, "Making up the bed."

"Why?" I yelled in distress.

When the nurse realized what we were thinking, she said, "No, dear, it's so that Randy has clean sheets when he returns."

I fell against Romano, and once again, we shuffled down to the waiting room to wait for Randy to be returned to his room. I awoke close to midnight, and the doctor shook Romano awake.

"What is it, doctor?" I asked as Romano stirred. "Is Randy going to be okay?"

"Yes, he had a tiny blood clot, probably from surgery. We were able to monitor it until it disappeared. Once he's awake, we'll get him up to walk every hour for the next day or two to make sure his blood is circulating without a hitch. This is more of a common occurrence than we'd like to admit. But it sometimes happens, especially when someone is unconscious for any time. But all is well, and we'll ensure it stays that way."

Watching and listening to Romano's sobbing of relief was hard for me. The doctor put his hand on Romano's shoulder and said, "Why don't you go home and get some rest? You, too, young lady."

"No, I'm not going anywhere. I'm going to spend the night here with Randy," Romano pleaded. "Please, doc."

The doctor studied him. "I'll make the arrangements."

After the doctor left, Romano turned to me. "Please go home, Rosie. I'm worried about you, for you need the rest too."

"If you're sure you're okay …."

He roughly pulled me toward him and whispered, "How can I ever thank you, Rosie?" He pulled back from me and searched my eyes. "This is better left between you and me, right?"

"Yes, that would be hard to explain to anyone. I love you, Romano. Let's talk tomorrow, or should I say later?" with an uneasy laugh.

I called Mike and explained what'd happened to Randy minus our seeing the death energy. "I'm going to stop off at the construction site. I want to view the hole while no one is around and see what comes to me psychically. I won't be long."

"I don't think that's such a good idea, Rosie. Why don't you just come home?"

"But …"

Knowing I'd already decided to stop there, he said, "At least call the guard to meet you when you get there."

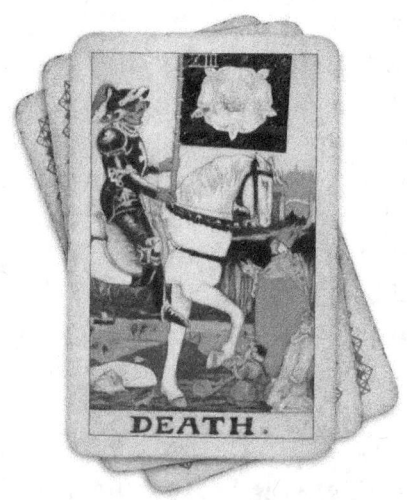

CHAPTER 31

When I got to the construction site, each building in progress had several large spotlights focused on them, so they appeared well-lit. I met the guard, who told me his name was Jacoby. He looked bored, and I couldn't blame him, for it wasn't easy to work the night shift, especially alone.

We chatted briefly, and then I headed toward the back where the skeletons had been found. The guard followed. His phone rang, and he stopped to talk. I pointed to the back and said I'd be right back. He nodded and waved me ahead with a finger up in the air, signaling that he'd be joining me momentarily.

I picked my way to the back and found the lighting so poor I had to bend closer to the ground to locate the hole. I was surprised that it hadn't been filled in and seemed deeper than before. I wondered if Mike and the police chief had decided to leave it open to entice the perp to return with more bones. I stood above the hole and closed my eyes to see if any psychic information would come to me.

I envisioned two women hanging onto each other, laughing, and weaving through a crowd in a drug-induced state. One of them spoke, slurring her words. "I can't believe you called yourself Martini Darling. How did you come up with that?"

Suddenly, my mind was jerked back to the present as I heard steps rushing toward me. Then I was falling, falling, until all went black.

I woke to Mike's frantic voice, "Where is she, Jacoby?"

"She was right here. Isn't she with you?"

"Why did you let her out of your sight?" Mike demanded.

"I heard someone running away, and I gave chase, but I wasn't fast enough to catch him," answered the guard, out of breath.

"Mike? I'm here," I called out, but my voice was barely above a whisper, for I couldn't seem to draw in enough air. I felt all around me until I found two rocks. Then, I clicked them together so they made a loud continual beat. I knew neither could hear me otherwise.

"Listen!" ordered Mike.

I continued banging the rocks together until I saw figures standing above me surrounding the hole. "Mike?" I croaked.

"Oh, my God! Rosie? What's going on?" He bent closer. "Here, help me lift her," he ordered the guard.

Mike jumped into the hole and picked me up from the bottom where I sat, and forgetting my broken ribs, he squeezed me until I gasped for air. "Mike, stop!" I said as I pushed him away to catch my breath.

"Rosie, you are going to be the death of me yet," he scolded.

"I don't want to talk about it right now," I stated firmly in a dismissive tone.

"Did you recognize who did this to you?" asked the guard.

I shook my head. "Not a clue. I didn't hear him until he was behind me, and it was too late. I never saw him."

"Why you, Rosie? What do you know that we don't?" asked Mike. "It's obvious this has something to do with you. What is it?"

"I wish I knew," I said, shrugging my shoulders in dismay. Nothing was making any sense, and my mind was rattled. "I just want to go home."

"All right, but you're riding with me. Jacoby, take her car keys and pull her car onto the site. Brian and I will get the car in the morning."

"Okay, boss," he said.

With Mike's arm around me, I trudged beside him, glad for his support. I climbed into the car in a funk, and my body ached. This incident affected me and my spirits, and I was subdued on the ride home. When we arrived home, Brian greeted us at the door, and I saw Mike shake his head at Brian, indicating not to ask what had happened.

When Mike started to walk me up the stairs, I placed my hand on his arm and said, "No, I need to be alone."

"Aw right, baby, whatever you want," he answered, concerned as I groaned with each step I climbed. I knew Mike would understand that I'd reached my limit. Now it seemed it was on me to figure out why the bones of those girls were tied to me.

Instead, all I could think about was the apparition Romano and I had dealt with earlier. Death waiting?

I'd known of others who'd said they had seen this same phantom in their own experience, but it was new for me. I couldn't get it out of my mind. I was drawn back to the question that Cal's mother, Lizzie, had asked me. "Do you think you can ask death to wait?"

Remembering back, my face warmed, knowing I had been cavalier in my response. I was happy that she had had the time to make amends with her daughter before she passed, but I would no longer be careless in my response if anyone asked me the same question again.

I knew it was essential to sleep, so I went to the medicine cabinet in the bathroom, reached to the back, and pulled out the pills the doctor had ordered for me. Instead of taking one, I took three and hoped I wouldn't remember anything for the next 12 hours. As I laid my head on my pillow, I smelled my grandmother's perfume and knew she was around to protect me. I gave her a half-smile and whispered, "Thanks, Gram," as a tear slid down my cheek.

CHAPTER 32

I felt Mike stir against me when it was barely light out. He kissed me tenderly, got out of bed, and said, "Go back to sleep. I don't want you to worry about a thing. I've got it covered. Just sleep, Rosie, I mean it. You need to take it easy."

I groaned and rolled over. Mike leaned down and kissed the back of my neck. "I'll check in on you in a bit. Love you, baby."

I nodded and hoped he'd know I loved him too. I awoke in the early afternoon, my joints so stiff I could barely move. As memories flooded in, I was tempted to take more pills to escape them, but returning to sleep wouldn't find the murderer. As I did most mornings, I meditated with my eyes closed for a few moments. When I flipped onto my side, Sweet Pea came wiggling toward me from her spot at the foot of the bed. She jumped on me and began to lick my face, making me laugh. I grabbed her, pulled her close to me, and nuzzled her. Her tail was on fast speed, wagging back and forth, and it was just what I needed to get me out of my slump.

"The house is mighty quiet. Where is everyone, Sweet Pea?"

She jumped out of bed, raced to the doorway, and waited for me to follow. I grabbed my robe and slippers and padded down the stairs into the kitchen. There was a note lying on the table. "Rosie, a sandwich is in the refrigerator for you, and coffee is ready to perk. Isabella, Brian, Cindy, and I've gone bowling, and we will be back with dinner. Love, Mike."

I chuckled at the thought of Mike and Brian bowling. Oh, to be a fly on the wall ….

I poured fresh coffee into a mug, grabbed my sandwich, and carried them into the office. I pulled my tarot cards from my desk drawer and shuffled them, and asked for any information to be the truth from the Universe. After I cut the cards twice, I needed to pick out three from the pile for an Oracle reading. *The first card was for the present problem.* I pulled a card from the deck and slowly turned it over. The Hermit deals with his problems when the time is ripe, and without trying to avoid the issue, he has the bravery to do the right thing. That made sense because the time to deal with what was happening relating to me was NOW.

The second card stood for the way out of the problem. I slowly pulled out another card and held my breath as I turned it over. The Emperor means facing the unknown undaunted, with personal self-determination; sound judgment. This second card gave me the courage to march ahead and seek out what I may have done in the past to connect me to the skeletons. Nothing came to mind right then, and I needed to leave no stone unturned and 'Follow the Dots' like the message advised.

The third card stood for the future – if you are prepared to take that path. As I hesitated to pull out the last card from the deck, I could have sworn that one slid forward and stuck out a bit. My hand hovered above it for a few seconds, and then I slowly pulled it from the deck. I half-expected it to be the Death card, so I was more than pleased to see The World card, its meaning to triumph in all endeavors, assured success.

I knew that many people did not believe in using Tarot cards. They thought the Tarot cards didn't indicate anything and were used simply as a crutch. But I knew everything was energy for me, so the cards offered a look into my energy, what was going on in my life, and the higher energy without linear earth time. That allowed me a glimpse into the future. So I was comfortable with the cards and the messages I'd turned up. Now I was more than willing to march ahead and unravel the mysteries waiting to be solved.

I sat in the plump chair in the corner of the office and went over things in my mind. Who had I irritated to the point that they'd want to hurt me? Or want to destroy what I was trying to do by constructing an office to help those victims of human trafficking? As I sat with my eyes closed, I counted backward the events that had taken place surrounding the Purple Passion Lounge. True, I'd irritated several people—Tony, Johnny, and Lorenzo for sure—still alive and who could be the culprits. Others—the former Chief of Police and his sister Mama—were no longer alive, as well as the murdered victims. So who was left who hated me enough to cause me all this trouble?

I felt a breeze and smelled my grandmother's perfume. *"Rosie girl, you need to have faith. Let things unfold as they are meant to."*

"You mean do nothing?"

I felt her smile. *"No, sweet girl, you know better than that. You need to do your part and then stand back. Let the Universe do its part too. Stop trying to control everything. All of your worrying is blocking your thoughts and clear thinking."*

"That's so hard to do."

"Tell me about it," she said with a slight chuckle. *"Love you, darling girl."* Off she went sending me red roses for love.

How had I gotten so far off track?

CHAPTER 33

I awoke and felt better than I had in days despite the stiffness in my joints and the pain in my taped ribs. I shifted, and Mike's arm automatically reached for me. He pulled me to his side and whispered, "How is my queen this morning?"

I whispered my response, and he smiled, pulling me closer. I never knew a man could make love so gently and tenderly. Between Mike showing me love in his way and my grandmother in hers, I knew no one in the world was luckier than me.

I showered and dressed with a new lightness of spirit. Isabella was up and dressed, eager for school to begin for the week. She wanted me to drive her there early so she could work on a particular school project. I was looking forward to it.

Once in the car, I saw how excited Isabella was to be going to school. "Isabella, how are you and Tiffany getting along?"

"She's not so bad. I think she likes me. At least she doesn't bother me anymore."

"Well, that's good, isn't it?"

"I guess," said Isabella.

"You know, sometimes the bullies are the most afraid."

Isabella studied me. "I know, right?"

Isabella never ceased to surprise me. She seemed to have an innate understanding of what makes people tick. I knew she had a lot to teach me. When we pulled to the school, Isabella readied herself to get out. She turned to me, worried. "You'll be careful, won't you, Mama?"

I reached where she sat and smoothed her brow with my thumb. "I promise."

I looked over Isabella's shoulder and saw a girl coming our way. When Isabella saw her, she said, "Mama, this is Amanda. She's in my class."

I lowered the passenger side window. "Hi, Amanda. How are you?"

"Hi, are you Isabella's mother?"

"Yes," answered Isabella before I could get a word out. I looked at Isabella's mischievous expression and shook my head. "Goodbye, lovey. Have a good day. Ride home on the school bus today like usual, okay?"

She nodded and walked away, not looking back. I sat there for a few extra minutes to ensure she went inside without trouble. Then, as I pulled around the limo parked ahead of me, I noticed that Tiffany had climbed out of the back of the limo and now stood outside, wiping away the tears her blond hair couldn't hide.

I continued to the library, where I wanted to do some research of my own. Cindy and Mimi were going to meet with Tony and Lorenzo to review the newspaper photos to see what they knew about the people in them.

Mike and Brian were researching the police records of cold cases to see what they could discover. Both were anxious to open up their western office for business. Later they would meet with a realtor to look at renting office space.

I'd thought about what my grandmother had said and determined to do my part by letting the Universe take over some of my worries, an idea had come to me. Mike was right in that the skeletons seemed tied to me, but I believed it might have nothing to do with the bones themselves. Instead, they had served as payback, but for what? What had I missed? As painful as it might be, I knew I had to go back to the time of Jeff's murder.

I entered the library, and when the librarian recognized me, she nodded to the back and said, "I'll be right there. I have to check out this book first."

I smiled, went to the rear of the library, and unloaded my things at the same table that Cindy, Mimi, and I had worked on before. The librarian hurried to where I sat, and after I told her what I wanted, she brought the microfiche to me and quickly returned to the main desk. I removed the film from the container, inserted it, and held my breath while waiting for the photos to come to life.

There was several days' worth of photos and articles about the drugs and Jeff's death. Interestingly, the two issues were never separated. They had been immediately tied together, so Jeff's death appeared to be the sole reason the department's drug dealing had ever come to light.

Looking at Jeff's photo, my heart became heavy and sorrowful. Not so much that I'd lost a love in my life because I'd come to terms with that. Instead, the sorrow was over the unfairness of it all. As I studied the picture of the former Chief of Police, I felt a wave of justice having been met at the thought of his death.

Eying the photo of the police chief once more, I became angry again at his leering face and those of the two goons surrounding him. I'd encountered those two then and more recently at the Purple Passion Lounge when they interviewed me about my former employer's suicide. I felt sick as I glanced through several other photos and reacted to the arrogance of the three of them as they stood together photo after photo, pretending to be innocent of any involvement with Jeff's death or the drug dealing scheme in place.

I felt a headache marching in, and I knew I needed to step away from what I was viewing and get myself under better control. I printed several photos, folded them, and stuffed them into my purse, disgusted with all that had happened.

I'd been at the library for barely an hour, so I decided I'd have enough time to drop in at the hospital and check on Randy. I felt edgy, and the back of my neck prickled the closer I got to the hospital. My heart beat faster, and I suddenly felt an urgency to see Randy and ensure he was okay. I speed-dialed Romano, and he picked up right away.

"Where are you, Romano? Are you at the hospital with Randy?"

"Yup, we're both here. Why? Are you coming to see us?"

"I'm on my way. I should be there shortly."

"Are you okay? You sound upset," said Romano.

"I guess with all that's happened, my nerves are rattled. Nothing to worry about, though."

"Okay, then. See you soon."

When I reached the hospital, goosebumps crawled across my body. I felt that someone was watching me. When I looked around the parking lot, several people had left their cars to head inside. There was an older couple who clasped hands and strolled toward the entrance. Another younger woman had a baby in her arms, and a toddler grasped firmly in her hand as he tried to pull away and escape. We got to the entrance simultaneously and took turns entering as an unkempt middle-aged man held the door for us. He had a hat pulled low with greasy hair escaping. He smelled as if he hadn't bathed in a while. I thanked him for his kindness and headed to the elevator.

Just as the elevator doors began to close, a dirty hand pushed through, and the doors automatically re-opened. It was the man who had held the entrance door to the hospital for me and the others. We were the only two in the elevator. I moved to the side and gave him space and a tight smile without looking at him. As the doors closed completely and we were ready to move, I asked, "What floor for you?"

He glowered at me and growled, "The same as you."

Then, he pushed me away and blocked me from reaching any buttons. I hadn't had a chance to punch in the number I wanted, and I watched in alarm as he pushed the button for the basement. He turned, looked down at me, and demanded, "You don't recognize me, do you?"

I glanced at him, and although he looked vaguely familiar, I couldn't identify him. "You have no idea the trouble you've caused me, bitch!" he sputtered angrily.

My heart pounded, and I began to panic. I lurched to the side and tried to reach around him to push the emergency stop button, but he blocked me. He withdrew his hand from his pocket and held a dirty rag toward me. Then, with one swift chop, his hand came down hard on my forearm, stretched toward the buttons, and I screamed in pain. Then all went black as he covered my face with the dirty rag.

When I awoke, it was completely dark. I lay flat on a hard surface, shivering in the cold air. The air was sickly sweet, and I was dizzy. My stomach churned, and I felt sick. I tried to sit up, only to bump my head against the top of the space. Both hands hit metal when I held my arms out to steady myself. My heart nearly stopped with fear. I knew exactly where I was. I heard a whimpering sound and realized it was coming from me as tears slid down my cheeks. I was in one of the chambers designated for dead bodies in the hospital morgue. I reached my arms behind my head to see if there was a way for me to unlock the door. Nothing.

I panicked and began to call out in a rasping voice, "Anyone here?"

My grandmother's voice echoed within, *"Rosie, stop! Lie back down and close your eyes. Send pictures of where you are to Isabella, Brian, and Mike. Tell them exactly where you are and tell them to hurry. You can do it, Rosie."*

"Gram, what has happened?"

"Just do what I say!"

I laid back down. I sent pictures of the hospital, the basement of the hospital, and the chamber I imagined I was in. I went over and over it again, like a mantra in my mind, accompanied by the word, "Hurry!"

What seemed like several hours later, when I'd just about given up hope, I heard movement in the room. I listened to the door of my chamber open and felt my bed begin to slide forward. It took all my resolve not to move and to lie still. Just when I was about to shout out, something told me to pretend I was still out cold.

"Shit!" my captive mumbled, irritated. "I can't move her like this. I'll have to come back."

With a quick movement, he shoved my bed back inside the chamber, and I heard the door snap shut. At that moment, I began to lose hope as I realized how impossible it'd be for Mike, Brian, or Isabella to find me before the cold overtook me. Despite my earlier resolve to remain still, I waved my arms and lifted my knees as far as possible to keep my circulation moving. Tears slid silently down the sides of my cheeks, and I began to wipe them away. My mind kept slipping back to Jeff's murder. I kept envisioning the photograph of the former Chief of Police with his two goons beside him. The longer I held that image in my mind, I knew there was something wrong with that picture. But what? What had I done to deserve this? Who was this maniac who thought I should know him?

I returned to my telepathic way of sending messages to Mike, Brian, and Isabella. I don't know how much time had passed, but I came alive when I heard the jangle of keys hitting the metal entrance door of the morgue. I heard Brian's annoyance as he demanded, "For God's sake, mister, move over. Give me the keys, and let me unlock the door."

"Hurry, Brian!" urged Mike.

"I don't know what you men expect to find. Nothing here but dead bodies" said an unfamiliar voice.

"Isabella said it was over to the left. I'll search there, and you start on the right, Brian," ordered Mike.

I was so stiff from lying in one spot for so long that I couldn't move. I hoarsely yelled out, "Mike!"

Suddenly, the door flew open, and Mike's head was above mine as he pulled me toward him. His tears mingled with mine as he tenderly lifted me into an upright position and then into his arms.

"Oh, my God!" said the unfamiliar voice. "What are you doing here?"

Mike crushed me to him. "Who has keys to this place?" he asked the security guard beside us.

"Just the pathologists and the security guards," he answered defensively.

Brian took his frustration out on the guard as he grabbed his shirt and shoved him backward. "Are you responsible for this?" he asked angrily.

"Nooo. I'm as surprised as you are!" he exclaimed, trying to loosen Brian's grip on him.

"Brian, don't! That's not going to help anything. We need to call Isabella and tell her I'm okay. I know she's worried," I said as Mike lowered me onto my feet.

We stood and stared at each other, trying to understand what had happened to me. I shivered, knowing it was a miracle they'd found me. The air stirred, making us look around for the source of the sudden breeze. I knew who it was. *"Good work, Rosie girl,"* my grandmother whispered.

I clutched Mike's arm in fear. "We have to get out of here now. He said he'd be back to get me."

"Don't worry, Rosie, I'll be waiting right here for him when he returns," said Brian. "And you there, Mr. Security Guard? You'll be waiting right here with me, too, understand?"

The guard's eyes widened. He didn't seem thrilled with the idea but looked unwilling to challenge Brian.

"Did you know that dude? Could you recognize him again?" Brian asked me.

"He seemed to think I should know him, but I don't."

"What did he look like, Rosie?" asked Mike tenderly.

"He looked pretty scruffy. I'm pretty sure he hadn't bathed in a while. He wore a black knit hat down low with black hair that stuck out. He was about 5'10" and had brown eyes." I was surprised I'd remembered that much about him because I'd acted like many when seeing someone in that condition. I hadn't noticed him until he asked me to identify him. Shame on me.

"Okay, we'll get him," said Brian.

Mike turned my chin up to search my eyes. "Are you sure you're okay to walk, Rosie?" he asked, covering me with his jacket.

I nodded, held onto his hand, and ordered my stiff legs to move forward. Mike turned to Brian and the guard as we headed to the door.

"We're out of here, then. After you capture that son of a bitch, you'd better keep him away from me. I'm unsure what I'll do to him if I ever get my hands on him."

Knowing what Mike was capable of, Brian ordered, "Just go. I'll see you back at the house later."

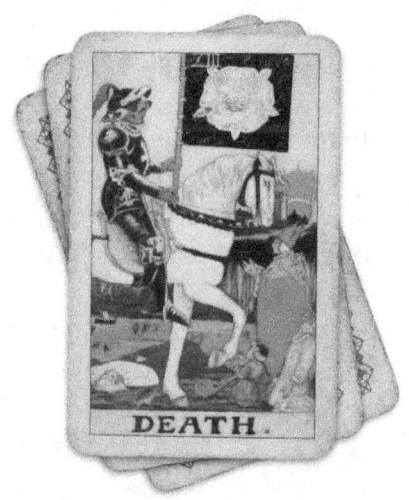

CHAPTER 34

I sabella was waiting at the door to greet us. She flung herself at me and said, "Mama, I was so worried about you. I knew this morning that something bad was going to happen. I should have warned you."

"But you did, darling girl. Remember?"

"Yes, but …"

I placed my finger across her lips. "Not to worry, Isabella. Sit with me in the kitchen. I'll have Virginia fix us a nice cup of tea."

"I'm calling in the police chief on this, Rosie. He needs to be involved," said Mike.

"I hope Brian catches him. If he doesn't, and that guy sees that the police are involved, he can go into hiding, and we'll never find him," I said.

"I don't know," called Mike over his shoulder as he headed to the office. "If Brian catches him first, it may not be good either ...."

I leaned on Isabella and limped my way into the kitchen. Virginia had already set out tea cookies and stood to wait for the kettle to boil. She looked at me with sympathy. She knew me well enough now not to ask questions and to let me speak when I was ready.

I was sore, upset, and irritable. I was tired of all that had happened to me. I rose from my chair and pushed away from the table. I kissed the top of Isabella's head. "Excuse me, please. I need to figure things out to stop all this madness."

I hobbled into the office where Mike sat at his desk. I startled him, and he looked up at me expectantly. "What's wrong? Are you okay?"

"Where did you leave those printouts of the double arrests?"

"They're right there on your desk; why?"

"I need to go through them, and I'm going to ask you to leave if you don't mind."

"Now?" he asked.

I smiled as I walked closer. "Yes, handsome, now, please."

He opened his arms wide, and I snuggled against him only briefly. I couldn't let anything disturb what I had in mind.

"Okay, my queen," he said with a sigh. "I'll shut the door on my way out."

I knew he was humoring me, for I'm sure he thought I'd been through enough that I deserved to do whatever I wanted. I eased down in my desk chair and tried to get comfortable. It wasn't easy. I shuffled through the pile of papers until I found what I sought. I pulled out a lined tablet and began to make notes. A pattern emerged as I went through the pages and wrote down the arrested individuals' names. Several months before Susan had disappeared, Allison was listed as one of several twosomes picked up for solicitation. The other person's name with her changed each time, yet I felt it was the same person simply using a different name as a front. A taunting of sorts. Martini Darling, Mary Delight, Marianne Dewit, Melinda Dearest. Stage names? Why the initials M.D.? I needed to have Mike and Brian check to see if the fingerprints matched.

I closed my eyes and rested against the back of my chair. I took psychology in school and knew we humans could be strange folk. I also realized that we often acted in passive-aggressive ways if we wanted to hurt another person. Two thoughts came to mind. I wanted to see if any missing person reports showed that a parent was a doctor or if a doctor had been the one calling in the missing person report. I frowned when I remembered that we didn't know if Susan's parents had even called in a missing person report, for that matter.

The other thought I had was to use social media as Cindy had suggested and see if any of these names came up in a search. I knew that sometimes dancers or prostitutes set up their own business without an agency or a John—at least some tried to.

Tomorrow, I'd flag those double arrests for Mike and Brian that I wanted them to follow up at the police station. I believed that if they downloaded the arrest photos, we'd find the same person—Susan—in all of them.

After eating, I asked Virginia if she would stay until Mike arrived. She came to me and placed her arms around me. "Of course, Rosie. I think it'd be a good idea for you to go to bed now, don't you?"

I agreed and held out my hand for Isabella, waiting for me to rise. I didn't want her out of my sight. After we both changed for bed, Isabella cuddled next to me while Sweet Pea created a spot for herself at the foot of the bed. I fell fast asleep until I woke up screaming.

CHAPTER 35

S omeone was heavy on top of me, trying to pin my arms to my side. Then I heard Mike's frantic voice. "You're okay, Rosie. It's just a bad dream. You can stop hitting me now. I'm right here, and you're safe."

Slowly his face became in focus, and I made out his worried expression. "Oh, Mike," I whimpered. "I was dreaming I was back in the chamber at the morgue, and this time I wasn't going to escape …."

"I've got you, baby. No one's going to do that to you ever again. I promise you," he vowed.

"Did Brian catch him? Who is he?" I asked, pushing away the thought that no one could promise anyone what Mike had said.

There was enough hesitation that I knew he hadn't.

"I'm sorry, sweetheart. Not yet." When I groaned, he added, "But don't worry, we'll get him."

As I lay in Mike's arms, I thought about what a miracle they had found me at the morgue. "Mike, how did you know where to look for me yesterday? Was it Isabella?"

"Yes. It's because of her we found you," Mike replied. "Isabella told the school she was sick and had to go home. Virginia called to tell me that when she picked up Isabella, she became hysterical and said you were in trouble. She said you were trapped in a dark place. Then Romano called me to see if I'd heard from you. He told me you'd said you would see him and Randy, but you never showed up."

"Then what happened?"

"As soon as Brian heard what was happening, he said we should head to the hospital because he thought you must be there. And is there any place in a hospital darker than the morgue?"

Upon hearing those words, I shuttered, and Mike pulled me closer. But as soon as he did, I reacted and began pushing him away, fearing being trapped. I guess it would take some time for me to release that fright. Mike seemed to understand as I moved further away from him.

"It's okay, Rosie. Go back to sleep," he said as he gently laid his arm on my hip. "I'm right here if you need me."

"I love you, Mike," I whispered as I closed my eyes, praying for sleep without dreams.

"I love you, too," were the last words I heard.

***

When morning came, I was glad to find myself in bed with Mike beside me. I felt energized despite all that I'd been through. This time the darkness that filled my mind was kind without visions. I knew every second counted to seek out the person determined to hurt me.

We had so many things to resolve—finding Martini Darling; the identities of the skeletons and who murdered them; the person who put the skeletons there and why, and the man who wanted to hurt me. I knew they were all tied together. Perhaps we could hone in and solve these mysteries with the plan I'd devised the night before.

As I started to get out of bed, I felt Mike's hand pull me back. "No, you don't, baby. You're not going anywhere. You need to rest today. You've been through enough," he stated in a firm voice.

"No, Mike," I said in a tone that matched his, "I'm getting up and calling the others to meet this morning. I've got a plan that I think will work."

"Why don't you let Brian and me handle things with the police? I think the more you stay put here in the house, the safer you'll be, and we all want that," he continued in an even tone of voice.

"You know I can't do that. There's too much to do, including me, and we all need to do our part."

He sighed. "Do you realize how much time we've spent rescuing you? If you can stay put in one place, maybe our time could be better spent solving these cases," he pleaded.

"Really?" I snapped in a frosty tone.

"Think about it, Rosie. Your running around puts you in danger and jeopardizes us solving these cases, and ...."

"Wait just a minute! Are you telling me that you haven't been able to solve these cases because of me? Let me remind you that because of my involvement, you at least know we are looking for a man who hates me ... and ... and ..." I sputtered and looked at him helplessly, tears filling my eyes.

"Look, show us your plan, and then we can discuss it with the others. How does that sound?" Mike asked in a pacifying manner. "You still have to stay put, though. Deal?"

"Okay," I said reluctantly, crossing my fingers behind my back, knowing I couldn't promise that.

I clumsily climbed out of bed and headed into the shower. Mike followed me in. We stood and gently washed each other without any sexual advances. We both were uptight and worried. He shaved while I blew out my hair, and then we dressed casually and headed downstairs. I smelled coffee and knew Brian had beaten us getting up even though it was still early.

"Good morning, you two lovebirds. How goes it?" asked Brian.

"Okay," we both answered unenthusiastically.

"Wow, bad night then?" he asked, eying us.

"Bad dreams," is all Mike answered.

"Here's some coffee, you two," he said, handing us each a cup.

"C'mon, guys, let me show you what I found." I was hurrying to show them what I'd discovered in my research the night before. I took my coffee and headed into the office.

I overheard Brian ask Mike, "Did you talk to her yet about staying put?"

When I looked back, I saw Mike shake his head and put his finger across his mouth. I just shook my head at the two of them. I sat at my desk while Brian and Mike pulled chairs close to me.

"Let's see what you've got there," said Brian.

I had carefully made notes with names, dates, and thoughts. Sometimes I even surprise myself with how organized I can be. The guys were impressed and agreed to follow up on Allison, the main person of the twosomes I'd listed.

"Mimi, Cindy, and I downloaded several photos of the former Chief of Police with Susan. If we could show those photos to the others in the picture, and see if any of the MD names resonated with them, maybe we can tie them all to one person—Susan."

"I agree," said Brian. "But that won't solve everything, for we still haven't been able to identify Susan."

"That's true," I said. "Mimi spoke with Tony, and what he said rang true for the little I'd learned while working at the Purple Passion Lounge. The girls often don't use their real names. They get fake I.D.s and sometimes don't need them to be hired. Some places don't care and pay them in cash, so there's no trail. But maybe you could talk to Tony and Lorenzo separately about the photos. You never know what they might remember when under pressure from you two."

Brian grinned. "That's true, huh, bro?"

"You know it." Mike's eyes twinkled.

I rolled my eyes and shook my head. Guys. "What do you think about the M.D. – doctor aspect?" I asked.

"Let's go with it," said Brian. "We'll have one of the guys at the station start on that right away."

"Anything else, Rosie?" asked Mike.

"The rest of us will go through social media and Google to see if we can come up with anything."

"Good, that means you can stay put right here. No need for you to leave," Mike said in a determined voice. When I hesitated, he added, "I think it might be a good idea to keep Isabella home with you today. She needs to be assured that you're okay and doesn't need to worry about you. What do you say?"

I was floored. It was a good idea despite realizing it was Mike's way of ensuring I didn't leave the house. "I agree, and I don't think she'd mind missing just one school day."

"Okay, then," said Mike with a wide smile. "Agreed."

"Let's get rolling, Mike," urged Brian. "We'll catch breakfast on the way."

"You'll get back to me as soon as possible, won't you?" I asked their retreating backs.

"You'll be the first to know," promised Mike. Then he halted, turned around, and said, "I love you, Rosie. Please keep safe."

I nodded, blew them a kiss, and watched them leave.

CHAPTER 36

I sabella padded downstairs, and I heard her frantic voice, "Mama? Mama, where are you?"

I stepped from my office and called, "I'm right here, sweetheart."

A look of relief crossed her face when she stepped through the doorway and saw me. I held out my arms, and she rushed to me. As I stood holding her, I felt such love for her. If only we could find Martini Darling, Susan, or whoever she was and straighten out Mike's marital status. We had only days now to do that, and I was already distraught with worry.

I'd called Santa Fe earlier to learn that Grandmother was well, as were Angela and Nica. Maria reassured me that she still supported me in becoming Isabella's foster mother despite all that had happened. "I lit a candle for us at church. Keep the faith, Rosie."

Upon hearing her words, I filled with love for her. If Maria believed in me that much, there was a good chance she was right, and things would work out. Her faith energized me to move forward.

Instead of meeting with Mimi, Cindy, and Romano, I placed a conference call with them. I filled them in on what Mike, Brian, and I were doing and asked if they'd continue researching the media and see if anything came up. In addition to Allison's name, I repeated the other identities used so they could write them down.

"Thanks so much to each of you for helping," I said as I held back my emotion. "I know with all of us working together, something will come up."

"We'll do it, Rosie. I know we will," confirmed Cindy.

"Hang in there, Rosie. It will all turn around—wait and see," said Mimi.

"Don't do anything foolish, Rosie. It'll work out. Just stay put," ordered Romano.

I had to smile at Romano's remark. Clearly, Mike had spoken to him about backing him up on that. "Thanks again. I'll let you know if anything breaks."

I entered the kitchen, where Isabella sat dressed, ready for the day, munching her cereal. I'd already explained that she wouldn't attend school that day and seemed content to stay with me.

"Is Virginia coming today?" she asked.

"Not today; why?"

"That means it's just you and me then," she said with a smile.

"Yes, it does, darling girl!" I said before I grabbed her and kissed her many times. I laughed along with her giggles while Sweet Pea jumped on both of us, wanting to participate.

"I've some work to do. Want to join me?" I asked.

"Really? I got my new laptop from school yesterday. Want to see it? I'll bring it down."

"Sure," I answered. I was glad each student received the same laptop as part of their school tuition, so there wouldn't be any competition or one-upmanship.

Isabella plugged in her computer, and connecting it to the internet was easy. She sat at Mike's temporary desk and began to type away. "This is so much fun working together, Mama."

"What are you doing?"

"I'm writing a story for English class. It can be about anything the teacher said, so I'm writing about Sweet Pea."

I laughed. "That should be interesting."

She continued typing for a few minutes and then turned to me. "What are you working on, Mama?"

"I'm trying to find something," I answered vaguely.

Isabella sat up alert. "Did you lose something?"

"Kind of," I replied.

"Then, why don't you go to the lost and found? At school, we go to the lost and found anytime someone loses something."

I stopped what I was doing and stared at her. My mind whirled. Why not go to the lost and found? It would simply be another way of finding the answers we were seeking. If the girls had been murdered and their cases were never solved, wouldn't the police still have evidence boxes for their cold cases? Maybe we could get into that storage area and look for a box with one of the names I'd circled. Why not try?

"Let's take a ride," I said to Isabella.

She hesitated. "Aren't we supposed to stay here?"

"Yes," I answered truthfully, "unless we have somewhere to go."

I had confused her, but she gamely said, "Okay."

I drove to the police station to discuss this with Mike and Brian and to demand that I be a part of the search. When we arrived, I discovered they weren't there.

I introduced myself to Roberto and told him what I had in mind. He said, "It wouldn't hurt to try that angle, but I don't have anyone on staff with the time to do that."

"Please, I'm happy to do that myself. If you'd show me the way …."

"Those boxes are old enough that they are at the old location. They're in a storage unit two doors down."

"Please, if you could just let us in there, we're happy to go through the boxes … and we'll be neat. We won't make a mess, I promise you."

"Mike and Brian know about this, right?" he asked.

"They will as soon as you let them know, okay?"

There was a long, silent pause. "I guess it wouldn't hurt to get you started on this. Come on, and I'll let you in myself." He ruffled Isabella's hair. "You're helping too, I see."

"Yup," Isabella answered proudly.

The storage room was dark but brightened when the hanging overhead lights flashed on. It was damp and smelled musty, but it held promise for what I was hoping to find. The chief showed us the filing system they used for the shelves of boxes, and he began to poke. "What year did you want to see? And what names?"

I told him.

"Martini Darling? What kind of name is that, huh?"

"How about Mary Delight, Marianne Dewit, and Melinda Dearest?"

He chuckled. "Only in Vegas. Here's where you can begin," he said as he pulled out a small box and pointed down the long row of cartons. These will take you to the end of the row."

His phone rang, and he seemed reluctant to answer it. I imagined his calls couldn't be that pleasant. He listened to what was said and grimaced.

"I've got to go. Good luck. Call the office when you're ready to leave so we can lock it up."

"Thanks, Chief. I really appreciate it."

After he left, we started down the aisle, checking the name and date on each box. I'd brought paper and pen with me, and instead of writing each name and date onto my pad, I realized that I was wasting time and began my search by running my hand across the boxes on the middle shelf—the shelf at eye level.

Isabella watched me in awe. "What did you lose, Mama?"

"Have you ever heard the expression 'like a needle in a haystack'?"

Isabella giggled and shook her head.

"It means that it would be like a miracle to find it."

"What is it you want to find?"

"A piece of paper with Mike's name on it. I think it's inside a box with Martini Darling's name. Or Susan's name or just about anyone else's name," I sighed.

"You mean our Mike's name?"

"Yes, our Mike … Mike Williams." A thought came to me. "Isabella, how did you know where to find me the other day?"

"Your picture kept coming into my mind, and I heard you speak. You said you were in trouble, and it was dark and cold. You said you felt trapped," Isabella said in a shaky voice. Her eyes watered. "It was awful."

I put my arm around her. "Do you want to try an experiment?"

"What kind of an experiment?"

"Let's see if we can communicate like we did the other day. I will close my eyes and concentrate on what I think the lost paper looks like with the name Michael Williams on it. Here I'll draw it for you. Then, I want you to put that image into your mind, okay?"

"What happens then, Mama?"

"We'll see what happens. After we meditate for a while, we'll put our hands on each box we've tagged to see if the box is warm."

"What happens if it's warm?" she asked, curious.

"That means the energy of our thoughts connected to the piece of paper, and we've found what we are looking for."

Isabella pulled her fist down in a sign of triumph— something she had learned at school.

We sat not far apart on the floor and closed our eyes to meditate. I wasn't sure how long we'd been meditating, but when I opened my eyes, I had stiffened up from sitting. Isabella still sat with her eyes closed and looked asleep. I lightly touched her arm and whispered, "Time to return to the room, Isabella."

Slowly, she stirred and opened her eyes. She looked at me and smiled. "I think I know where it is, Mama."

"You do?" I asked in astonishment.

She got up and pointed to a box on the middle shelf. The name on it was Lucinda. I dragged the box off the shelf, hurriedly brought it to the floor, and opened it. Isabella's face creased in disappointment as I plowed through it and came up with nothing. I was uncomfortable going through things that belonged to a dead girl, and I carefully put things back in place and hoisted the box back onto the shelf.

"Don't be upset. We'll try again." I comforted Isabella.

A slight breeze moved the air, and I heard the word PERSPECTIVE as if it had been shouted. Isabella must have heard it, too, because she asked me, "Mama, what does 'spective mean?"

I thought about the word and what it meant. I watched Isabella approach the box we'd just pulled from the shelf, and then it hit me. Of course! The box in her reverie was shoulder high to her, but it wasn't shoulder high to me. I walked to where she stood and raised my hand to the box above it. As soon as my hand touched the box, I felt its warmth. The name on the box was Meredith Susan Dodge. My hands trembled as I pulled it from the shelf and lowered it to the ground. Isabella's eyes were wide as I ceremoniously removed the lid and looked inside. Things were chaotic and in disarray. Papers were everywhere as if tossed carelessly inside. I carefully separated them, and when I picked up the last one in my hand, I felt the heat emanating. I cried when I saw it was the signed paper for annulling Mike's marriage. I sniffled as I handed the paper to Isabella to hold. I began to put things back in place when I heard the door open. "Mike, Brian, in here! We found it."

I stood up to see their smiles when we told them the good news. The man approached the corner, and it was not Mike, Brian, or the police chief. It was the man from the elevator. "What have you got there?" he asked. Isabella grabbed the letter and turned away.

"Run, Isabella, run," I screamed.

The man's eyes never left mine. He didn't seem to care that Isabella had escaped. He held an iron wrench and advanced toward me with menace. Strangely, the man stopped and pulled off his hat. He glowered at me.

"Still don't recognize me?"

I shook my head, and then I gasped.

He jeered, "Ahh. Now you recognize me, don't you?"

I couldn't believe anyone could change so much. "My God, Jerry, what's happened to you?"

"You mean besides losing 60 lbs. and being unable to work because of you?"

"Unable to work because of me? What are you talking about?"

"At the time of Jeff's death, didn't you think it was odd that no one interviewed me? Who doesn't interview a cop's partner when a cop is killed? You were like everyone else who only thought about what had happened to Jeff and not about what happened to his partner," he proclaimed bitterly.

"What did happen to you?" I asked, curious.

"You couldn't leave well enough alone. You kept yammering about Jeff being murdered, and when I challenged the chief about it, he said he could no longer trust me. He removed me from the precinct and let it be known that I was a cop who couldn't be trusted. Before long, word got around that I wouldn't make a good partner for any cop. No one wanted me, and I was without a job. The only thing left for me was to be a security guard at the hospital," he said disgustingly. "And it all was because of you," he spat angrily.

"But ..."

"Just shut up, bitch. You've no idea what I've been through. You got to live your comfortable little life without troubles while I was left with nothing!" he shouted. "You even got your name in the paper—a heroine. Why should you have everything and I have nothing? It's not fair, and you're going to pay."

"I'm so sorry, I really am. But you're accusing the wrong person of what happened to you. Think about it. None of that would have happened if the precinct were clean and you were doing the right thing and not dealing drugs there. Didn't any of you realize it would only end up badly?"

"Don't go preaching to me! Everyone was in on it, even your boyfriend. Don't think for a minute he wasn't involved …."

"Then why was he killed?" I hollered, furious.

"Someone had to take the fall." His mouth drooped, and he looked sad. Then he jerked his head up and glowered at me. "I lost everything because of you. That wouldn't have happened if you hadn't made such a fuss."

"Are you sure about that?" I challenged.

He stood still and contemplated what I'd said. He smelled like alcohol, and I think it was difficult for him to sort things out. Suddenly, he snapped to attention and rushed toward me. I kicked the box still on the floor before me as hard as possible, jamming it into him. He lost his balance, tripped, and fell. His head resounded as it hit the floor. He lay there, out cold.

Led by Isabella, the police chief came running into the storage area. He looked at Jerry on the floor and raised his hand to salute me. "Good work, Rosie."

Isabella threw herself at me, and I wrapped my arms around her. We heard a car screech outside the door, and two pairs of feet slapped their way to where we were huddled around Jerry. Mike and Brian looked at the scene, looked at each other, and shook their heads in disbelief.

Then Mike stepped forward and reached for me. "Are you okay, Rosie?"

"Better than that ... I found the paper for your annulment," I grinned.

"Let me see," he said excitedly.

"Not on your life, buster. I'm taking no chances. I don't want anything to get in the way of this marriage getting annulled."

"Fair enough," agreed Mike.

"So, who was the real Martini Darling?" asked Brian. "Meredith Susan Dodge," I said as I pointed to the box.

"Isn't that one of the names we found whose father was a doctor?" asked Mike.

"So it worked then," I said, excited that my idea had brought about results. "What about Allison? Did you find out anything about her?"

"Not yet, but Cindy called and said she had some good news. We're to meet the rest of the gang back at the house," said Mike.

"Who is this deadbeat?" asked Brian, lightly kicking the man with his foot.

"Jeff's former police partner. He saw my picture in the paper at the time of the girls' escape, and it brought up old resentments of me raising a stink at the time of Jeff's death. He said I was to blame for losing his job back then."

"After all this time, he's getting back at you now?" asked Mike.

"None of us knows when we meet a person whether we'll have a lasting effect on them. And we never know how someone else interprets our actions. I never thought about Jerry when I complained about Jeff's treatment by the police, which seemed to be eating at him, too."

Brian and Mike shook their heads in dismay.

Death Returns

"Everything cool, Roberto?" asked Mike. Roberto waved us away. "Okay then, let's head home," said Mike, putting his arms around Isabella and me.

CHAPTER 37

We sat around the table in high spirits. We raised our glasses and toasted. It was a glorious moment for each of us because together, we'd come up with the identities of both girls, found the annulment paper, and discovered who had wanted to injure me and why. The only thing left to discover was who murdered the girls and whether more bodies could be found. I had my fingers crossed that between Jerry and the two police goons in the photos with the former police chief, and perhaps even Tony and Lorenzo, the truth would come out. So far, no one has been talking.

Cindy and Mimi had contacted several of the people in the photos, who confirmed that it was Susan in the picture and also named Allison as one of the other women in one of them. Cindy and Mimi had found more information about Allison on social media. Allison's sister was still seeking her, and it was through social media that she periodically sent out requests for any information regarding her sister. Now that we knew her full name, additional information on her was available in the police records as well. The new chief had already called the parents of both "Susan" and Allison.

Jerry had the rest of Allison's bones in the trunk of his car, and we all agreed it was time to bury both girls with some respect. Our sentiments moved Romano because he felt that society had let Susan down with all its unrealistic demands of a person. Her way of living had been her recourse to rebel against her father, as her pseudo names suggested. I was sure there was an unpleasant story behind that.

Cindy decided to fly out the following day back to the life that awaited her with her new boyfriend. Mike and Brian offered her a job, and she was considering working for them again—doing research work offsite. I thought it would be a good move for all three of them.

Mike had arranged for a celebration dinner to be brought in. Romano would join us for cocktails and spend the rest of the evening with Randy. They were excited because Randy was leaving the hospital at the end of the week with a nurse hired to come in daily to help until he was stronger and could do things for himself. That was going to take some time, but their spirits were high.

Isabella called her sister-friends in Santa Fe, reassuring them we'd be there in a few weeks. Although Maria and I had spoken the day before, we talked for nearly two hours as I filled her in on every detail of finding the annulment papers and all that'd happened. I was blessed to have her in my life; I knew our friendship would continue to deepen as we raised our girls.

The only thing left to be resolved was the hearing with the judge regarding Isabella and me. The next day, Jacklyn called and told us she'd meet us at the courthouse. She wanted to be there in case the judge had any questions.

Once there, Jacklyn patted my shoulder consolingly and whispered, "Don't worry. It'll be okay."

My stomach churned, and I kept telling myself to relax. Isabella kicked her feet back and forth as we sat in the pew, waiting to be called forward. It was the only sign she was nervous. She smiled at me. "Is it our turn yet, Mama?"

"Not yet. But soon," I whispered back.

The time came, and our names were called. Isabella and I rose and held hands as we stepped forward to face the judge. He was a kindly older man who peered at us over his wire glasses between reading each of the papers about our case that sat before him. The silence was deafening while we waited.

When he finished, he smiled at us. "This is a rare case in that all the parties involved want the two of you to be together. I am pleased to see you stand before me today. In each of your roles, I encourage you to love and honor each other for the role you will play in the other's life. Do I make myself clear?"

Isabella looked up at me as I gazed down at her, and we smiled. "Yes," we said in unison.

"Isabella Rodriquez, do you accept Rosalie Bennett as your foster mother?"

"Yes, please."

"And Rosalie, do you accept Isabella Rodriquez as your foster daughter?"

"More than anything, Judge. We belong together."

"Then, this court declares that you, Rosalie Bennett, are bound by the State's covenants to follow the rules of the foster care system. Jacklyn Wilson has requested to act as your advocate in helping with the transition. Do you understand?"

"Yes, Judge. I do. Thank you."

Isabella faced the judge. "Can Mama and I please go home now?"

The Judge peered down at her and smiled. He stamped several papers and said, "Next."

We left, smiling. Mike kissed me and then Isabella. "I'm so proud of you both."

I turned and hugged Jacklyn, "Thank you so much for all your help. That wouldn't have happened without your support, and I'm forever grateful."

"And we are for having Isabella well cared for by you and Maria."

That night after many celebration calls and a celebratory dinner, I tucked Isabella in for the night, Sweet Pea by her side. I leaned down and kissed the top of her head. "Goodnight, my darling daughter. I love you, Little One."

Her hand reached for me and pulled my head closer to hers. "I love you too, Mama. I always will."

I was touched by her sentiment that sounded beyond her years. She was a deep well of all that was good, and I knew the future held so much for us to love and learn together. And I was grateful.

I went to join Mike downstairs. As I neared, his phone rang. He picked it up and mouthed, "It's Cal."

After the call ended, I asked, "Mike?" My heart dropped. Did Cal want Mike back in Boston?

"What, baby?"

"What did Cal want?"

"There's another young girl here in Las Vegas who has gone missing, and it doesn't look good. Are you up for it?" he asked, knowing how unwittingly I seemed to get involved in his cases.

Was there no end to missing persons? Dead bodies? Or murder? Apparently not. As long as there were people, there were deaths—that was life. I knew that together Mike and I, along with Brian, would never end our quest for justice for those murders yet to be solved.

Sensing my worry, Mike came to stand behind me. He wrapped his arms tightly around me and nuzzled my neck. He whispered into my ear. "Do you know how much I love you?"

I smiled. "Perhaps you'd better show me just how much."

"A wonderful idea. Come, my queen, and let's begin."

ACKNOWLEDGMENTS

To all of you who have picked up this book to read, I thank you from the bottom of my heart. I hope you enjoy every page and, even more so, find this book difficult to put down. That's what a good mystery is all about.

I thank my early readers and reviewers – Doreen Ping, Nancy Burger Eberhard, Maya-Sofia Geissendoerfer, and all my other ARC readers. Because of your time and reviews, you help an author succeed. I appreciate your time and effort. A special shout out to Elizabeth Frenette and Donna Stockwell for their honest input.

What makes a good book great? Editing. So with great appreciation for her editing, I thank Summer DuPree for helping me tie up loose ends.

I was blessed the day I contacted Kelly Martin to be my book cover designer. Thank you, Kelly, for your creativity and artistic talents. I love your work and you!

Thank you, Jake Naylor, for designing my website, being my layout person, and so much more. You're a marvel! You're the best and a blessing to me! I love you.

J.S. PECK

Joan was reared in a family of readers in small-town Elmira, New York. When she was growing up, each Sunday afternoon was a special time when each family member relaxed with a good book. "It was when I began reading the Nancy Drew series that mysteries intrigued me."

To me, the fun of reading mystery books is to become so involved with the story it becomes impossible to put the book down. A good mystery has often caused me to stay up all night to finish it to see whether I can figure out whodunit. For anyone hooked on reading mystery books, there's nothing better than that."

In addition, Joan was raised to be open-minded and understood that we are all connected energetically and can communicate with others who have passed on. She brings that idea into her Death Card series by having the spirit of Rosie's grandmother pop into her life with advice or loving messages. Rosie is portrayed as a psychic, meaning she has visions of what is yet to come.

Joan also writes books under the name Joan S. Peck, and that website is www.JoanSPeck.com.

I hope you enjoy reading this book and the entire Death Card series. If you did, please help other readers discover it by leaving a review on Amazon.com. I thank you for your kindness.

—*Joan*

BOOKS BY J.S. PECK

THE DEATH CARD SERIES
- Book 1: *Death on the Strip*
- Book 2: *Death at the Lake*
- Book 3: *Death Returns*
- Book 4: *Death in the Shadows*
- Book 5: *Death on the Run*
- Book 6: *Death Comes Calling*

A HOLIDAY ROMANCE SERIES
- Book 1: *Santa Baby*
- Book 2: *Presents from Heaven*

ROMANTIC MYSTERIES
- *Angels Out of the Dark*
- *The Waiting Room*
- *The Boston Fiasco*

BOOKS BY JOAN S. PECK

- *The Seven Major Chakras – Keeping it Simple*
- *A Simple Approach to Living a Successful Life*
- *What You Need to Know to Live a Spiritual Life*
- *Prime Threat – Shattering the Power of Addiction*